Storm Over 4

For All at

4

JEREMY ISAACS

Storm Over

4

A PERSONAL ACCOUNT

Weidenfeld and Nicolson

LONDON

First published in 1989 by
George Weidenfeld & Nicolson Limited
91 Clapham High Street, London SW4 7TA

British Library Cataloguing in Publication Data
applied for

ISBN 0 297 79538 4

Printed in Great Britain by Butler and Tanner Ltd, Frome and London

Contents

Illustrations

(*All photographs by courtesy of Channel Four Television Company Limited, unless otherwise stated*)

Between pages 86 and 87

Advertising by BMP for Channel 4's opening night
Ian McKellen as *Walter*
Richard Whiteley presenting *Countdown*
Anna Carteret, Sue Jones-Davies and Fanny Viner in *The Raving Beauties In the Pink*
The cast of *The Comic Strip Presents – Five Go Mad in Dorset*
Cartoonists' views of Channel 4's early problems by Marc, Mel Calman and Alan Parker
Channel 4's early headlines (courtesy of Associated Newspapers plc, Express Newspapers plc, Times Newspapers plc and Thomson Newspapers Ltd)
Edmund Dell, Channel 4's Chairman until 1987
Justin Dukes, Managing Director and Deputy Chief Executive until 1988
Paul Bonner, Channel Controller and then Programme Controller until 1987
Liz Forgan, Senior Editor, Actuality
Mike Bolland, initially editor for Youth Programmes, later Senior Editor for Entertainment
David Rose, Senior Editor, Fiction
Naomi Sargant, Senior Editor, Education
Peter Sissons, original presenter of *Channel 4 News*
Max Headroom (courtesy of Chrysalis Visual Programming)
Jonathan Ross at *The Last Resort*

Acknowledgements

This is my account of my time at Channel 4, and my part in its making. It is not history. I am aware of how much I have omitted. I have written of what I remember now, and think significant. I hope all those whose contribution is understated here, or omitted altogether, will understand. That must apply to colleagues and, particularly, to programme-makers whose work is not mentioned. But everyone who worked at Channel 4, and everyone who made a programme for us, counts and has a place in this story just the same.

I am grateful to all those who have helped jog my memory, and who have taken trouble to answer my questions. Christopher Griffin-Beale has been meticulously helpful in researching fact and checking detail. Anthony Howard read the typescript and made tart, useful criticisms. John Lucas, Fiona Maddocks and Liz Forgan also read it and made helpful comments. Allegra Huston, at Weidenfeld, too, has been a constructive critic. I warmly thank them all. For all imperfections, and particularly for opinions expressed in this book, I alone am responsible.

The indomitable Gritta Weil took on the heroic task of translating the text from longhand manuscript, i.e. illegible scribble to immaculate typescript and for sending it via her floppy disks on to the printer. To her, and the eagle-eyed Sheila Colton who assisted, I am ever beholden.

I am grateful to Miles Kington for a daily dose of laughter, and for permission to quote from the *Times* of May 1983. For their cartoons I thank Mel Calman, Alan Parker and, through Anna, Mark Boxer.

Fred and Barbara Zollna at the Blue Waters Inn, Speyside, Tobago, helped me get started by providing space to write in on a happy stay there.

Gillian Widdicombe prodded me to begin, kept me at it, put up with me while I wrote, sustained me throughout. My loving thanks to her.

I

Debate

On 31 December 1987 I cleared my desk at 60 Charlotte Street, and prepared to leave Channel 4.

The cartoons and the pictures that had hung on my walls were packed and gone. Mel Calman's little man hoping the new channel wouldn't be too good for him. Mark Boxer's smoothies pondering: 'I suppose this audience of one Channel 4 is down to must be Mrs Whitehouse.' Alan Parker sympathizing: 'Running a sodding, effing, blinding TV channel isn't easy you know.'

Gone from the walls was Tom Phillips' portrait of Elgar with Union Jacks, which my colleagues gave me the day we went on air, and the framed letter of encouragement and good wishes the Home Secretary, Willie Whitelaw, sent me that same morning.

It was New Year's Eve. Last New Year we had broadcast at midnight from Newcastle a horror of a live programme in which everything that could go wrong had gone wrong, and a desperate Ruby Wax, hearing nothing coming back to her from the studio audience, had become more and more loose in her language, descending in panic at the end into the obscenities of the club circuit at its earthiest, and worse. Leon Brittan MP was in the studio to take part. The Foreign Secretary, Sir Geoffrey Howe, switched on to watch him, and could not believe what he saw and heard. He wrote to the Chairman of the Independent Broadcasting Authority (IBA) in protest. Two senior staffmen at Tyne Tees Television narrowly escaped the sack. There were apologies, from me, all round.

This New Year it would be different, very different. I had asked John

McGrath to give us from Scotland a quiet and civilized Hogmanay. There would be poetry from Norman MacCaig and others, and Gaelic songs. The idea was to be reflective, to dignify the passing of the old year and the coming of the new. I had little thought when I commissioned the programme, nearly a year before, that in the middle of it, as the year turned at midnight, I would cease to be Chief Executive of Channel 4, seven years to the day after formally taking up the job.

* * *

The debate on the nature of the fourth television channel had meandered on for nearly twenty years. In 1962 the Pilkington Committee castigated ITV and recommended the setting up of BBC-2. It envisaged also that the fourth channel might eventually fall to a reformed and restructured ITV, allowing the commercial system too to provide a full range of programmes.

The spectrum used to be the scarce resource in broadcasting; a quality signal depended on careful allocation of space on the airwaves. In the United Kingdom the available wavelengths had always been strictly rationed; to be charged with their use was to be entrusted with a large public responsibility. For decades the BBC alone received this trust, but in the Fifties their monopoly was broken, and ITV set up, in a commercial interest, over against them. The companies enjoyed a lucrative monopoly of advertising revenue. But ITV was also given public responsibilities and was placed under a regulatory authority, the ITA. A national consensus, across governments of different political hue, insisted on the need to police broadcasters, and to set them high standards. Through the Board of Governors of the BBC, through the members of the Independent Television Authority, Britannia would rule the airwaves too.

Space in the broadcasting spectrum was scarce, but not that scarce; there was one unused button on the television set. There was room for, there could be brought into being, another national television channel. Only an act of political will was required.

BBC television strikingly demonstrated what an effective service two complementary channels could provide – introducing grand documentary series, generous arts programming, and adventurous drama and comedy, for which singlemindedly popular programming on BBC-1 left little room. Still smarting from Pilkington's strictures, and spurred on by the sacrifice in 1967 of a franchise or two *pour encourager les autres*, ITV moved to enlarge its programme ambition and extend its range. In this ITV was, by general consent, successful. Now, it sought to expand. So what sort of channel should the fourth channel be? Crucially, who should control it?

For years the regulators of commercial television had assumed that, if ever a second commercial service was introduced, the ITV monopoly would be broken. Any such service would be competitive with ITV; the 1963 Broadcasting Act stipulated that the Authority should ensure, where practicable, that any second set of programmes be supplied by different contractors. At the end of the Sixties, the Act was amended so that the Authority was required only to ensure that 'the same kind of subject-matter is not broadcast at the same time in different programmes'. Complementarity of programming, as practised by BBC-1 and BBC-2, now took priority over competition as a goal. For another decade it remained the general view that competition for audiences and revenue would lead to a lowering of standards, and was to be avoided.

That was not, however, the view of everyone. I vividly remember, as a current affairs executive at A–R Television, attending in 1965 a lunch given as one of a series to each of the broadcasting contractors by the Conservative Party, newly in opposition, seeking their views on future policy. At a round table in a Park Lane hotel I sat next to James Prior; over the beef we chatted. How long, after his election defeat, would Alec Douglas-Home stay on as Leader of the Opposition, and of the Party? Opposite us Martin Redmayne in the chair called on Paul Adorian, Managing Director of A-R, an engineer and an influential pioneer in ITV, to speak. A-R had survived a shaky start as Associated Rediffusion, the first ITV contractor. The 'Associated' element, Associated Newspapers, panicked at the early losses and withdrew. A-R was now the largest and the most profitable company in ITV. Speaking from a prepared text in his slightly accented English, Adorian said simply that all was for the best in the best of all possible worlds; the service given by BBC and ITV to the British public could not be improved upon; viewers were happy; the public interest was well served by the present dispensation. To introduce competition would do irreparable harm. Let well alone.

As he spoke, Iain Macleod, the best debater in the Tory Party, a future Chancellor, scribbled a note and passed it along to Martin Redmayne. 'Iain has something to say,' said Redmayne. One hunched shoulder forward, Macleod rose. He had never, he said, encountered such brazen impertinence. 'It was for you,' he said, 'for the ITV contractors, that a Conservative government broke the BBC monopoly. I never expected to hear from the very beneficiaries of our action that the monopoly you in your turn now enjoy should be for ever sacrosanct. I will not be party to it.'

I left A-R, where I edited *This Week*, when I was invited to the BBC to edit *Panorama*. My stay was short-lived. I tried to turn *Panorama* into a single-subject programme, and did not quite make it stick. I left, to return to A-R. When in 1967 the company, confident to the end, reapplied for its London weekday franchise, it lost, and after a shotgun wedding was merged with another contractor which had a weekend franchise in the North and Midlands, ABC Television – ABC having the controlling interest. The reluctant partners gave birth to Thames.

In the early 1970s no high priority attached to a fourth television channel. Before deciding, Government set up a committee to inquire into the future of broadcasting. Noël Annan was appointed to head it in May 1970. In June, slightly to Harold Wilson's surprise, Labour was defeated at the general election. The new government of Edward Heath promptly stood the Annan Committee down.

Did this mean a further postponement of the introduction of a fourth TV channel? Or would a new Conservative government, skipping the stately process of public consultation, act of its own volition? It would not go short of advice.

ITV now sensed an opportunity to argue hard for ITV-2, hoping perhaps to find a sympathetic ear in Edward Heath's government – soon deprived by his death of Iain Macleod's courageous persona. The ITV companies believed that they should run the fourth channel, controlling its air-time and output, emulating BBC-TV in the complementary scheduling of two channels. They would allow some space to the product of the smaller ITV companies, the regionals excluded by the Big Five from the network schedule; they would allow rein to the talents of programme-makers among their own staffs, now denied scope within the constraints of a single schedule. To him that hath should be given, was their argument.

Others took a different view. The ITA – it became the IBA in July 1972 – was now itself under scrutiny, notably by the House of Commons Select Committee on Nationalized Industries. Had it secured for the public the best service from the ITV companies? Had it secured for the Treasury a proper return on profits made from a public asset, the airwaves? It would need, in formulating policy for the fourth channel, not simply to serve the interests of the companies, but to take note of and respond to the views of other parties to the argument. These now came forward.*

Credit for the idea that added most to the mix of British broadcasting in the 1980s, if it is to go to a single individual, should be given to the author of an article in the *Guardian* on 21 April 1972, advocating a National Television Foundation. This was the broadcaster, author and academic Anthony Smith. The ITV companies fought their corner; advertisers demanded a market to buy time in; producers and directors, freelances or dissident staffmen, sought wider opportunities; the BBC hoped the status quo would not be disturbed against them; the Open University asked that the fourth channel should be given to the Open University; the audience, who had most interest in the outcome, was silent. Anthony Smith had an idea: broadcasting should aspire to the pluralism of publishing.

Smith had been an effective editor of *24 Hours*, a nightly BBC-1 news magazine. Later he was to be a hugely successful Director of the British Film Institute. Now he is President of Magdalen College, Oxford. Smith has a lively turn of speech, expressive gestures, altogether a buzz about him. He was too critical of the institution he worked in, and too prone to speak his mind, to be happy long at the BBC, or for his employers there to be happy with him. (I well remember in the Sixties one respected BBC figure telling me – it was a time of upheaval and some threatened dismissals in the current affairs group at Lime Grove – how much he longed 'to get rid of that shit Tony Smith'.) Outside now, Smith took a critical view of broadcasting institutions. Hierarchical, self-important, necessarily embodying an ethos that informed all their action and utterance, they were licensed by the state to fulfil a conformist and consensual role. Competing with each other in theory, in practice their output converged towards a norm. The institutions, unconsciously almost, schooled their staff to think safe and produce predictable work; bureaucracy lay heavy upon them. What was wanted was not to give more power to the present institutions, nor to set up others like them, but to extend broadcasting's range and the modes in which it might serve its publics by inventing an institution for broadcasting which would not itself create the work it broadcast. Broadcasting was at the same early stage of its

---

*A detailed account of the to-and-fro of argument on the fourth channel from 1970 to 1979 can be found in Stephen Lambert, *Channel Four: Television with a Difference* (BFI, 1982), and in the chapter 'The Empty Channel' in Jeremy Potter, *Independent Television in Britain, vol. 3: Politics and Control 1968– 80* (Macmillan, 1989).

development as, in the eighteenth and nineteenth centuries, the taxed and licensed publishing of books and newspapers had been. Now publishing was free; broadcasting should be reshaped like publishing.

Specifically Anthony Smith proposed that a National Television Foundation should be created to act as an electronic publishing house, to which any author, documentarist, dramatist, pamphleteer, individual or interest group might bring offerings. On it they might claim air-time; from it obtain resource.

The National Television Foundation would exercise editorial judgement merely in deciding whom to allow on the air. Its role was not to make programmes, nor, in approving them, to reshape them. Its function would be to broadcast. The object was diversity, to let thousands of would-be programme-makers, amateur and professional, catering for a plurality of interests, flourish. The great broadcasting institutions, BBC and ITV, in looking to the future, served always their own interests first. What was needed, in a Britain in which urgent voices were going unheard, was a new structure which might give new ideas expression.

But how fund such a structure? A pluralist broadcasting house, Smith thought, should depend on several sources of funding, not just one. He made a list: sponsorship by companies, by trade unions, by ministries; government grants; block advertising, presented not in 'natural breaks' but in one large nightly slab; publishing ventures and programme sales; existing broadcasting organizations would make grants for experimental work; viewers would pay subscriptions.

In the critical moments of the debate that were to come, as argument yielded to action, this diversity looked chancy. The National Television Foundation's Achilles' heel was to be its financing. After all, if publishing was the analogy, neither books nor newspapers cast their net so wide. So many different prospective sources of revenue suggested insecurity for a television channel committed to broadcasting fifty-two weeks of the year.

But if, in the end, the National Television Foundation never saw the light of day, something of what it stood for remained and had a lasting influence. Smith questioned the broadcasters' prevalent practice. Why need transmission schedules be fixed and repetitive? Why need programme durations conform to regular slot lengths? Why could no programme express a point of view? Why should all broadcasting aim at an audience of millions, and not reach out to small self-selecting audiences? Why, above all, if we were to extend the volume of British broadcasting, should we be offered more of the same?

Smith's ideas found some support, at least among the workers. The National Television Foundation idea had the backing of the BBC house union, ABS. The Union which organized in ITV, ACTT, for long remained opposed. Understandably. Their members' prosperity had long depended on a profitable ITV; for years they and the ITV companies had divided the spoils of monopoly. ACTT members in ITV had safe, well-paid jobs. Working to an outdated national agreement developed in the days of live television, inapposite now to the practices of film-making, of stop-and-start video recording or of continuous round-the-clock trans-mission, they were used to racking up vast overtime to augment their substantial basic pay. The ITV companies basked in the profits that were the fruit of monopoly. Time and again ITV managements bought their way out of trouble. Many ITV workers earned comfortably more than nurses, teachers, junior doctors; year on year they never had it so good. Independent production would bring with it, the Union feared, desta-bilization. Bolstering permanent employment was its habitual objective; casualization of the industry to be avoided as the plague. ACTT's television members believed they had as much a vested interest in sustaining the status quo as anyone. But ACTT also had members in the film industry who were already freelances, and often out of work. They argued the freelance case, and eventually won it.

In October 1972 a new Minister of Posts and Telecommunications revived interest in the fourth channel. One of Britain's most distinguished broadcasters, Sir Hugh Greene, the Director-General who had led the BBC forward under the onslaught of ITV's popular programming in the Fifties and in doing so had given us its finest hours of programme creativity and broadcasting élan, delivered a Granada lecture at the Guildhall. It was only fair, he argued that in competing with the BBC the ITV companies should have a second channel, and on their present form they deserved it. But ITV should not have the whole of it. Could not the National Television Foundation share it with them? This intervention on the side of ITV carried weight. ITV now began to modify its outright bid for sovereignty.

Sir John Eden, at the Ministry of Posts, invited ideas for the future of the fourth channel. John Birt and David Elstein, two young programme executives, made a lengthy submission to the Minister advocating more

7

room for the creative talents within ITV. They argued for an ITV-2, but under a single IBA-appointed programme controller, freed from the constraints, the habit of mind and the horse-trading that characterized the Programme Controllers Group in ITV. I, too, sent a brief paper to the Minister in June 1973, though I had completely forgotten it until I found it again years later. Those who then ran ITV were not, I thought, the right masters for a channel that would offer a different service.

In my note to the Minister* I urged a fourth channel that extended viewers' choice; that allowed space for programme-makers from within ITV and from outside; that was funded by ITV but not controlled by it.

Government played for time. In 1973 a White Paper proposed to extend the then current broadcasting arrangements from 1976 to 1981. There would be change thereafter. The Conservatives lost the general election of February 1974. Harold Wilson's Labour Government recalled Lord Annan and his committee.

Anthony Smith was to have been a key member of the reconstituted Annan Committee. He was taken off it at the last moment at the Prime Minister's personal insistence. His offence had been to criticize some remarks by the Prime Minister that were propitiatory of the repressive regime in Czechoslovakia. Roy Jenkins, then Home Secretary, nominated to the committee Phillip Whitehead, then Labour MP for Derby North, already an old hand in the broadcasting argument and a severe critic of the structures of ITV and BBC alike. The Hon. Sara Morrison, Vice-Chairman of Edward Heath's Conservative Party, was made a member; she later resigned her political post after Margaret Thatcher defeated Edward Heath for the leadership. Also appointed was Tony Jay, an experienced broadcaster and future author of *Yes, Minister*, capable of casting a cold eye on any pretentious proposition and, as it turned out, on the BBC.

In March 1977 Annan recommended that the fourth channel be entrusted to a new institution, an Open Broadcasting Authority. The principal idea that had fermented like yeast in the committee's deliberations was Tony Smith's proposal to add a pluralistic variety to our broadcasting: the publishing house analogy. 'He gave us the dough,' Annan later told the House of Lords, 'we baked it to a turn.' But the principal proposal Annan made was not Smith's but Whitehead's, and that was for the setting

*Reproduced as Appendix

up of another broadcasting authority. Publishing, the committee thought, at least on the airwaves, necessarily involved the exercise of editorial and regulatory powers.

A plurality of suppliers by all means, but no free-for-all. The OBA was to be a new institution, but with the same controlling editorial powers as the old. The trouble was, as Annan slightly ruefully later came to confess, they never thought through how to fund it. A new authority with new staff and premises and new expenses, but no new clearly identified source of funding; Achilles' heel again.

Handed this half-baked hot potato – yet enshrining a most valuable idea – James Callaghan's Labour Cabinet split and fumbled. Eventually it proposed, without satisfying the Treasury on funding, to set up the OBA. But, at Anthony Wedgwood Benn's insistence, it added to its proposals a dottier than usual scheme to add a layer of external interventionist management to the superstructure of the BBC.

In the House of Commons, the Conservative Opposition was critical. But the criticism carried with it a wish to see a fourth channel somehow established. It came from the substantial figure with an equal claim to be the practical founding father of Channel 4, Willie Whitelaw, Shadow Home Secretary. Whitelaw welcomed Annan's vision of a distinctive new development in our broadcasting, and wished, somehow, to implement it. He saw the broad case for ITV-2, but did not wholly trust the dominant Big Five ITV companies; it is significant that his Westmorland constituency was not in one of the central company franchise areas but in that of Border Television, one of the smallest of the regionals. Above all, Whitelaw was unconvinced by Annan's, or Labour's, proposals on financing a fourth channel. Simpler, surely, rather than set up a new and penniless authority, to hand the fourth channel to the IBA, and let ITV fund it.

On 3 May 1979 the electorate voted Mrs Thatcher into power. It would take time to prepare legislation to implement the more radical proposals on her agenda. With parliamentary time available, a Cabinet composed equally of what came later to be known as wets and dries – of the wets but a couple remain today – looked favourably then, as it never would now, on bringing a new public-service broadcasting institution into being.

On 12 May the Queen's Speech stated: 'Proposals will be brought before you for the future of broadcasting. A Bill will be introduced to extend the life of the Independent Broadcasting Authority, which will be given responsibility – subject to strict safeguards – for the fourth television channel.'

The debate on the fourth channel was nearly, but not quite, over. The time for the final decisive choices, and for acting on them, was near.

2

A Job Application

IN the summer of 1979 I was practising my trade as a freelance and would-be independent television producer.

Years earlier, a wise colleague, Cyril Bennett, discussing the hazards of the shaky ladder that led in television to executive promotion, had got it into my head once and for all that, if pitched off it, the thing to do was simply to return to one's basic skill and earlier job. And that is what I had had to do.

As Controller of Features – documentaries and current affairs, that is – at Thames Television until 1974, I kept my hand in as a programme-maker, producing a film on the river Thames, *Till I End My Song*, and a documentary series on the Second World War, *The World at War*. As work on that ended, suddenly Thames was looking for a Director of Programmes, responsible for the schedule and for all programming. There would be a place on the ITV Programme Controllers' Group, and a seat on the Thames Board. Thames's Chairman, Howard Thomas, now to move up to Chairman, had lost an able Director of Programmes, Brian Tesler, by failing to appoint him Managing Director. Tesler had gone off to London Weekend Television. Now with a new Managing Director, the former Sales Director George Cooper, at his side, Thomas asked every one in town to be Director of Programmes. Bill Cotton, Stella Richman and others turned him down. I had been Controller of Features, I thought, long enough. I asked for the job, pointing out that although I had no track record in light entertainment or drama, on which the company's success in the ratings battle depended, I was capable of working with those who did. Thomas and Cooper assented. I backed the Controller of Light Entertainment, Philip Jones, and hired a new Controller of Drama, Verity Lambert, and got to work. We never looked back.

Thames was ambitious to excel; it had spare cash to spend on programmes. It had a fair wind from the IBA, which had brought it into being. In an otherwise enthusiastic mid-term report, the IBA had offered one note of criticism; drama and entertainment programmes were too predictable. Could we not be a little more daring, some of the time?

Philip Jones and I set about replacing one set of comedy hits with another. In drama, Verity Lambert pushed the boat out. We seized audiences with series like *Edward and Mrs Simpson*, and political and critical attention with Trevor Griffiths' *Bill Brand* and Howard Schuman's *Rock Follies*. In two years, Thames, unprecedentedly, won three Italia prizes – the most prestigious international television award – one in each available category. The drama prize-winner was *The Naked Civil Servant*, an account of the life of the effeminate homosexual Quentin Crisp, written with point and brevity by Philip Mackie, directed by Jack Gold. Crisp was played with a marvellous dignified flaunting air by John Hurt. The script had been turned down by every film producer in London, and by the BBC. It was as good a script as I had ever read. I persuaded George Cooper that we must do it. Gallantly he agreed. The IBA, too, had to be persuaded; the Broadcasting Act gives the IBA the ultimate editorial say over any programme in the schedule. After wearisome argument, the IBA insisted on cuts, one serious. *The Naked Civil Servant*, to which in the full version no one except at the IBA ever objected, won much applause.

There were arguments, too, over programmes on Northern Ireland. *This Week*, reporting on the fight against IRA terrorism, made a corner through an able reporter, Peter Taylor, in stories on the methods used by the security forces. More alarums at and excursions to the IBA at Brompton Road. These minor irritations apart, all went swimmingly. Or nearly all. At one point I overdid the pursuit of excellence – in peak time; with *Bill Brand*, a documentary series *Destination America*, and ATV's *Clayhanger* at 9 pm, Thames won plaudits and lost audience share on three of its four evenings. The advertisers, with nowhere else to go, paid more for less. But other major commissions redressed that balance. The company looked set to have its franchise renewed and to enjoy a profitable future, as indeed it has.

But Howard Thomas determined to find a new Managing Director to take Thames forward. On a Monday evening in July 1977, I retired to bed, whacked out, in my Chiswick home at 10 pm. The telephone rang. Would I take a call from Peter Fiddick of the *Guardian*? No, not tonight. Next morning, on the doorstep, the *Guardian*'s front page told me that Bryan Cowgill, recently Controller of BBC-1 but now reshuffled up and sideways, a programme executive of a combative temper, was to be Thames's new Managing Director. Cooper was out. Fiddick had picked up the news the previous evening at Guildhall – another Granada lecture – from BBC personnel he met there, who were reeling slightly at the move. Howard Thomas apologized that I had not learned from him of this drastic change. Cooper knew nothing of programmes, Cowgill a great deal.

I gave it a day and rang Cowgill at his home; he had cleared his desk already and was out of the BBC. I congratulated him and wished him well. I would work with him, but we needed to talk. Could I buy him dinner? We met at the Brompton Grill. 'I want only one thing clear,' I said. 'I am Director of Programmes at Thames, and am responsible for programmes, and for the scheduling of them. Is that agreed?' 'Yes,' said Cowgill. 'In that case,' I asked, 'what are you going to do?' There was a long, long silence as he prepared an answer. Eventually: 'I shall make it my business to look after the welfare of 1500 people.' 'Good,' I said. 'Let's drink to that – it needs doing.' But I didn't believe him. The silence spoke louder.

Bryan 'Ginger' Cowgill had – and why not? – very much his own ideas for programmes at Thames. He bought Morecambe and Wise away from the BBC. He tried to buy on Thames's own, and without the ITV network's financial consent and partnership, ten runs in ten years of *The Sound of Music*. He became apopleptic with fury with me because the BBC had bought, and we had not, a minor heavyweight boxing match. Eventually, long after I left, he bought *Dallas*, again without the ITV network, away from the BBC. The IBA, in an extraordinary liaison with the BBC, humiliated Thames and forced the company to give it back.

In January 1978 I had had enough. In the Beverly Wilshire in Los Angeles, where we'd gone on a film-buying trip, Cowgill sewed up, by telephone, the Morecambe and Wise deal – £250,000 a year guaranteed for four shows over two years, cheap, by the way, at the price. We ate one night at Palm, a restaurant which serves lobster and steak, surf and turf. The house's prize exhibit, the stuffed carapace of a monster crustacean that must have weighed over twenty pounds, was wheeled out and put in front of us. In spite of this horrid sight, we each ordered lobster and then meat. Over the steak, I told him I could not work with him. He was giving me no room to move. I must, and would, leave Thames. There was a ghastly pause, and an explosion, not of voice, but of vomit. In a solid, curving arc he spewed up over the table towards me what he had eaten. It turned out later, though this could scarcely have explained the timing of it, that each of us was suffering from some bug. Almost tearfully, he begged me not to go; not to do that to him. We agreed to leave it awhile.

A few months later, as Thames approached the time at which it must reapply for its franchise, I came near the end of my contract as Director of Programmes. Plainly, they must either renew it to take us through the franchise procedure, or let me go, and go on without me. I wanted out; they asked me to stay. It was agreed that Cowgill and Thomas and I would meet on a Friday morning in June 1978 to sort it out. The previous evening Thames was involved in a broadcasting fiasco, brought about by the law which gives the ultimate power to decide what is transmitted not to the ITV broadcaster, but to the regulator, the IBA.

Peter Taylor, for *This Week*, had prepared a programme on the findings of a forthcoming Amnesty International report on the treatment of suspects by the RUC at Castlereagh interrogation centre in Northern Ireland. The IBA ordered us in advance not to screen our programme until the Amnesty report was formally published, and ministers had had a chance to comment in the House of Commons. What the rationale was for this extraordinary ukase, I never discovered. The Amnesty report was extensively quoted in the *Guardian* on the Monday of that week, and later on BBC-1's *24 Hours*. To all our pleas to publish the IBA remained adamant. The full Authority backed its officers on the Thursday morning, the day of *This Week*'s transmission. That afternoon the Secretary of State for Northern Ireland referred to the matter in the House of Commons. Surely, now, the IBA would alter its view, at least if logic meant anything? They would not. I ordered a substitute programme but rather than put it out the ACTT members in Thames's Euston Road headquarters blacked the screen for its half-hour duration. Understandable, but an illiberal act. Cowgill and I were equally angry at the result of the IBA's intervention. The following morning, as I prepared to discuss my future, BBC Television's early evening news magazine *Nationwide* asked to use some of the banned material. I agreed it could be made available to them. At the meeting in Thomas's office I said that, not having room to work freely, I preferred to leave Thames. 'I know just how you feel, love,' said my friend the actor and comedian Jimmy Jewell. 'It was the same for me in *Nearest and Dearest* with that Hylda Baker. There just wasn't room for two of us.'

1978 was a good time to be free. The ITV franchises were coming up. (Some friends and I developed a project, but packed it in.) The Labour Government was dickering with the future of the fourth channel. There might be work for me – there would need to be – as an independent producer.

Like many freelances, I took on too much work at too little reward. The BBC asked me to work with Robert Kee on a television history of Ireland. I said yes, and enjoyed it, but settled for a modest fee. I asked Bill Brown at Scottish Television if his company would collaborate with mine in making a fictional film on the life story of a convicted murderer, Jimmy Boyle, then in the Special Unit of Barlinnie Prison in Glasgow. They would and did, at their considerable cost. I waived my fees to split the sales proceeds with STV – there were none. My company – my wife Tamara, myself and a letterhead – hired the producer Tom Steel to work with us on a film for New Zealand Television on the Battle for Crete to be ready for the fortieth anniversary in 1981. The film cost NZTV £80,000 to make. I hoped to recoup some of that for NZTV and for my company also by selling it in the UK. The BBC would only pay £3000 for it, take it or leave it. The life of an independent producer, it was salutary but unsurprising to discover, was no bed of roses.

Another experience had other useful lessons to teach. Early in 1979 I became a governor of the British Film Institute (BFI), and chairman of its Production Board. Once the Experimental Film Fund, the Board had a commitment to new and different work that could not be funded in the commercial sector. It had funded Kevin Brownlow's *Winstanley* and Bill Douglas' trilogy on his bleak Scottish childhood. But now it had, in the view of the governors, become too esoteric in its preferences. Many of the members were heavily into semiology and film theory. Some were avant-garde minimalists, some oppositional leftists. All assumed that the theoretical intention of the script or the interest of its techniques of representation were a guarantee, somehow, of its worth as a film.

The Chairman of the Governors of the BFI, Sir Basil Engholm KCB, once Permanent Secretary at the Ministry of Agriculture and Fisheries, asked me to take this lot on and see if I could not find support for more accessible films which might find audiences in cinemas.

Coming from the shelter of ITV, I found myself in culture shock. The names of Barthes and Lacan were on every lip, and on nearly every script. The movies that resulted were often of a tedium that was almost comic. The Board, which included representatives of the Independent Film-makers Association (IFA), was riven by faction. At the first meeting over which I presided which would actually allocate our tiny store of funds, cabals kept forming and reforming as members horse-traded, coalescing to stop X in return for support for Y. In the heat of the argument one charge of betrayal rang out that has stuck with me: 'You are an opportunist, and when I use that word I do so in its strictly Leninist sense.'

I brought new members on to the Board. We put emphasis on verve and viewability – anathema to the ideologues – in some of what we funded. Under me and my successors, the Production Board began to make low-budget feature films. Some were rather good, some excellent. It is to the BFI that we owe Ed Bennett's *Ascendancy*, Peter Greenaway's *The Draughtsman's Contract*, Terence Davies' *Distant Voices, Still Lives*, Derek Jarman's *Caravaggio*. And it is to my time at the BFI that I owe an education in the values of 'independent cinema' and of an 'independent film practice'.

Here were serious people, working outside the commercial cinema and outside television, for which they had for the most part a lofty contempt. They had something to say, and were struggling in some cases to find a new film language in which to say it. Surely the best of their work had some claim to be seen on, and to be funded by, a new television channel? Bill Douglas' masterly autobiographical trilogy, *My Childhood*, *My Ain Folk*, and *My Way Home*, was screened by BBC Television. But Kevin Brownlow's remarkable *Winstanley* was rejected. To the suggestion that work of this calibre deserved a showing, the response of BBC-TV's Managing Director Aubrey Singer was that it was not good enough, and never would be. The BBC knew best. Independent film-makers wanted a fourth channel on which other standards prevailed.

The Queen's Speech of 1979 gave the channel to the IBA, 'with strict safeguards'. But what safeguards? Would these be designed to protect the quality of programmes? To take some account of minority interests? To provide opportunities for independent producers? There was no joy for the advertisers; it looked as if ITV would sell the time on both channels, and with the same sales force. The monopoly the advertisers so resented would not be broken. They wanted two competitive services, 'but must forgo this,' said the IBA's Director-General Sir Brian Young in a speech on 26 June, 'in the interests of the viewers at large'. Advertisers' deep grievance at this constant cold shoulder found no echo in the Downing Street of those days.

It was on the precise construction of the new channel that most work remained to be done. Who would own it? Who would control it? How would it relate to ITV? Would it be run by committees which would attempt to reconcile the various conflicting interests that might be involved? In his June speech the IBA's Director-General seemed still to be saying it would.

Lady Plowden, Chairman of the IBA, an energetic public servant who had already been Vice-Chairman of the BBC Board of Governors, welcomed the opportunity given to the Authority to show what it could do. She gathered the voices of independent producers, and was impressed by their numbers, their abilities, and their confident claim to be able to provide a large share of the new channel's output. She concerned herself with the role and status of women in the industry, and urged improvement. And, with her long concern for the nation's schooling, she would insist on a sizeable educational element in the channel's programme provision. I went to an IBA consultation on drama at St Andrews in July to which, perhaps to show that though I had left Thames I was not forgotten, I was particularly bidden. I made a brief contribution. Socially, putting at risk all hope of preferment, I took on the Chairman of the IBA at table tennis and beat her 21–7. Bridget Horatia Plowden took it like the good sport she is.

The Director-General Sir Brian Young applied his mind to structures, and rationally laid out options for the future. He was fond of the algorithm as a device for guiding thought; thus many of us learned a new word late in life, if not a new technique of planning. Young was no creature of the ITV companies, and would ensure they had no roughshod ride over others' interests in the settlement to come.

The detailed work of planning, and of liaison with Shirley Littler at the Home Office – she later became Deputy Director-General of the IBA – fell to the IBA's Director of Television, once Secretary to the BBC Board of Governors, Colin Shaw. If the inspiration was Tony Smith's and the clout was Willie Whitelaw's, much of the staffwork that finally determined

the form and temper of the new channel and shaped its destiny we owe
to the Home Office, to the IBA and to Colin Shaw. Passed over to succeed
Brian Young as Director-General, Shaw never received the credit that
was his due. In the dining room of the Charing Cross Hotel, once a haunt
of Betjeman's but now a carvery, one evening that summer, he and I –
but Colin was the soul of discretion – exchanged ideas. I was preparing
to speak on 'TV in the Eighties' at Edinburgh at the end of August. Colin
was obviously hard at work consulting with the Home Office. Was ITN,
owned by the ITV companies but under its own editor, a model for the
new channel? Perhaps. Or something like it. We drifted off, separately,
into the night.

*   *   *

On the afternoon of Bank Holiday Monday, 27 August 1979, I arrived
with Tamara at the George Hotel in Edinburgh to deliver the James
MacTaggart Memorial Lecture at the Television Festival. We came from
Aberawen, our second home at Ceibwr in north Pembrokeshire. The
summer days had been spent partly, as usual, walking the narrow switch-
back of the coastal path and the broad sweep of the Preselis, partly hunched
scribbling over the kitchen table.

We had interrupted our quiet time in West Wales – work as ever
intruding – to take the ferry from Fishguard to Rosslare, en route to
Londonderry and Belfast. As an independent producer, I was then making
Ireland – A Television History for the BBC, and was to film the annual
Apprentice Boys' March in Londonderry and a Sinn Féin parade up
Belfast's Falls Road to Roger Casement Park. The procession through
Catholic West Belfast straggled its way in a Sunday downpour on to the
football field. Most of the audience for the speeches took refuge from the
heavy rain in the stand, leaving only the cameramen on the platform
erected opposite it, and a thin line of supporters beneath gazing up. I,
too, ducked in out of the weather and was received into a small partitioned
space in the centre of the stand, a sort of directors' box, where I looked
out at the banners in Gaelic – Sassenachs Go Home, Brits Out – and at the
dark green and black berets of the paramilitary stewards, one Palestinian
Khefiyah among them, in a solidarity of nationalism and violence. The
speeches lifted spirits and tempers. A man with a microphone came up
the stairs beside me and sang; the Irish people would not be defeated till
the British had gone. The IRA had arms still, and would fight on. As he

ended two hooded figures stood suddenly in his place, brandishing Sten guns, a man and a woman at my right shoulder, received with acclamation, in whose eyes I read hate. They vanished into the crowd. Later there was some stone-throwing; no one was hurt.

In Edinburgh, a fortnight later, the Television Festival's organizing chairman, Paul Bonner, greeted me. Had I heard the news? Lord Mountbatten, on holiday with his family on the coast of Donegal, had been murdered with others by an IRA bomb. The lecture on 'TV in the Eighties' would go ahead. In the Physicians Hall in Queen Street I began to speak.

'In Wales, if they are not written in the right language, they knock the signposts down. In Ireland they tend to put roadsigns at or after the crossroads, not before.' Here I was, putting up signposts to 'TV in the Eighties' just before we entered them. Much of what I had to say dealt with the BBC and ITV. I had worked for both, and was now independent of either. What the audience was waiting for was what I had to say about the fourth channel. I tried to sum up what we knew; it was to the IBA that the government had entrusted responsibility for the fourth channel; that meant it would be ITV-2, and would be called ITV-2. (In this I was, in the end, mistaken.) We were not to have an OBA; those who fought for it had won the argument but lost the vote. The idea of the OBA, the broadcasting institution as publisher, not author, would remain, and influence our practice. But the new channel was placed under a regulatory authority, it would not disseminate its offerings through a liberal publishing sieve. Nor would the channel compete all out for audience with ITV-1; that was what the advertisers wanted, but they were to be disappointed. The consensus was still against arranging broadcasting in their interest.

What sort of fourth channel did we want? I asked. And answered:

> We want a fourth channel which extends the choice available to
> viewers: which extends the range of ITV's programmes; which caters
> for substantial minorities presently neglected; which builds in to its
> actuality programmes a complete spectrum of political attitude and
> opinion; which furthers, in a segment of its programming, some broad
> educational purposes; which encourages worthwhile independent
> production; which allows the larger regional ITV companies to show
> us what their programme-makers can do. We want a fourth channel

that will neither simply compete with ITV-1 nor merely be complementary to it. We want a fourth channel that everyone will watch some of the time and no one all the time. We want a fourth channel that will, somehow, be different.

Could these objectives be realized on ITV-2? 'I believe they can, although I have to say I would not be optimistic if the channel were to be run by the IBA's proposed planning group, or by the Companies Programme Controllers' Group enlarged. If the channel is to have a different flavour it needs a different chef . . . ' I was making a general point, not merely staking a claim. But, having said it, I could not complain when some wit tagged my speech 'The MacTaggart Memorial Job Application'.*

The speech that really mattered came two weeks later, on Friday 14 September, at the Royal Television Society Convention in Cambridge. The Home Secretary, Willie Whitelaw, spelled out the Government's intentions. 'I start from the position that what we are looking for is a fourth channel offering a distinctive service of its own.'

The IBA, Whitelaw made clear, would run it; finance would come from the sale of spot advertising, but not from selling time competitively against ITV. That would lead inevitably towards 'single-minded concentration on maximizing audiences, with adverse consequences for both of the commercial channels, and before long for the BBC as well.' There must be 'programmes appealing to and, we hope, stimulating tastes and interests not adequately provided for on the existing channels'. It was wrong to call these 'minority' interests since the proportions of the population thus appealed to 'may in some cases be numbered in millions'. It would be, except for Wales, a new national programme service with, at first, no regional opt-outs. The service should start as soon as it could be transmitted to and received by a substantial proportion of the population throughout the country. (Rather than creep in slowly as had BBC-2.) It was not to be dominated by ITV's Big Five; there should be a substantial contribution from the ITV regional companies. The news was 'clearly a job for ITN with the resources to do it, and its admirable record'. (An honest view; but Whitelaw had been well lobbied here.) This would be an opportunity for 'far more extended treatment of news'.

*The MacTaggart Memorial Lecture for 1979 is printed in abridged form in the *Listener*, 6 September 1979, pp. 298–300.

Of critical importance, the Home Secretary laid down that programmes were to come not just from the ITV companies but from independent producers. They must receive a fair return for their products. They should supply 'the largest practicable proportion of programmes on the fourth channel'. In Edinburgh I had suggested that independents should start small and grow; Whitelaw was saying they should punch their full weight, the fullest possible weight, from the start.

The Home Secretary spoke from years of involvement in the politics of broadcasting. He reaffirmed his and the government's support, citing Annan, for the principles that had determined the structure of British broadcasting in a free society:

> that broadcasting services should continue to be provided as public services, should continue to be the responsibility of public authorities, and that these broadcasting authorities should be independent of government in the day-to-day conduct of their business. Furthermore, that the broadcasting authorities should continue to be responsible for the content of programmes, for ensuring that the services are conducted in the general public interest and are in accordance with the requirements and objectives which Parliament places on each authority.

Authorities accountable to Parliament, Parliament to the electorate; that was the British way.

Whatever the skill of the various hands that helped in its drafting – and Shirley Littler's at the Home Office was the most prominent – it was the speech of a statesman. Whitelaw's utterance conveyed a profound understanding of what broadcasting can mean in a democratic society. It was marked also by a practical common sense. It was wise 'to leave a wide measure of discretion to the broadcasting authorities'. On the other hand, the IBA 'is entitled to a reasonably clear indication of what it is that the law expects of it'.

All governments wrestle with the contradictions inherent in deciding whether to control broadcasting or set it free. Whitelaw's Broadcasting Bill would get the balance between prescription and licence exactly right.

In November the IBA declared its hand. It would set up, and in the end own, a non-profit-making company to run the new channel through a board appointed by the IBA; the board of twelve or fourteen would contain four members from the ITV companies, while 'five others would be able to speak on behalf of other potential suppliers of programmes'. The Chairman, Deputy Chairman and two executive directors would make up the numbers. The funds would come from the ITV companies. The IBA would oversee programme schedules and ensure complementarity with ITV. There would be no quotas governing the supply of programmes. The ITV companies would sell the advertising, and retain the proceeds. A new transmitter network, already ordered, would carry the new channel's signal to 80 per cent of the United Kingdom in two years' time.

In February came the Bill. It spoke still of ITV's 'Service 2'. Later this was changed, in committee, to the 'fourth channel service'. The qualitative objectives the Bill set out for the channel were its most remarkable feature, and were to become a matter for study, envy and emulation by other broadcasters worldwide.

The IBA was required to ensure that the fourth channel service would contain 'a suitable proportion of matter calculated to appeal to tastes and interests not generally catered for by ITV'. The IBA was required to see to it that 'a suitable proportion of the programmes was of an educational nature'. The channel was to be required by statute, uniquely among the world's broadcasting institutions, 'to encourage innovation and experiment in the form and content of programmes'. The channel was to have 'overall, a distinctive character of its own'.

Set beside this determining rubric, all details of structure and finance and governance, though crucial to the operation, were but means to an enlightened and potentially exciting end.

ITV welcomed the Bill, and what it proposed, without qualification. When it came to it, their monopoly of advertising was to be sustained and extended. The independents welcomed the Bill also, and the provision the Bill made for them to act as suppliers, but, suspicious of ITV's welcome and concerned to change the channel's name, they lobbied hard to improve it. The winter wore on.

I had a living to earn, work to do. In the BBC cutting rooms at Kensington House, I helped squeeze into shape thirteen episodes of *Ireland – A Television History*, marvelling anew at Robert Kee's unerring ability to marry the word to the image as he sat in the cutting room, writing. The writing of the film and the making of it, he had taught me – the best lesson I had in television – are the same process. Now he made that maxim good again. The first six episodes, taking Ireland's history from the mists of antiquity to the end of the nineteenth century, were agonizingly difficult; we, and the director Jenny Barraclough, made bricks without visual straw. There were no photographs, no newsreel film. The last seven had the benefits of newsreel aplenty; eyewitnesses to the 1916 Rising, eyewitnesses to the War of Independence in 1919, and the Civil War that followed it, still living; eyewitnesses, and the camera's witness, to the events of 1969 onwards in the North, still living and still dying. These later programmes posed an easier task. We had to go as high as Sir Ian Trethowan, Director-General of the BBC, to receive permission to include statements by IRA men in the final programme, 'Prisoners of History'. The story could not be well or fully told without them. In the Republic, the law preventing their being quoted on television was waived to see us clear.

On the freezing streets of Maryhill in a Glasgow winter, I worked with Peter McDougall, the writer, John MacKenzie who directed, cameraman Chris Menges and an STV crew to film *A Sense of Freedom*. This was the story of convicted murderer Jimmy Boyle's nasty, brutish and short life in the streets, and of his long years in brutal solitary in Peterhead and Inverness, foreshadowing but not delineating his growth and rehabilitation. Popping in to see him, between takes, in the Special Unit of Barlinnie Prison, I was offered crusty home-baked bread and excellent salads; the prisoners in the unit had won the right to buy and prepare their own food. Glasgow, or some of it, was up in arms over our film on 'Scotland's hardest man', as they persisted in calling him. We needed room to film in. Glasgow's councillors repudiated the short leases we had negotiated on premises they owned. Scottish Television successfully injuncted the Council to compel performance. The *Daily Record*, a lively, leftish tabloid, had it in for us, the news editor daily urging his reporters to find evidences of shock or horror at our presence and intentions. After days of headlines – 'Residents Outrage at Murder Movie' sort of thing – the *Record* finally gave way gracefully. Eight days into filming, on an inside page, the demure crosshead appeared: 'Quiet Day on Boyle Film'. The media fires of Glasgow were to stand me in good stead later.

In May to Crete for the film for New Zealand, commemorating the heroism the two island peoples had displayed under the German airborne invasion in 1941. Interviews with combatants in the villages, orchards, hay meadows above Maleme airfield; the ceremony of proud remembrance at Galatas; boozy reunions. The shepherd George Psychoundakis, who served the resistance as a runner, had astonished his commander Patrick Leigh Fermor after the war by producing a clear, simple narrative of all he saw and did, which Leigh Fermor translated and had published in English as *The Cretan Runner*. Now, with a harsh irony, Psychoundakis tended the graves in the German war cemetery above the Maleme road. There he autographed copies of his memoir and, for me, of his translation of the *Odyssey* into Cretan rhyming couplets. The *Iliad* was to follow. We sniffed the thyme and oregano on the mountains and drank deep of ouzo and good fellowship.

*   *   *

The IBA now announced it would set up a panel of consultants; they could not be constituted as a board to run Channel 4 until the Broadcasting Bill had passed into law. They appointed a Chairman and Deputy Chairman; these were to be the Rt Hon. Edmund Dell, an ex-Labour Minister for Trade and Industry and Paymaster-General, now Chairman and Chief Executive of Guinness Peat, and Sir Richard Attenborough, actor and film-maker, brother of David, the BBC's admired natural historian and author of *Life on Earth*, and once the pioneering Controller of BBC-2. Attenborough knew of me through David. Dell, when he kept reading my name touted as a possible to run the channel, made clear he had never heard of me. 'Who is this Jeremy Isaacs?' he asked a friend. As is not unheard of in major broadcasting appointments, he did not then possess a television set.

Some appointed to the panel knew television, and me, better; they included Anthony Smith, and another freelance producer on the independent ticket, Roger Graef; and, from ITV, an old Thames boss, Brian Tesler, now of LWT, and Bill Brown, Managing Director of Scottish Television, with whom I was still working on *A Sense of Freedom*. In July the two jobs of the executives sought to run the channel were advertised. From my point of view, an absolutely critical decision had been taken as to which was to be the senior. I was, first and last, a programme person, an editor. But I wanted now to be in charge. The panel was not looking for a Managing Director with the editorial figure, a Director of Programmes, reporting to him. The advertisement was for a Chief Executive who would be responsible for the procurement of all programmes, with a Director of Finance under him. After much debate, on the grounds that the new channel was about programmes or it was about nothing, they had decided that the editorial, the creative figure, was to have ultimate authority. They had put on offer the job of my dreams.

At first, bemused by the too-good-to-be-true attraction of it, I did nothing. A message was conveyed; did I mean to apply? If so, would I please write. I wrote, setting out my priorities. They were:

> To encourage innovation across the whole range of programmes;
> To find audiences for the channel and for all its programmes;
> To make programmes of special appeal to particular audiences;
> To develop the channel's educational potential to the full;
> To provide platforms for the widest possible range of opinion
> in utterance, discussion and debate;
> To maintain as flexible a schedule as practicable to enable a
> quick response to changing needs;
> To make an opening in the channel for criticism of its own
> output;
> To accord a high priority to the arts;
> If funds allow, to make, or help make, films of feature length for
> television here, for the cinema abroad.

I received an impersonal acknowledgement. Eventually I was summoned to an interview in Brompton Road. 'Thank you, Mr Isaacs, that will be all.' Silence. Rumours that others were favoured – John Birt, Brian Wenham (but had he applied?). There was a dark horse; but who? Another summons, another interview. Tamara drove me on a Friday morning in late September to the IBA. 'How do you find and put together a schedule of programmes? How can you ensure they are of any interest?' 'You say yes to good ideas; no to bad ones.' 'Last question' (from Dell): 'How should a chief executive relate to a chairman?' 'He should keep him informed of anything of moment, consult him and seek to carry him with him in any major matter.' 'Thank you.' And out. We drove back to Chiswick, lunched in a pub at Strand-on-the-Green, came home, went to bed. At half past three the telephone rang. It was Edmund Dell. 'We have resolved unanimously to offer you the job. Congratulations. Can you come and see me now in my office?'

3

Ready Steady Go

EDMUND DELL received me in a cool, bare office, with the tidiest of desks, at Guinness Peat's headquarters at St Mary at Hill. We agreed on a five-year contract, to start formally on 1 January 1981. I offered to work till then without fee if I could have a fortnight's holiday early in the New Year. And we agreed on salary. He mentioned £30,000 a year; the level had been set by the IBA and would have to bear some relation to what was paid at Brompton Road. I asked for £35,000. He thought he was, or could be, authorized to go so far.

'One other thing,' he said, 'which I put to you not as a condition of contract but as the very strong wish of my colleagues on the panel. At the interviews they have been very impressed by another candidate, Paul Bonner. We want you to consider taking him on to work under you on the programme side.' I was taken aback but did not hesitate to say yes. Paul Bonner was Head of BBC-TV's Science and Features. He had consulted me earlier that summer – we were both working at BBC's Kensington House. Over a Chinese lunch in Kensington High Street, suitably alcoved against prying ears, Paul had confided to me that he was thinking of applying for the fourth channel job when it came up. 'Of course,' I said, 'you must.' He had done so, and done well, impressing the panel with his large competence, and his experience of 'access television' – he had run the BBC's *Open Door* and its Community Unit. He had been the dark horse at the interviews, nipping in ahead of the other serious short-listed candidate, John Birt of LWT. Birt had come forward, I found out later, with a plan for perpetual diversity, every programme

aimed at a particular self-selecting interest group – birdwatchers, motor-
cycle enthusiasts, gardeners, anglers – the whole backed up by bulky
research into specialized print magazine circulations and readerships, on
the lines of a lecture he had given in Edinburgh the year before.* What
he offered was his vision, not mine. But I thought instantly that Paul
Bonner and I could work together. I was not willing, I stipulated, to cede
authority over programmes, but a role, and a title, could be worked out.
I undertook to see him over the weekend and confirm whether we could
agree or not.

Paul Bonner was a programme-maker and had a basic grasp and understanding of certain essential practicalities of television that have always
totally eluded me. I can, just, change an electric light bulb; even, in dire
necessity, mend a fuse. There my understanding of the applied science of
broadcasting begins and ends. Cameras point at things in studios; there is
gadgetry; signals – but how? – leave that space and whizz through the air
or down a line to a transmitter, whence they whizz through the air again
to a receiver in your home or mine, arranged in zillions of dots on 625
lines, looking, miraculously, something like the picture the camera was
taking in the first place. If, as a television producer, you are trying to
concentrate on what information – I use the term in its non-technical
sense – that picture should contain, it is a great relief never to have to pay
attention to how it is going to enter, via an aerial on someone's roof, the
back of a television set, and then, arranged in these little lines, move on
to the screen at the front. For more than twenty years I had been content
to leave all that to others. But now, in charge of a channel, I should have
to take overall responsibility for the whole of this process, and for a new
channel with a new, purpose-built transmission system to boot. Paul
Bonner understood these mysteries. He was likely to prove – indeed did
prove – essential to the enterprise. Over a celebratory drink in Chiswick –
it was my birthday that Sunday – we sealed it. I jibbed at Programme
Controller for his title, being determined to have my way there, which
the advertised job description had provided. We agreed on Channel
Controller as apt and suitably grand.

Corks popped. Friends were let in on the hard-to-guard secret. Rumour
rippled. On the Tuesday morning the IBA planned a press conference for
Edmund Dell, the Chairman of the Panel of Consultants which was soon

*'Freedom of the Broadcaster', *Listener*, 13 September 1979.

to be the Board of the Channel 4 Television Company Ltd, and myself, its Chief Executive. I had thought their press statement would do it, but I found myself, over the breakfast table that morning, inventing and dictating into the telephone a statement of my own. It was taken down and faultlessly reproduced by a bright-as-a-button secretary to the Secretary of the Consultants, Susan Crowson. The new channel, I hazarded, would be 'lively, responsive to viewers' changing needs, useful, fun'.

Edmund Dell introduced me, a trifle ruefully, as someone whose appointment had been 'extensively forecast in the press'. Paul Bonner could not be there that morning. There was later some adverse comment that his post had been filled without its having been advertised.

At the press conference I reiterated that there would be no supply quotas; no one would have programmes accepted 'as of right and willy-nilly'. I challenged the ITV companies to extend and improve upon the service they already provided; the independents to demonstrate the quality of their work; and innovators and newcomers to the screen 'to speak to television audiences in a language they will understand'. The channel would serve and represent a broad spectrum of opinion, from extreme left to extreme right. But there must be selection. There would not be room for everybody; 'there will not be room for loonies'.

There is, and has remained, a large measure of agreement between those most closely concerned as to what ends the fourth channel should broadly fulfil, however fiercely at times there has been dispute over particular means to those ends. Channel 4, as we shortly decided to call it, was not, *pace* Isaacs in Edinburgh, to be known as ITV-2. More importantly, it was not to be ITV-2. It was not owned by ITV. But neither was Channel 4 the OBA of Annan's recommendation. It was to be owned by and regulated by the IBA. It was indubitably part of the ITV system. Whoever ran it would have to get on with those who ran ITV, as well as with the new breed of independent producers challenging ITV's dominance. The channel was asked to be different, to provide a distinctive service. But the channel, as was made clear in the parliamentary debates that determined the final wording of the Bill that brought it into being, would also be expected, sooner or later, to pay its way. Leon Brittan MP, Minister of State at the Home Office steering the Bill through Committee, thought three years was about right for that; Channel 4 would about then be expected to return to ITV in advertising revenue the funds ITV would put up by subscription to finance it. That meant the channel's programmes, however innovative, would need to reach and hold audiences.

At Edinburgh, when asked how different Channel 4 might be, I had replied, and been magisterially reproved for the timidity of the reply, 'different, but not that different'. But I knew I was right. An artist – writing, painting, making music – can be, can afford to be utterly true to the singularity of his or her vision, almost irrespective, at least for a time, of whether that particularity is communicated to others or not. Such an artist is not dependent on reaching audiences, except to pay the bills. Broadcasting, though it can certainly be a medium for artistic expression, is not a solitary art. If the channel were to carry innovative work, and that was its explicit purpose, it must somehow find audiences for that work either by the work itself reaching out to viewers, or because other more familiar work the channel broadcast brought in those audiences and dared them to expose themselves also to the shock of the new.

Since my earliest days in it, I have been sure that broadcasting is not for broadcasters but for the audiences it serves. That is why my job application set out as its highest priorities both the statutory need to innovate and the no less urgent need, required not by statute but by common sense, to reach and serve audiences with the programmes we would put in front of them. To realize ideals there must be practical means. There needed to be work on Channel 4 different from anything produced at the BBC or in ITV. But it need not, could not, wholly overlay and colour the channel's output. Art for art's sake, and a place for it on television; but broadcasting for audiences' sake.

A new fourth channel must extend viewers' choice. It must entice new viewers to television; call disenchanted viewers back. It must serve viewers, or fail. To offer nothing familiar, to house only experiment, would be a brave way to die. We were not licensed, as was *l'Institut National de l'Audio-visuel* (INA), in France, to cater for an hour or so only for connoisseurs of invention. We had been handed a larger, public trust; would spend many millions of pounds each year; would broadcast for maybe fifty hours a week.

The programming would be a mix, as cunning a mix as I could contrive, of the familiar and the challenging. It would relate to various socio-political goals: women's rights were, and wanted to be, in the air; Afro-Caribbean and Asian Britons' claims were on the table, and had the IBA's backing. Young people watched little television; they had better things to do. But they deserved a service. There was a need for a longer, slower, more analytic news programme. The fourth channel had an obligation to educate. These were not ends that could be met by broadcasters' or would-be broadcasters' self-indulgence. The channel must connect. But, against the habitual conventions of broadcasting, the channel ought not to count its audiences only in tens of millions or millions. Most of those tastes were catered for elsewhere. Above all, the fourth channel should not think of itself as addressing only one audience, a single undifferentiated mass, a country-wide agglomeration of nuclear families. The audience was also a single person in a single room.

Advertisers used ITV to reach mass audiences. They easily targeted millions of housewives. With more difficulty they found men watching sport. I had for four years been a member of the Programme Controllers' Group that arranged ITV's schedule. That schedule aimed programmes only at audiences of millions, and tens of millions. Nothing smaller was of interest. ITV's comedies – Thames's hugely successful output had been a prime example – eschewed specialization of any sort in favour of broad appeal.

At A-R, as Head of Children's Programmes in the late Sixties, I had come up with *Do Not Adjust Your Set*; in it, produced by Humphrey Barclay, there first flowered on television the talents of Terry Jones, Michael Palin, Eric Idle. It also featured David Jason and Denise Coffey. Broadcast in children's time, adults left work early to get home in time to see it. But there was no place for it in Thames's peak-time schedule – too risky. Jones, Palin and Idle teamed up with John Cleese and Terry Gilliam to create *Monty Python's Flying Circus* for the BBC. Later, as Director of Programmes at Thames, it took me three years to find a slot for Kenny Everett's brand of anarchic rudery, though my son John fell off the sofa laughing when he saw it, particularly at the naughty bits. 'The family audience' for ITV came first and last. High millions mattered; low millions hardly counted; hundreds of thousands counted not at all. *The World at War* found favour because it did find and hold audiences of many millions for twenty-six consecutive weeks. *Black Man's Burden*, an expensive documentary on poverty in Africa (expensive partly because the crew insisted on staying in a five-star luxury hotel at some distance from the location) was another matter. I persuaded my predecessor as Director of Progammes at Thames, Brian Tesler, to schedule this, against his wiser judgement, at 9 pm instead of after *News at Ten*. *Black Man's Burden* resulted in the steepest drop of peak-time ratings ever recorded, a blip of altruism in

Thames's invariably immaculate scheduling. More than a million watched the programme, and may have benefited from it. But that was not the point. It was the many millions who switched over or off that mattered.

Channel 4 would cater for millions, but for smaller audiences also. It would approach the viewers it sought to reach not as *the* audience, but as disparate, differing audiences, each composed perhaps of hundreds of thousands – as many, I used to point out to doubting colleagues, as would fill Wembley Stadium several times over. And each audience had individual tastes and preferences, each made choices of their own. The few viewers eagerly looking out for avant-garde minimalism were certainly an important audience. But, given the need to pay our way, repeats of *Upstairs, Downstairs* would also be deployed to find audiences vital to survival.

Channel 4 would not be just for self-selecting minorities, but for all of us, at least in some of our viewing time. I would work with ITV and with the most innovative of independents to reach and satisfy the audiences we were jointly to serve. The two horses threatened to pull apart, of course, rather than together. But this bareback rider would attempt to ride both, and in the same direction.

In the press, the talk was all of money. How could the channel provide a decent service on the short commons it was to be allowed? Television's managers were then applying, for the first time, total costing techniques to programmes. They shuddered at the figures; entertainment, news and current affairs, the expensive categories, were running to over £100,000 an hour, drama at thrice that. (Michael Checkland, then the BBC's Controller of Planning and Resource Management, gave an impressive analysis of cost realities at a Royal Television Society conference at Southampton in early November; he was reportedly offered three jobs in ITV.) The fourth channel was to operate on far smaller funds than those available to the most economical of its rivals. How could it possibly provide anything other than a feeble shadow of a service at an average cost of £30,000 an hour? At those figures, some wondered if it could ever be worth watching. But the sums never worried me. The IBA had calculated that the subscription it would levy on the ITV companies, who would soon be reapplying for their profitable franchises, might provide about £70 million in a full year. We would get by on that.

Of course, if one thought of all the channel's output as commissioned programmes, the total cost of whose production was to be covered, it was difficult to make the sums come out. But much of what we would broadcast

I knew, but was not yet saying, would be acquired material, foraged from the bazaars of the world. And some would be repeated material, picked up at a mere fraction of its total original cost, and still likely to find new audiences. (Many of today's satellite services will offer little else.) And some would be provided below full cost by ITV companies who retained rights in their material while allowing us the two UK transmissions we needed. No; whatever budget was ultimately granted us, we would stay within it and provide a service.

At Southampton in November 1980 I was asked what the channel would be called – the Fourth Channel, Channel 4 Television, or what? I said Channel 4, and, ultimately, 4.

Others at the conference had other preoccupations. Our hosts were Southern Television. We were greeted thus: 'Good morning. My name is Michael Barrett. I am Master Carpenter here. It is my great pleasure to welcome you all to our studios here at Southampton. I now hand you over to someone who some of us think would be better fitted, but fortunate, to be employed here as a tradesman, Mr David Wilson, our Managing Director.'

David Wilson's hospitality culminated in a grand seaside binge. Southern's Head of Light Entertainment, Bryan Izzard, his ample figure clothed in velvet and lace, invited the guests to join in singing Victorian ballads and sea-shanties. They ended with 'There'll Always Be An England'.

There was not always to be a Southern Television, however. Eight weeks later the company heard from the IBA that it had lost its franchise, and in a year would be out of business.

Channel 4 had a franchise, and would soon have adequate financing. It did not have much time to make its mind up what to do. Government and the IBA wanted the new service to start as soon as possible. The IBA was building, at a further charge levied on the ITV companies, a new transmission system which would ultimately cover the country. To reach all parts of the United Kingdom would require the construction of fifty-one main transmitters, on sites shared with ITV and BBC, and about 850 other transmitters and booster relay stations, carrying the signal up hill and down dale to communities of as few as 250 souls. It is one of the beneficent conditions of public service broadcasting as we understand it in Britain that coverage should be universal, with provision for all. Satellite and cable obey no such categorical imperative. Channel 4's coverage would spread as rapidly as equipment could be supplied, and as the IBA's large, but unaugmented, labour force of engineers could build. It would not spread evenly, and would not, as previous transmitter systems had done – ITV, BBC-2 – spread slowly out of London, covering the most densely populated areas of the country first, its most remote fastnesses last. On this occasion it was intended to favour Wales, which was now, after a U-turn, to have a fourth channel service of its own, and even the Highlands of Scotland, before the blessing of a Channel 4 signal was brought to all of the prosperous South-East, or to the South-West. Some of those ITV franchisees, therefore, who contributed most to the cost of the new channel – TVS in the wealthy South-East is the best example – would, in the earliest days, receive the least benefit. And those cultivated and affluent viewers in, say, Surrey, who might be expected most to welcome a sophisticated new service, and whom advertisers were most eager to reach, would have to wait longest to receive us.

Channel 4 would enjoy one advantage denied to all its predecessors. It would be able, on its first day, to address the larger part of the nation. At our start coverage was 87 per cent, and 99 per cent four years later. In our case, when local transmitters were in place and on beam, all viewers needed to do was first to make sure that the set was tuned to receive our signal, then push the unused fourth button, usually marked ITV-2, on the set.

In the most inconvenient cases, it might be necessary to fit a new aerial. We must persuade our public to be ready to do that. But the set was there already; the signal soon would be. At the launch of BBC-2 in 1964 the signal crept slowly out of London, taking nineteen years before it reached 99 per cent of the United Kingdom. To receive it at all, in 625 lines on UHF, viewers had to buy a new television set. A snail's pace by comparison.

Channel 4's task in pleasing and keeping audiences might be more difficult than BBC-2's – there were already three channels vying for attention. But Channel 4's task in reaching those audiences would be infinitely easier, thanks to the IBA's transmitter-building programme.

The IBA ordered that transmissions should start as soon as coverage amounted to 80 per cent of the prospective audience; that was expected to be, if the building schedule held, two years away, in November 1982. We would go on air as early in that month, therefore, as possible. An incidental advantage, I thought, for ITV who would sell the air-time, would be having us on air in the bonanza months for advertising before Christmas. January was always bleaker.

Another broadcaster would be keen to start also in November 1982 – simultaneously, if they could, with us. In December 1981 Peter Jay's TV-am had been awarded a breakfast franchise on the ITV channel. They asked to launch jointly with us. My colleagues were adamant they should not share the limelight; we needed a head start. The ITV companies against whom they would compete for revenue were also opposed. The IBA agreed, and held TV-am back. They were to play a different role in our affairs.

There was no time to lose. The IBA, in a decision which more than anything else was to characterize the structure of the new channel, following Anthony Smith's publishing house model, had laid down that we were to make no programmes of our own but were to acquire them from others. To do so we would need, I argued, to employ intermediaries who would, as did editors in publishing houses, commission work and see it through to publication, in our case on to the air. Their choices would in the end govern what we did. The channel could only be as good as the judgements of those who worked for it. So far, there was Paul Bonner and there was me. I was set on determining the flavour of the first mix myself. But help was urgently needed.

I brought in immediately, on funds the IBA provided, to a flat above the offices at Brompton Road, as general fixer and organizer an old colleague and fellow refugee from Bryan Cowgill's Thames, Joyce Jones. She found me a secretary who was already at the IBA, and who won golden opinions there – Susan Crowson. I asked John Ranelagh, a sharp intellect of formidable energy then working with me at the BBC on *Ireland – A Television History*, to join me as Personal Assistant. John Ranelagh had previously been employed in the Conservative research department. He played a key role throughout his time at Channel 4 though, in the end, not so big a role as he would have liked. Paul Bonner, too, hired a secretary, the dauntingly down-to-earth Phoebe Roome.

To commission television programmes, through every stage from the evaluation of ideas through research, pre-planning, production, to post-production, entails long lead times. (Unlike the institutions, we had also to agree the terms of contract between supplier and purchaser.) We had to get on. I must, as soon as possible, gather senior colleagues round me who would help send out scouts, map out the territory ahead, agree strategies, block volumes of requisite material, begin the process of purchase and commission.

Without consulting the Board to which I answered, but believing they would approve, I set out myself to make three key appointments. I proposed not to advertise vacancies, but to hunt heads. There was little time to go through the processes of advertisement, response, interview, selection. I had only modest salaries to offer. I thought I would do better to identify the individuals I wanted and persuade them to join me than to rely on the response in open competition of those in television who fancied a change. Besides, in recruiting for a channel providing a distinctive service, I was certain I had to find some future colleagues who had never worked in television at all, and to whom it may never have occurred that they ever would. We should avoid the pitfalls of predictability of an ITV or BBC house style: 'the way we do this is'; 'same again please, only more so'. 'I asked you,' a famous ITV executive once said, 'for a pound of apples. You have brought me a pound of pears. Take them back and bring me a pound of apples.' This bald and simple commissioning utterance enshrines a great truth of the supplier/purchaser relationship which Channel 4, in its turn, could not in the end avoid barking its shins on. But I thought we needed, at least some of the time, not apples but pears, and uglies and kiwi fruits. I wanted to ensure that, somehow, new ideas, wonky ideas, maybe even by conventional wisdom bad ideas, anyway different ideas, honed and sparked in other disciplines, would be put forward as to how we should operate, what we should put on air. I was after a combination of professional experience, of relevant but disparate disciplines, and of innocent inexperience if there was invention to go with it.

Three broad areas deserved early appointments: fiction, news and current affairs, and education – the IBA required educative material to constitute 15 per cent of our output. In the beginning I attached no similar importance to entertainment; everyone agreed the channel was to offer a more serious mix in its programmes than did ITV. Again, whatever brave face I put on it, money would be tight; there would not easily be ample funds for every programme category. I would buy in entertaining programmes cheap, as there was nothing to stop my doing, and save my pennies for the fare that would make the channel's reputation. In any case, fiction, documentaries, debates are entertaining. So are the arts. Channel 4 could, I thought, be entertaining enough without too lavish expenditure on the canned laughs of conventional 'light entertainment'.

I began with fiction. Channel 4 would not only make no programmes itself, or virtually none; it would have no studios in which to make them. We would not own expensive electronic gear waiting to be employed in putting drama on to video. We could, if we chose, cause much of our drama to be made, expensively but elegantly, on film. We could commission not plays, but films. We would call the work not drama but fiction.

At that time films were initially made either for the cinema or for television, not for both. There was hand-to-hand fighting ahead, but in the end we managed to break through the tangle of restrictive practice that hedged around cinema exhibition in Great Britain, and bring films into being that could be shown both in the cinema and on the television screen also.

To take charge of Channel 4's fiction, I first approached a fine director, a former Head of Plays at the BBC then working at the National Theatre, Christopher Morahan. I found him in a vast rehearsal room there. 'No,' he said. 'Tempting, but when I finish here I have a long commitment to something for Granada, in India, the Paul Scott tetralogy – do you know it?' He was to produce *The Jewel in the Crown*, under Denis Forman, whose cherished project it was, and to direct episodes himself. He was looking forward to it. So, no. 'Had I thought of David Rose? One of the pioneers. Produced *Z Cars* and *Softly, Softly*. Face never quite fitted at Television Centre. He's at Birmingham now, doing some marvellous things. Due to retire soon. Could be looking for a change.' 'Marvellous things' indeed. I knew. I had seen the films which, using BBC's regional resources, he had managed to make there; David Hare's *Licking Hitler* and more recently *Dreams of Leaving* stuck in the mind. And there'd been a silly row about a pickled penis in a bottle in a little play produced by W. Stephen Gilbert from an Ian McEwan short story, that the Controller of Pebble Mill had unnecessarily banned. And there was work with Asian and West Indian writers to his credit. He could be just the man. We met two days later. He was.

For factual programmes I wanted someone from outside television. If there was one slice of subject-matter in which new initiatives, new attitudes were needed it was in news and current affairs. In conventional broadcasting objectivity – the aspiration to it and its achievement – was all. No room for the personal opinion, the subjective view, the representation of sectional interest. Air-time was scarce, and properly, therefore, controlled.

The Broadcasting Act, to which Channel 4 would also be subject, insisted on 'due impartiality in matters of current political or industrial controversy'. It was not for the broadcaster to editorialize, only to convey, giving both sides always of contentious questions, a balanced impression of objective reality. This was the iron rule. It was one thing though to prevent Max Beaverbrook or Sidney Bernstein using a public franchise for propaganda. Beaverbrook never had the chance; Bernstein, a little reluctantly, accepted that he could not. (Let them, in the Nineties, try to stop Rupert Murdoch.) It was quite another to prevent an experienced journalist conveying, even by a curl of the lip or by an adjective, what he thought, say, of apartheid or of the IRA. I had never forgotten an occasion when a journalist I knew and worked with but who had no cause to love me, Kenneth Allsop, was reproved by that old dreadnought Grace Wyndham-Goldie for some failure of 'balance' on a nightly news magazine. I wrote in the *Listener* that Allsop was not Kennedy, was not Day, not Kee, not Mossman, but was himself. Why employ so many varied talents, I asked, if mouthing automata were all that was needed? There was value in variety. Allsop wrote to say how much, feeling a touch beleaguered, he appreciated that word of understanding. Robert Kee's *Ireland* series conveyed his view of Ireland's history, not mine, and certainly not the BBC's. Now was the time, surely, to accept that a variety of journalistic voices would serve us better.

On television most journalism tended to a generalized norm. Specialized interests were barely catered for. There was a *Money Programme* on the BBC, but none on ITV, and no programme on trade union affairs on either. Trade unions believed that, pulverized in a popular press which knew no inhibitions, they were entitled to a fairer deal in publicly accountable media. Women had no particular voice. Nor did black Britons. Nor did a critical left. Nor a radical right, though they were ideologues to those who were now in power. Nor – hardest to target and deliver – a questing centre. Yet all such views of the world could contribute grist to the consumer of information's mill. Newspapers could contain such multitudes, and be the better for it. As well as would-be objective news reporting, newspapers found space for features, for the unsigned editorial, for columnists' opinions. On inside pages, untendentiously, they serviced particular interests; fed a hunger for information on money, housing, fashion, food, travel, on the music that moved particular age groups, rock and pop and classical, on gardening and yachting. Television could feed specialisms also. It would help, I thought, to bring a writing journalist's editorial judgements and perspectives to our task. And could this paragon be a she? Women complained of how, demeaningly, they were represented on television, and how meagrely they were represented in the decision-taking echelons of male-dominated broadcasting institutions. Why not a woman editor of factual output at Channel 4?

Liz Forgan, editor of the *Guardian*'s Women's Page, asked to interview me on my plans for the new channel. At Edinburgh a year earlier I had said that I hoped, in the Eighties, to see 'more programmes made by women for women which men will watch'. Was I serious? What did this mean? What was I going to do about it? The *Guardian*'s Women's Page was readable, lively, consistently varied and consistently, but to my mind unstridently, provoking. I agreed to be interviewed.

A brisk, cheerful, plump – but if I put plump, I learned to ask myself later, would I have used such a description of a male? – business-like person introduced herself. I said I would answer her questions if, at the end, she would answer a question of mine. The interview over, I asked her if she might be interested in taking charge of all Channel 4's news and current affairs output, of all its journalism. Indeed, I invited her to do just that. A couple of days later, we had another brief chat in a pub: 'You are serious about this, are you?' 'Yes.' She accepted. I never for a moment regretted it.

Two down; one to go. For education, risking the self-inflicted wounds of the old pals act, I had an idea closer to home. Naomi Sargant was the wife of one of my oldest friends, Andrew McIntosh, briefly, before being shafted by Ken Livingstone, Labour Leader of the GLC. Naomi was a trained market researcher who had been in at the birth of the Open University. There she was now Pro-Vice Chancellor with responsibility for student relations. We needed someone who knew broadcasting's educational potential, and how it might be fulfilled. We needed someone who knew her way around in the woods of educational politics, since we would be hedged around by advisory bodies who would require careful handling. Perhaps some further lateral thinking would have been in order, but I decided to ask Naomi. Her birthday and Tamara's were on successive days in early December. At a noisy dinner *à quatre* in a bistro in Shepherd's Bush, I quietly – the racket was such you could not hear your neighbour speak – popped the question. Amazedly, Naomi responded. She was understandably reluctant to give up the tenure and seniority her Open

University post afforded her, but after some heartsearching she agreed to the adventure.

At the December Board meeting I told the Board. The Board was not pleased. The ITV people understood what a catch David Rose was, and that an advertisement might not have lured him. Anne Sofer, a formidably able SDP mind, did not take kindly to Naomi Sargant's appointment; she knew her as a leading figure in Haringey's Labour Council, and did not admire her. But her qualifications did seem relevant. Some astonishment greeted my choice of Liz Forgan; the *Guardian*'s Women's Page, was this the best we could do? Edmund Dell, whose idea of the person to take charge of the channel's journalism would have been something between a Harvard professsor of economics and the editor of the *Financial Times*, was particularly put out. Besides, and understandably, where was the Board in all this? Was the Chief Executive, though I had notified him of my intentions, not even going to consult the Board in this sort of matter? A newspaper editor of course need not have done. But in a public broadcasting service? Passing over the question of whether the jobs ought not to have been advertised – for, of course, Paul Bonner's, at their behest, had not been – what was the Board for? If time was, as I argued, of the essence, I could promulgate and announce these appointments on this occasion. For the future, the Board thought it would wish to approve all commissioning editor appointments. And Edmund Dell set himself to define in writing the role and responsibilities of the Board of the Channel 4 Television Company Limited. As well as commissioning editors, the Board would approve all appointments at a salary of over £20,000 a year. It would approve all individual commissions of a value of £300,000 and over (later revised to £500,000). It would be consulted on and approve all other commissions of any special sensitivity.

The advertisement, meanwhile, for a Director of Finance, placed in July, had so far failed to bring results. Perhaps because of uncertainties over our funding and future, perhaps because we simply seemed a puny child, no one of real weight, ambition or ability had come forward. No one interviewed was up to it; no one up to it had applied. Towards the end of January 1981, word reached us – Roger Graef was the conduit – that someone who was something at the *Financial Times* might be interested in taking on the senior managerial job at Channel 4. This was Justin Dukes, Joint Assistant Managing Director there. I saw him at his house in Gibson Square. He was not an accountant, not interested in being

Director of Finance. In newspapers there was an editorial side – the editor in charge – and a business side. Channel 4 was a business; he would take over the business side. He wanted the title not just of Managing Director but of Deputy Chief Executive also. But the demarcatory line between us would be clear; as at a newspaper, I would have unfettered editorial responsibility, be left solely in charge of programmes; he, Pooh-Bah-like, would have charge of absolutely everything else, and particularly what he foresaw as the business development of the company. In one important respect this distinction was artificial. Programmes once used could be further exploited in other markets, which might, if allowed weight, affect what was commissioned in the first place. So the separation of powers was not at every point absolute. But the clarity and emphasis with which Justin stated the distinction made a strong and lasting impression on me. We shook hands. I told Edmund Dell he was the right man for us.

Numerate, much interested in gadgetry and systems, given to diagrammatic tutorials on his intentions, ignorant of television and its politics, sceptical of the ways and values of ITV, intolerant of the checks that constrain publicly accountable bodies, nobody's patsy, fierce defender of our interest at all times, shy and private but unafraid to speak his mind to anyone, Justin Dukes was a godsend.

Paul Bonner and I had tried to forecast to the Board the likely future organization of the channel. At one point, I recollect, with reckless caution, we decided that the right number of staff needed for the channel to operate efficiently was forty-eight. The ITV managing directors on the Board were jealous, as paymasters should be, for our husbandry. But even they were prepared to go beyond that. No more pottering; Justin Dukes would bring order and system, and ensure there was adequate staff for what we intended to do. Economy, I insisted and we all agreed, was crucial; if resource was scarce it would be unforgivable to spend more than we need do on ourselves. The channel would always pride itself on its low overheads. These were never allowed to rise to more than 10 per cent of income. All the rest would be available to spend on programmes. So we skimped, mistakenly, on secretaries and assistants. Too many colleagues worked far too hard in the back-breaking start-up period in consequence.

Paul Bonner found a Chief Engineer, Ellis Griffiths, whom I remembered warmly from a night of hands-on crisis management at Thames. He had since helped design and build an advanced studio and transmission centre for South African Broadcasting in Johannesburg. Ellis Griffiths promised us a state-of-the-art computer-driven, lowest-possible-man-power, fail-safe transmission system on air, on time. He delivered.

Paul Bonner and I selected, in interview, Pam Masters from BBC Television to be our Head of Presentation. For coolness, common sense, power of command, she stood out above the other applicants. Pam Masters was to rule our Presentation Department with an icy efficiency. Unfortunately she and Ellis Griffiths never got on. But, somehow, with Paul as referee of their quarrels, this dangerously dotty disagreement never blew our fragile craft out of the water. Like Ellis, though, Pam Masters gave us, in our on-air symbol and station identification signals, the best the current state of the art could offer. The visuals were created by Martin Lambie of Robinson Lambie Nairn, the music that accompanies the ident by David Dundas. The whole was computerised into graphic mobility in Los Angeles. Our particoloured four, the components representing our pluralist diversity, was a practical but dazzling device that marked us as as up to the minute as any television channel anywhere on planet earth, the very pineapple of perfection, the envy of our peers.

Paul Bonner and I appointed Eric Flackfield, ex-LWT, an experienced planner, to run the schedule. His knowledge of ITV systems proved invaluable. Later, when he retired, we were fortunate to replace him with the meticulous and expert Gillian Braithwaite-Exley.

We needed, too, to hire, this time with the Board's approval, another swatch of commisioning editors. I decided not to specify responsibilities, and fly-fish in different rivers for single trout or salmon, but to trawl deep, and see what we could find.

DO YOU KNOW A GOOD IDEA WHEN YOU SEE ONE?

Television production experience may be an advantage but is not essential. Whether your passion is angling or cooking, fringe theatre, rock, politics, philosophy or religion, if you believe you can spot a good idea and help others realize it on the screen, we are looking for commissioning editors, and would like to hear from you.

We got six thousand replies. And read them.

We were trying to find people whose talents and abilities, whatever their interests or experience, somehow matched the strands of subject matter we already knew we would want to explore. And we hoped to find people whose potential ability was so striking we must hire him or her regardless, and rethink our categories in consequence. The main impression on me, ploughing through the letters, was of unbounded creativity locked up in the teaching profession, and bursting to get out. But we hired, in the end, no teachers. (One we turned down became a Conservative MP.) From the applicants we selected fifty for interview, and agreed on six. One other got away.

Mike Bolland, a wisecracking Glaswegian cherub not so young as he looked, whom Paul knew from the BBC's Community Unit, would give us programmes for younger viewers, for teenagers and up, but not for your granny. He would then go further.

Our educational output in volume alone would be too great for any one pair of eyes, ears, hands. Carol Haslam, a documentarist at BBC's Open University Productions, suggested herself, by sheer force of personality, to work alongside (she never willingly worked under) Naomi Sargant.

Andy Park, recommended to me by Gillian Reynolds who knew about radio and the talent in it, was sought out by me in his Programme Controller's office at Radio Clyde. He had never worked in television, but agreed to apply. A live wire, at the interview he came on strong, himself a composer, as a polymath in music. I was keen; we had him.

Sue Woodford, a sparky current affairs producer at Granada TV, was part-Trinidadian. We were to cater for Britain's ethnic minorities, and would look silly trying to do so without input from someone whose skin was darker than that of the rest of us. Sue Woodford was to prove a tough in-fighter in a good cause. She did not stay long. She laid foundations that lasted.

Cecil Korer was an old hand in BBC Light Entertainment, nearing early retirement there. Unprepared to make a large investment in comedy, but wanting to acquire some on the cheap, I cruelly offered Cecil the job of finding us light entertainment programmes without ever intending to give him the financial means to do it on anything like a substantial scale. He did find some good things, including one treasure, *Treasure Hunt*. With my blessing and approval he brought us some bloody awful things also; *The Gong Show* from the US syndication market, the *Cut Price Comedy Show* from TSW. He never had a proper chance because the chance to upgrade our comedy output, when it came, I offered to someone else. Cecil Korer was a good man in a hole. I put him there. I owe him an apology.

Alan Fountain I had known as a member of the British Film Institute

Production Board. He applied, and I was glad of it. The Independent Film-makers Association had played an active role in the debates that led to the Channel, fighting hard to keep it out of ITV's clutches. The film and video workshop movement, claimed as of right a share of our finances. We repudiated the claim, but wanted to see the best of their work on our screen, and we were prepared to make a contribution to funding the infrastructure that produced it. Channel 4 needed to deal with them. Alan Fountain struck Paul Bonner and me as just the person to do it; calm, courageous, intellectually honest, he was to give us two lasting strands, *People to People* and *The Eleventh Hour*, on each of which our claim to encourage innovation, particularly in programme content, would partially rest.

We offered the job of commissioning editor in the arts to a young woman wholly inexperienced in television, Susan Richards, but David Puttnam also offered her a job. She chose Enigma.

John Ranelagh, already with us, I asked to take responsibility for our religious output, an obligation there was no escaping. The IBA required us to offer one hour a week. And John Ranelagh was charged also to bring us work from Ireland, the near neighbour with whose peoples, culture, history and politics we were inextricably linked. I invited Paul Madden, then television archive officer at the BFI, and an informed enthusiast with an independent mind, to advise on the use of archive programmes. Later, I asked him to take responsibility, when a gap appeared, for single documentaries.

After a pause, we made two further appointments, commissioning editors for sports programmes and for the arts. It soon became obvious we could not do without sport. We had no contracts in it, and did not want merely to operate the fag-end of ITV's. But someone would have to deal with it, and with them. Anyway, sport was part of life. I invited Adrian Metcalfe, Olympic silver medallist, now an ITV athletics commentator, to give us sport on television that was different. Since we had no contracts, and since the BBC was sewing up nearly everything in sight, that was our only course. Adrian brought both a committed professionalism and a spirit of adventure to *Sport on 4*. We failed to snitch New Zealand rugby or one-day cricket from the BBC and the stay-close-to-nurse conservatism of its administrators. We plumped instead for the healthy family image of British basketball. Later we watched it resolutely refuse to take off. We agreed to share ITV's snooker. This we both resented, Adrian strongly. But on this, for the sake of our partnership with ITV, I had to insist. I pretended not to notice the hike it always gave our ratings. Later, when ITV dropped it, we disagreed on whether or not to take over ITV's horse-racing contract. But I wanted an outdoor feel to the channel, and liked the idea of the green of the track, the most restful of colours, on our screen in the afternoons. Besides, if pluralism counted, the horsey interest also deserved to be catered for. So we took over ITV's racing. Adrian and his team made a good thing of it. For our prize goodies we looked abroad. *American Football* appealed to us both as a fierce new addition to British sport and as an exotic spectacle.

Someone suggested Michael Kustow for the arts post. He had run, and been run out of, the ICA, and had been since at the RSC and at the National Theatre. 'Strong on ideas,' Peter Hall told me on the telephone from Glyndebourne, the unsaid bit casting some doubt on Kustow's ability to realize them. But his internationalism was attractive. He had to be approved by the Board, so I wheeled him in to Edmund Dell, warning him not to go on at too great length. His answer to Dell's first question ran twenty-three minutes. Bemusing us both, he got by. We often disagreed, but Michael Kustow was to make a considerable mark.

The commissioning team was now all but complete, half from television, half from without; two other vital procurers were already on board. Derek Hill came to sell me foreign-language films; I asked him to buy for the channel. Leslie Halliwell bought for ITV; it was never our interest to bid against them. I agreed to use Halliwell's offices to buy American films and television material for us also. He was much more than a buyer. Leslie Halliwell was a film buff, a walking encyclopaedia. Leslie had a lifelong love for the golden years of Hollywood. He wanted not just to purchase material for us, but to help schedule it, which he had never been able to do satisfactorily for the ITV network. Eagerly he got to work on our behalf, chasing rarities, diverting goodies from ITV's vast store, earmarking interesting new work as 'obvious Channel 4 material', constructing themed series for our schedule. Leslie Halliwell's selection of 1930s' Hollywood movies – black and white, but billed as golden oldies – was to give many great pleasure.

We found premises in Charlotte Street, Soho. The building was occupied by National Car Parks. The site was that of the old Scala theatre. The rake of the old stalls gave sufficient height for our presentation studio in the basement. I liked the idea of Peter Pan – Barrie's play had been

performed there every Christmas for decades – helping us on. Dickie
Attenborough was particularly approving of the choice. And I liked
Charlotte Street, where I first saw Londoners eating out-of-doors. Camden
Council gave permission for light industrial use. In the bowels of the
building, as Ellis Griffiths got to work and transmission neared, I kept
finding tangles of little coloured wires waiting to be introduced to other
wires. I was worried. Ellis was not.

Justin Dukes was recruiting also: a Head of Programme Acquisition
from the BBC, a lawyer, Colin Leventhal; after a hiccup, an accountant
from Peat Marwick as Controller of Finance, David Scott; a Head
of Marketing from LWT, Sue Stoessl; a Head of Administration and
Industrial Relations from the *Financial Times*, Frank McGettigan.
Justin was determined that Channel 4 should not be held to ransom
by television unions. Newspapers, including the *FT*, were an awful
warning.

There was a tenseness in the air as the new men and women on the
business side moved in. Programme people, as ever, were suspicious of
them. They wore suits, carried attaché cases, were sticklers for form,
contract, propriety. They were there to service programmes, the company's be-all and end-all, yet they declined to see themselves in a sub-
servient role. As one, head low, clumped past, I remember wondering if
the business tail was to wag the creative dog. It was an unjustified
concern. These colleagues were of outstanding ability, and they conducted
themselves with tact and a real care for creative susceptibilities. Of course,
our suppliers, on the receiving end of a budget negotiation or studying
the pages of fine print that constituted a contract, did not always see them
in that light.

Commissioning, as 1981 wore on, began. Long term we planned and
plotted. Short term we snatched. There were plenty wanting to sell to us.
Suggestions poured in. Nowhere was one safe from the programme
proposal. I was accosted twice one afternoon by men with scripts between
Warren Street and Tottenham Court Road, and followed by another,
treatment at the ready, into the urinals at Brompton Road.

Where to start? I sent a facility company to record Max Wall's music-
hall act in its entirety at the Garrick Theatre. An absurdly young man,
Colin Callander, proposed to me that we should record the Royal Shakespeare Company's nine-hour-long *Nicholas Nickleby*. We did. (The bill was
enormous because we bought world rights in the actors' performances for

each of nine separate hours of work. Some bought their first homes on the proceeds.) Anthony Morris, a skilled salesman and influential lobbyist for the independent interest, had been shocked to hear me say there would be no nature programmes on Channel 4, because I thought there were quite enough elsewhere. We owed it to independents to be a market for good work, he argued. Now he sold me *Fragile Earth*, studies of the world's ecology produced by Michael Rosenberg, some stunningly photographed by Phil Agland. Peter Montagnon, maker of *Civilization* with Kenneth Clark for the BBC all those years ago, had found City money to fund a major documentary series on China, something of a breakthrough. We acquired UK rights in *China: Heart of the Dragon* at a knockdown price, which his backers must later have regretted. Thames Television, though we took long to agree terms, offered David Rose a four-part fiction set in a rundown hard-worked hospital, *The Nation's Health* by Gordon Newman; the scripts, he told me, were just what he was looking for. At Wheeler's in Old Compton Street David Puttnam offered me *First Love*, a series of shortish films, later to be stretched together with their price, dealing with just that touching aspect of all our lives. I accepted. The first finished and first to air was Jack Rosenthal's study of calf love and Test Cricket, *P'tang Yang Kipperbang*.

In January 1981 I gave a marathon address to would-be independent producers at the Royal Institution in Albemarle Street. After it, a sallow, dark, hollow-eyed fellow in T-shirt, jeans and dirty sneakers came up to me. He asked if it was true that, in the interests of realism, I was prepared to allow language in television dialogue that others would not countenance. 'Yes. That's right,' I said. 'Good, I've got something for you. You'll have it in a few weeks.' This was Phil Redmond, author of the BBC's *Grange Hill*, set at a comprehensive school, and of serials that caught the moods of streetwise teenagers facing unemployed futures. Redmond now wished to become an entrepreneur of television production, and in his native Liverpool. What he offered was *Brookside*. David Rose, reading the treatment when it came in, agreed that Channel 4 should have a soap opera of its own.

It took six months to negotiate a contract with ITN for Channel 4 News. It took a year to agree a deal with Redmond. These matters were taken in hand by Justin Dukes, and were referred for detailed scrutiny and approval to a formally constituted, and carefully minuted, Programme Finance Committee (PFC). I could chair PFC by all means but it was no longer on, it was intimated, for the Chief Executive, pleading urgency and the need for quick decisions, to commit the Channel's funds in restaurants, bars and gentlemen's lavatories.

Meekly I allowed myself to be corralled by the sterner method and cooler heads of PFC. Ours were public funds to disburse. We must deal, and be seen to deal, justly and prudently.

Justin Dukes and I set out to promote Channel 4, to tell the world of our intentions. We explained who owned us, where our funds came from, and what we were going to do with them. But it is very hard, I found, to offer in advance any understanding of the raw ingredients of a service whose flavour can only really be savoured when cooked. A promotional road show, begun in February 1982 at the Barbican, rolled on around the country. I went with it to Exeter, Belfast, Edinburgh. Sue Stoessl, in the weeks before we went on air, did twenty more presentations in other cities. Our advertising agency, BMP, successfully helped us urge the nation to tune their sets to 4. But, for all their skills and courteous professionalism, they never found one simple slogan to promote us. (Their rivals for our business, Gold Greenlees Trott, had suggested 'Television That Turns You On'.)

It was not BMP's fault. The channel, I insisted, was not a homogeneous entity. It was for all of the people some of the time. You might like some of it; you could not possibly warm to all of it. Nor was it to be represented by any one programme or category of programmes. Yes, there would be American football, but American football was not Channel 4. BMP agreed that they would promote not a channel, empty of meaning, but the progammes in all their disparate diversity. The result, the day we opened, was a scatter shot of different ads, calling attention to a dolly mixture of programmes. It had little impact.

The compilation page, pulling all the ads together, does credit to the vast ingenuity of their creative department's artwork, and to our own scope and variety. But it was free publicity, press editorial coverage friendly or hostile, that made us known.

The day of our first transmission neared. The Channel 4 test card, to which you could tune your set, was very popular with viewers. The public wrote to say how much they enjoyed the music we played behind it. They enjoyed it so much, they wrote, they never wanted it to go away, never wanted programmes to replace it. (There's a clear case, I knew then, for a national round-the-clock classical music radio channel.) Now the test card gave way to the news that programmes were imminent. We began to count viewers down the days to the launch.

A supply of programmes was to hand. We published a first schedule, for the first few weeks and for our first day on air. We chose Tuesday, 2 November 1982. S4C, the Welsh language fourth channel, we agreed would go first on 1 November, All Saints Day. (I sent a message of goodwill in Welsh, learnt parrot fashion.) There would be no phony ceremony at Guildhall or elsewhere, just a normal transmission pattern. I decided not to start with the bigger bang of any particular programme at any particular peak evening time. That would be to risk having the part, whatever we started with, taken for the whole (but avoiding this was perhaps a mistake all the same). We would start at 4.45 pm, with a normal schedule. The first programme screened would be *Countdown*, copied from the French *Des Lettres et des Chiffres*, a participatory game. *Channel 4 News* would be in its proper place at 7 pm, *Brookside* after it. We had a strongish film, *Walter*, denounced in advance in the press as a shocker, at 9 pm. Then, from Mike Bolland, a Comic Strip spoof of Enid Blyton, *Five Go Mad in Dorset*. Last that evening, *In the Pink*, a tart, entertaining feminist review. That was the mix; take us as you find us.

The programmes were to be separated and interrupted by commercial breaks. But there might be no commercials, because of a bitter, recalcitrant dispute, outside our control, between the Institute of Practitioners in Advertising (IPA) and Actors' Equity over repeat fees. And some ITV companies were still in dispute with their employees over manning levels in their new Channel 4 control room, so some parts of the country might go without our service. The Channel itself was locked in argument, still unresolved, with the IBA over parts of a polemical film I had scheduled for Thursday the 4th, two nights later. Our posture, someone said, was all too reminiscent of Foch: 'My flanks are in retreat; my centre is giving way; I shall attack.'

Willie Whitelaw, the Home Secretary, our onlie true begetter, had lunched with us some weeks previously on his way to the Conservative Party Conference. 'Castrate the muggers,' he confided, 'that'll be the cry this year.' Now, on the morning of 2 November 1982, he wrote:

THE HOME OFFICE

Dear Jeremy,
    On the day on which Channel 4 goes on the air I send to you and

all at Channel 4, from all of us concerned with broadcasting in the Home Office, warm good wishes for the success of an exciting new venture. It gave me great pleasure as Home Secretary to carry through Parliament the legislation setting up the Fourth Channel, after such a long period of discussion about the form it should take. Now I shall watch with interest the development of this latest addition to our system of public-service broadcasting.

Yours,
Willie

Telegrams, messages, bouquets, champagne by the bottle, the magnum, the jeroboam, were delivered. As the minutes ticked away I sat, glass in hand, with Edmund Dell in my office, overlooking Charlotte Steet. The test card vanished. To my horror – of course I should have foreseen it, but I had not, no one had warned me, and my heart lurched – the test card was replaced not by our ident but by black. A black hole; black night. In the office next door Paul Bonner looked calmly at his monitor. This must be intentional. It was going to be all right. Then from the black came our call sign, an announcer's voice, a seductive montage of promotional images created by Tim Simmons, our signature music over. We were on the air. I reached over and shook Edmund's hand.

4

Under Fire

START as you mean to go on; in its first days and weeks on air Channel 4 offered as wide a selection as we could lay our hands on. A television channel trying to be different needed to show, it seemed to me, as many attractively different individual programmes as it could. Others, building audiences, cementing loyalties, constructed schedules by placing familiar series at familiar times. But all our stuff was unfamiliar. We would follow a different course; not for us the viewer who tuned in and stayed tuned as habit-forming favourites succeeded each other. We would be a channel for the choosy viewer, selecting a particular chocolate from the box, leaving the rest to others.

That was the idea. In any case, at this point of the channel's life there was little alternative. We had plans to make some series. Not many, but some. But none of them was ready. At one time I had thought that our first commissioned drama series, *The Irish RM*, would be available in time for our launch. But the RM, Peter Bowles, fell off a horse and hurt himself. Completion was put back. We would have to wait a little longer for those genial misadventures of the English among the Irish. *Countdown* in the afternoons was later to become a cult, but was hard for viewers to find. *Brookside* was there, but would take months to get into its stride. So was *Channel 4 News*, which could have made a better start but, nervously, did not. Something about all new news and current affairs shows compels them to begin by making the same elementary mistakes their predecessors have made. *Channel 4 News*, in the wrong set, its capable presenters ill at ease, was no exception. No need to despair; the brief was agreed, the talent was there. It would come good in time. (I had once been responsible for a daily magazine, of whose early editions the critic Francis Hope justly said that there was nothing wrong that firing the entire production team could not put right. *Today* ran for ten years.) *Channel 4 News*, in any event, was never intended to be, never would be, a crowd-puller. But, apart from one acquired drama series, *Six Feet of the Country*, based on Nadine Gordimer's South African stories, virtually everything else we played in our first peak schedule would be a singleton, not a run.

As a come-on I front-loaded the first ten evenings with good movies; some of our own making, *Walter* and *P'Tang Yang Kipperbang* and *Remembrance*; some from Hollywood, *Network*, a satire on commercial television, uncensored, unbowdlerized; and Burt Reynolds in *Semi-Tough*, also, to our cost, unbowdlerized; from the archive, first television showings of Howard Hawks' *Scarface* and *Hell's Angels*; for polemical oomph, *The Animals Film*, and from the Cinema Action workshop the moving *So That You Can Live*; from the independent American cinema, a personal favourite, Henry Jaglom's *Sitting Ducks* – hilarious rudery, but latish in the evening who noticed? They noticed the language in *Network* all right, and from Faye Dunaway, too; and in *Remembrance* from a drunken bunch of tars ashore, consciously scheduled close to Remembrance Day; and they noticed the foul-mouthed locker-room badinage of *Semi-Tough*. I noticed too, but too late. I saw the film, for the first time, on air at 9 pm on Tuesday, 9 November. I nearly fell out of my armchair.

Leslie Halliwell had offered me a movie starring Burt Reynolds that had not been seen on British television. I was delighted. And there was a bonus: the movie was about the Lardner-type low life of American football, and would serve to introduce our Sunday coverage of that sport. It never occurred to me in my innocence that there must be some good reason why neither ITV nor BBC had snapped it up long before we came along. Now, gawping, I understood. Coach and team effed and blinded from one mundane moment of their day to the next. All this at 9 pm. No warning given. The *Sun* was counting the obscenities. It needed a calculator.

On 31 July that summer Maggie Forwood of that paper had nicknamed us 'Channel Bore'. Later she refined this to 'Channel Snore'. Now, with the *Sun*'s inventive splash subs warming to their work, it became 'Channel Swore' and 'Channel Four Letter Word'. In one week, with *Brookside* chipping in its modest quota, the word count was 173. And this was unintentional. Some found that hard to believe.

The movies did their job; none gained a huge audience, but they demonstrated effectively our will to entertain. Our share of viewing, boosted by sampling, was 6.6 per cent in our first week. (Had we been able to maintain that schedule indefinitely we should have hit our audience target earlier.) And there were other goodies, too. Lots of them; *Nicholas Nickleby*, in three long slabs, graced successive Sunday evenings. Tom Keating, the forger, blew the gaff on himself, and showed how to make your own Monet in *Tom Keating on Painters*. The first two in the series *Fragile Earth* – 'Korup', a Cameroon rain forest, and 'Pantanal', a swamp in Brazil, were each entrancing. *The Little Waster* was a one-man show, by the Geordie stand-up comic Bobby Thompson, his accent one in the eye for those who sneered we were a Hampstead channel for Hampstead people only. His timing alone had the mark of a performer blessed by genius. Baryshnikov and Shirley MacLaine did their thing. And Luciano Pavarotti popped up in *Idomeneo* from the Met.

Watching it come over by satellite on our first Saturday night in the makeshift monitor area, I was amazed to hear not Mozart but commentary on an American football game. Instead of Idomeneo meeting Idamante on the Cretan shore, here were heavy men in padded suits and helmets wrestling each other for a football. Someone at the New York switching centre had pressed the wrong switch. We were recording for transmission the next day, and had the Met's crew send Act One over all over again. Viewers in Germany and Austria got picture and commentary live. Many telephoned to inquire the final score.

Some programmes had a particular Channel 4 sheen to them, such as a documentary series on reggae, *Deep Roots Music*. *Voices*, chaired by Al Alvarez, began with a rather waffly edition on 'The End of the Jewish Example'. Claus Moser, Chairman of the Royal Opera House, wrote a card to say it was just the sort of thing we should be doing. *A Personal History of the Australian Surf* was an enchanting, understated account of his childhood by Michael Blakemore. And there was *The Life and Times of Rosie the Riveter*.

Against ITV's annual hugely popular but sexist *Miss World*, I thought special scheduling was called for. I had purchased for that purpose a camp and draggy *Alternative Miss World*. *Rosie the Riveter* told how, when the US war economy needed women in factories, women were trained to do men's jobs; but, with the war over, women lost out and went back to being housewives. *Rosie* seemed the better option. Overegging the pudding, we offered later that evening *Soldier Girls*, Joan Churchill's and Nick Broomfield's pulverizing account of female GIs in training for the US Army. Each documentary stood in sharp enough contrast to the frivolities of *Miss World* to make a point; together they sledgehammered it home. And between them, unremarked, in its regular place in the schedule, was an episode of *Six Feet of the Country*. And this too, as it happened, showed an Asian woman in Johannesburg, in an active political role, resisting apartheid's impact on her family.

The feature writers took aim. Channel 4, they charged, is getting at us; not content to call a spade a spade, it hits us over the head with loaded shovels. The channel was pushing ideas and opinions down their throats, and they objected to it.

I had never doubted, thinking too much television too unthinking, too bland, that Channel 4 would broadcast programmes that put, as forcibly as possible, a forcible point of view. I had not appreciated, and still find hard to understand, how offensive to some this turned out to be. People had no objection to an opinion strongly expressed in a newspaper, in a railway carriage, in a saloon bar. Why object to opinionated television? Perhaps they only enjoyed reading their own opinions in newspapers, and not the other fellow's at all. Did they only ever take one newspaper, and never read one that put another view? Perhaps they accepted an opinion in print, whether they went along with it or not, but valued precisely the absence of such provocation on the television screen.

First thing in the office each morning I read the note of viewers' telephoned comments in the previous evening's duty log. The nastiest reactions to Channel 4 were racist: this is a white country, we don't want blacks on our television. Despicable; easily ignored. But viewers objected also, at first, to the expression of opinions they disliked.

In our earliest days we seemed, in bringing stuff from all sorts of sources to the air, to have taken the lid off a pressure cooker. People crowded forward with what they were eager to say; too much of it, perhaps, was of a particular muchness.

Someone at the BBC had invited the historian E. P. Thompson to give the 1981 Dimbleby Lecture, in memory of the great broadcaster Richard Dimbleby. He accepted. The BBC changed its collective mind at the highest level and stood him down. Thompson, the author of *The Making of the English Working Class*, was of the left, a supporter of CND, a gifted

pamphleteer, lecturer, critic. I wrote to *The Times* to say that had we been
on the air Channel 4 would have been happy to offer him a platform, as
we would be happy to offer it to all shades of political opinion. I asked
for, and John Ranelagh caused to be executed, a series called *Opinions* in
which speakers would address viewers by addressing a camera, speaking
a carefully scripted, prepared text, uninterrupted, for half an hour. No
visuals, just a talking head; the best visual of all. *Opinions* proved excellent
viewing. I had written to Thompson inviting him to contribute. He
accepted, and delivered an eloquent harangue against media complicity in
'power systems' evil ways'.

Naturally, given the BBC's change of heart, Thompson would be first
up as *Opinions* commenced its run in our second week on air. *Channel 4
News*, for an hour each night save Fridays, would conscientiously follow
the precepts and practice of objectivity in broadcast journalism. So would
A Week in Politics. So would *Face the Press*. But some programmes,
carefully placed in the schedule, would make a variety of partisan points.
Opinions was one example. What I did not appreciate, until late, was that
other of our programmes intended to fulfil more general purposes might
also, according to the editorial judgement of those who made them, come
up on a particular day with messages that might unbalance the whole.

Broadside, current affairs edited by women, offered an early portrait of
the women of Greenham Common, E. P. Thompson fans, every last one
of them (those at least that accepted the possibility of benignity in the
male). *Whatever You Want*, a series aimed at youth and presented by a
talented maverick, Keith Allen, wanted as its first guest in that same first
week Anthony Wedgwood Benn. At the risk of feeding his paranoia about
the media I vetoed his appearance. In a later *Whatever You Want* Keith
Allen, reporting with great style on a to-do in a GLC old people's refuge
that did no credit to the managers or to the TGWU personnel involved,
ended, or wanted to end, by announcing that the demo to protest against
these events would be in Berwick Street on Saturday at 2.30 pm: 'Be
there.' That was cut. Some weeks later we were offered a young Trot's
view of unemployment for which the TUC, as in the Thirties, must share
responsibility. 'Mobilize the unemployed,' he argued, 'and bring down
Thatcher.' This was too much for Mike Bolland and me. That went, and
so did, voluntarily, Keith Allen. We were criticized for banning a perfectly
unexceptionable programme, as some thought. But the whole mix mattered more.

Some viewers rang the duty office to tell us of their gratitude that we had allowed E. P. Thompson to present his eloquent *Opinions*. 'We never expected to see the day,' one told us, 'that he would be allowed on to the air in this country.' That was gratifying; but did they think there was freer speech in China, or East Germany? When Edmund Teller's *Opinions* in praise of nuclear deterrence followed, and Paul Johnson's defence of market economies, the same viewers telephoned to complain. 'We never expected to see that man on *our* channel. Be ashamed of yourselves.'

The most contentious polemic of our first week, and the horridest, was *The Animals Film*, an onslaught, not finely focused, on capitalist man's abuse of animals, an attack on forced feeding, factory farming and the fast food industry, with anti-vivisectionism and a smack of animal liberation thrown in. The film was so horrible in parts that this squeamish Chief Executive could not bring himself to watch all of it, except with the aid of the fast forward button. I scheduled *The Animals Film* deliberately on our third evening partly because I knew many would want to watch it, partly to cause a stir, and partly because I thought it right to confront the IBA at the word go with the channel's intention to broadcast provoking opinion. The principle was accepted. After some argument, in which Edmund Dell represented the view of the Board, the IBA and its lawyers accepted the film-maker's right to lambast those who profited by our meat-eating, and were satisfied that defences could be offered to possible actions for defamation. They pointed out, however, that some murky scenes at the film's end, portraying an animal liberation raid on a vivisection laboratory, constituted an incitement to violence and could not be broadcast. Channel 4 reluctantly accepted this. But the film-maker Victor Schonfeld for long refused to allow his film – seen in cinemas without any prosecution resulting, it must be stated – to be cut by a single frame. For him this broadcast represented either an unvitiated opportunity to convert a nation, or the promise of instant martyrdom. Between regulatory authority and authorial authoritarianism the peacemakers padded to and fro. Eventually, with the cuts the IBA demanded, the film went out. No film Channel 4 ever broadcast better pleased its target audience. Those that agreed with what it said endlessly urged us to repeat it. 'Play it again,' the write-in campaigns demanded, and still do. The world goes on eating hamburgers. Meanwhile, rather than risk finding myself at home having to watch *The Animals Film* on air, I had arranged that its transmission should coincide with our launch party at the Riverside Studios at

Hammersmith, where a good time was had by all who could get in. Hundreds could not.

I would do it the same way again, choosing the 'shocker' *Walter* over *First Love* for our first night, and trailing our polemical coat with *The Animals Film*, or something like it. 'I greatly admired *Walter*,' wrote Herbert Kretzmer in the *Daily Mail* under the banner 'The Cosy Days of TV are Over for Ever'. 'It offered a compassionate glimpse into the lives of people called "God's mistakes" and was graced by two movingly observed and self-sacrificing performances from Ian McKellen and Barbara Jefford.' And the mix of the first few months was about right too, given the limitations of what we had to hand. The channel gained 6.6 per cent of the audience, and was well sampled, in its first week. That fell to 4 per cent shortly, and over Christmas dangerously to as little as 3 per cent. But, if we had started blander, jollier, easier on the eye, and that had failed, we would have had nowhere to go except further downstream in pursuit of popularity. As it was, having put our cards on the table and marked out territory as our own, we could build for the future without ever having to apologize for being sombre, or abrasive, or over-intellectual, or too way-out.

On our first afternoon our programme signal left Charlotte Street and instantly reappeared on our TV sets. When it came to the first commercial break I looked anxiously at the screen. Would the IPA/Equity dispute mean no commercials, a hole in our output? From Thames there popped in punctually a commercial for the new Vauxhall Cavalier; no actors, no voices, music over picture only. The agency, unable to resist being 'First on Four', had found an ingenious way of solving a difficult problem, how to make a commercial without using actors. The agency was Wasey Campbell Ewald, I later discovered. Its creative director was my brother-in-law, Tamara's brother, Leonard Weinreich.

Our screen was enlivened by those few advertisers with commercials ready for Channel 4 which did not use actors. They bought time at knockdown prices. Indeed, there was so much of it to spare, much of it was given away. 'Glints' jauntily commended itself for the hairstyling of the young in heart not once, nor once and again, but, like the young lady of Spain, again and again and again. In another toiletry ad, the nation learned of an exotic new substance, jojoba oil, from the jojoba nut. A useful device, which made some faces familiar, was 'be your own presenter'. But it was a thin crop. The result for us was monotonous and depressing; a succession of commercial breaks empty except for music, our ident, and the message: 'Next Programme Follows Shortly'. We varied this later to make clear that the dispute that wreaked this deprivation was beyond our control. It was none the less damaging for that.

Our screen was blotted and blotched by these holes, like dry rot in woodwork. Each gap to me seemed endless. Many the viewer, half-tempted to sample our wares, who must have been deterred by these sad blanks.

In newspaper previews, which influence many viewing decisions, journalists pointed to programmes of interest on Channel 4. This was another good reason for cramming in single programmes of merit. It was heartening for us to see, in a previewer's choice for the week ahead on all four channels, five or six or even more of our programmes out of the dozen recommended. Critics, too, gave their honest opinion of what we did, praising and blaming as judgement dictated. No complaints there, barring a bone or two of argument to pick later. But the feature writers and news editors, pleasing editors by drumming up matter for dreamed-up headlines, were something else again.

The British, some say, like nothing better than to take a look at something new and beat the hell out of it. Perhaps it is just that 'Newcomer falls flat on face' makes better journalistic copy than 'Newcomer makes fair start; may thrive and prosper'. Perhaps newspapers did take just an honest look, did not like what they saw and said so. Howsoever, when Channel 4 started, the press had a field day. I learned, and my family learned, what it is like to live in the eye of the media, where anything you do may be taken down, blown up and used against you. The clamour against us was noisy and at times seemed unrelenting.

The *Sun* I could cheerfully live with, perhaps because I could never take it all that seriously, and perhaps because whatever the paper came up with was done with relish and a sense of fun; Channel Bore begat Channel Snore and Channel Snore led on to Channel Swore as easily as daylight does to dusk.

The newspaper that seemed to make most of a dead set at Channel 4 was the *Daily Mail*. Something of what we were doing seemed to get the *Mail*'s editorial goat. The *Mail* stood for Queen and family and Mrs Thatcher and pride in achievement; Channel 4, they thought, did not. Mrs Mary Whitehouse's strictures on our offerings were treated as the sum of all wisdom. *Mail* feature writers fell over each other to explain that we were polluting the nation's morals with liberalism, feminism, Irish Republicanism, inverted racism, and many other 'isms' that *Mail* writers devoutly wished were 'wasms'. And, particularly on thin days for news, their headline writers went to town. You and I might think that the world was revolving snugly on its axis, the barometer set fair, most people busy with a pint or a cup of tea, or putting the children to bed or the cat out. The *Mail* was quite sure that these appearances were deceptive. In fact, trouble, big trouble, was brewing; batten down the hatches, a storm was coming up. The *Mail's* subs dealt in phenomena I called 'Stormovers'; these were, at any moment, likely to break over Channel 4's deserving head; 'Storm Over TV Language'; 'Storm Over IRA Film'; 'Storm Over' (this was a clincher) 'Gay Film'.

Four weeks after Channel 4 started, with things rumbling along quite nicely, it was time to tell the press about our programmes for the Christmas and New Year holiday, and for the winter schedule that would follow. On 30 November we did so. Included in our presentation were clips from the loveliest programme the channel ever produced, *The Snowman*, an animated film based on Raymond Briggs' delightful children's book, now an established Christmas favourite. Each reporter, in a crowded studio, received a fat press pack. It listed in all seventy-five new programmes on twenty-four pages of text, beautifully written as usual by Christopher Griffin-Beale, our Press Officer. The programmes listed included a season of popular Indian cinema; *Citizen 2000*, a documentary series which is following assorted babies born in 1982 through to their attaining the vote and citizenship; a Granada series on *The Spanish Civil War*; Jonathan Miller's mafioso *Rigoletto* from the English National Opera; *Treasure Hunt*, a popular pleasantry in which contestants steered a helicopter over the British countryside to find a trail of clues to treasure, against the clock; *The Irish RM*, rustic jollity in County Cork. The press pack also included news of a single programme on homosexual lifestyles scheduled for transmission at 11 pm on New Year's Day, and, somewhat eccentrically, entitled *One in Five*. *Mail* hacks were present, and went off with the info.

The next day the *Daily Telegraph*, in a single-column item down an inside page, singled out *One in Five* for mention, making rather less of its title than it might have done. That morning the *Daily Mail's* show business editor, Nick Gordon, presumably emerging from conference, rang Chris Griffin-Beale to ask where the *Telegraph* had obtained this startling information. Griffin-Beale told him it was in the press pack all the lads had got yesterday, and that went for the *Mail*'s brightest and manliest. He could find it listed, among the seventy-four other items, on page 22 towards the bottom. The *Mail* rang off. The shock horror machine ground into action.

'Party for gays starts new row,' the *Mail* led its front page next morning. And, very big, 'BAN TV4 DEMANDS ANGRY MP'. Under this the TV editor, Joe Steeples, a decent enough chap, reported:

> Channel 4 provoked a new row yesterday when it announced it was to screen a homosexual entertainment programme. [It was the day before actually, Joe, if your lads hadn't been asleep; it was the *Telegraph* that had it yesterday.] For Tory MP John Carlisle this was the last straw – and he is trying to get the new TV network closed. ...
>
> The MP for Luton West, who has been critical of Channel 4 for carrying too much bad language, said: I am horrified at the thought of this programme. This is TV for minorities indeed, and I hope the majority will show their contempt for it by switching off in their millions. [At 11 pm at night, Mr Carlisle, the millions will have switched off already. But let that pass.] A large section of the public is already thoroughly disgusted by the low standards on Channel 4, and now I feel it is my duty to protest in the strongest possible terms at this latest departure. The channel is an offence to public taste and decency, and should be drummed off the air forthwith.

Steeples included a description of the programme: 'the first ever to even begin to show what it means to be positively gay'. Over the page, he quoted the IBA: 'Channel 4 has been specifically instructed to cater for minority audiences and in providing a programme for the gay population is merely following its brief.' Bravely said. I was quoted also: 'Channel 4 chief executive Jeremy Isaacs said he was sure *One in Five* will be in perfect taste – "though I haven't seen it yet".'

That day Geordie comic Bobby Thompson came to Charlotte Street for the preview of our programme of his act. He could have told John Carlisle MP a thing or two about how many sorts it takes to make a world. What is the Geordie for 'There's nowt so queer as folk'? In the evening I went, as did the Prince and Princess of Wales, to the premiere of Dickie Attenborough's *Gandhi*. I gave no interviews, declining, among much else, to appear on *The Jimmy Young Show*.

Next morning, as I left my home in Chiswick for the office at 8 am, I was greeted on the doorstep by a *Mail* reporter, Peter Sheridan.

'Mr Isaacs, are you going to resign?'

'No.'

'Do you now regret your programming policy?'

'Absolutely not.'

(I am relying on Sheridan's story for this, by the way, and may have got it wrong. But I remember the next question.)

'Can I have a lift into town?'

He didn't get the lift. But he did, doggedly, get to my office almost as soon as I did. And he did, and will, go far.

These shenanigans seem now a source of harmless amusement. Yet is it right for newspapers to drum up this sort of rumpus by thinking up an answer that will make a headline, inventing the question that will provoke it, and finding a helpful Member of Parliament to sing the duet with? I later asked a *Scottish Daily Mail* reporter whom I met in Glasgow how he justified this habit of using Mr Rentaquote MP to make a story. 'You don't understand,' he said. 'If the news editor is after you, if you haven't much time, and you want to make the front page, there's nothing like having an MP handy to give you a quote. That's your story. Reporting from Glasgow,' he added, 'hasn't been the same since Teddy Taylor lost Cathcart and went to Southend.'

Newspapers, to achieve their effects, become expert at generating synthetic indignation on your behalf and mine, without ever asking whether we are actually in the least bit indignant at what they say, hypocritically, is so exercising them.

Meditating on the role of the newspaper-generated 'Stormover' in my life, I came to feel a new sympathy and understanding for rock stars, football managers, politicians, for all those who live their lives in the constant glare of publicity. However hard you try not to let it get to you, it does do something to you. I defined the neologism 'Stormover': 'A stormover is a conversation between a journalist and a Member of Parliament in which the journalist tells the MP something he does not know, and the MP calls for the banning of something he has not seen.' I have hopes that one day this useful word, its etymology well established, may appear in the appendix of recent usage to the Oxford English Dictionary.

One in Five was duly transmitted, on schedule, to an interested 858,000 souls, without further fuss or pother.

Over Christmas, with nothing much else around, the *Star*, on Boxing Day for publication the day after, cobbled together: 'Secret shake-up to save Channel 4. TV CHIEF FACES SACK. Exclusive.'

It was exclusive all right: someone made it up. A secret Christmas conference of ITV chiefs had determined that I must go.

It has been decided that:
* Idealistic Mr Isaacs, the man pledged to turn ITV audiences on to highbrow shows, must go.
* Minority programmes will be cut back and the Channel 4 soap opera *Brookside*, plunged into controversy by the use of four-letter words, will be scrapped.
* New schedules of hit shows, including the return of many old favourites, have been drawn up.

Anxious – though I doubt it – they may have been. Certainly the chairmen of companies, reporting their results to shareholders and resenting the subscription, tended to go for us a bit. One claimed we were draining the life-blood of the system. But ITV chiefs do not meet or confer over Christmas. The telephone, as other newspapers followed up the *Star*'s 'exclusive', interrupted the rest of Chris Griffin-Beale's holiday. But the ratings were not that worrying, though they verged on being so. Although few understood this, the 10 per cent share of audience we were after had never been expected overnight, or even within a year. Three years was the span we thought it might take to get there. In fact, it took nearer five – but that lateness hardly mattered; we were financially viable at a lower audience share anyway.

With hindsight, too – though our Head of Marketing Sue Stoessl saw this clearly throughout – November and December were by far the toughest months for a new channel to make inroads into viewing habits. The other three channels were at their very strongest, halfway through their autumn schedules. And Christmas viewing habits, with popular blockbusters abounding, were equally hard to dent.

We expected the share gained in our opening week, boosted by curiosity, to fall. Four per cent seemed respectable, just. Three per cent we might get away with, just. Two per cent, as anxious, supportive telephone calls to me from Dickie Attenborough indicated, would have been grim news indeed and would perhaps have compelled drastic change. 'Assistant Heads will roll,' the cry goes up at the BBC after *débâcle*. In fact, Assistant Heads only move sideways because, in the BBC version of musical chairs, when the music stops they put another chair in. But at Channel 4, if we did hit disastrous rock-bottom, only one head would deserve to fall – mine.

Every Friday morning we gathered round the video display screen in Sue Stoessl's office to look at the ratings up to the previous Sunday night. The screen showed numbers against each time slot, for each channel; 5 for BBC's *Money Programme*; say, 20 for ITN's *News at Ten*; 40 for *Coronation Street*. Some, sometimes many, Channel 4 programmes got zeros, noughts, little round o's. This was dispiriting, but not the end of the world. If each rating point meant 300,000 viewers then a zero could mean 250,000 viewers, and that was not too bad, was it? And some of our programmes already got numbers representing some millions. The crucial thing, for which on a Friday we always had to wait a few hours more, was the breakdown of weekly audience share by channel. What would it be this week, a satisfying 4 per cent, a worrying 3 per cent, or worse?

Here crudity came to our aid; in those days the figures were given correct to one decimal point but were then rounded, for presentational purposes, up or down to the nearest whole number. 3.9 per cent, therefore, was shown as 4 per cent; so was 3.6 per cent; 3.5 per cent also was, generously, rounded up to 4 per cent. Whew! Breathe again. 3.4 per cent, though, was shown as 3 per cent. And, but not to allow oneself to think of it, though 2.6 per cent would be shown as 3 per cent, 2.4 per cent would be seen as an irrefutably accusing 2 per cent. Dickie Attenborough hoped it would never happen. The lowest we fell, in fact, was to 2.8 per cent (shown as 3 per cent) in the week of 26 December 1982.

In January Tamara and I, leaving little local difficulties behind, went away for a fortnight's holiday to Sri Lanka, just weeks, as it turned out, before grave local difficulties between Sinhalese and Tamils erupted in communal bloodshed. We saw Anuradhapura and Pollonaruwa, and climbed Sigiriya. We went up into the Highlands to the Scots baronial tea planters' resort of Nuwara Eliya. On the way down, we passed tea plantations with names like Wavendon – our London home was in Wavendon Avenue. On the balcony of our hotel in Kandy I read in the local paper: 'West London Buddhists Protest Residents Bias'. A planning argument over whether Buddhists could build a meeting place – with parking for twenty cars – in the leafy back garden immediately behind and abutting on ours was making the headlines here in Kandy. I put the paper down, and called for whisky. And we bathed in the Indian Ocean.

I came back to England to calm, and to a long scheduled conference of

Channel 4 staff and the Board at Berystede, near Ascot. This was to be the third such weekend get-together to be held. At our first, held in July 1981 at Lane End in Buckinghamshire, much used by BBC middle management, it was primarily a question of getting to know each other. At the opening session I held forth, solo and, I regret to say, at numbing length. Next day the commissioning editors – most of whom the Board had never met – each gave an account of his or her intentions. Andy Park, I remember, made a dazzling impression.

On the Saturday evening we dined in a circular pavilion at The Bell, Aston Clinton. Channel 4, unlike some other broadcasters, never lived high on the hog. But this seemed a proper occasion for a blow-out. I chose the wines. The sauternes was particularly luscious. There were sore heads in the morning. There came, months later, a bulky transcript of the proceedings, replete with gaps, literals and hundreds of thousands of words. I doubt whether anyone ever referred to it.

The second was held at Minster Lovell in Oxfordshire in the spring of 1982, as transmission neared. Here there were programmes to show – 'Korup', the Cameroon rain forest, was well liked. Most of the talk in the corridors was of negotiations with ACTT; could we refuse to recognize the union? If we did, would we end up in thrall to it? Could we, setting the national agreement with ITV aside, arrive at an understanding that would suit our particular needs? We found a path forward.

Now, in January 1983, we were due to meet for a third time, three months after going on air, to review progress and consider what lessons were to be learned. A touch on the tiller?

This time it was for the chief executive to listen and respond. Brian Tesler, Managing Director of London Weekend Television, started off. For him it was, almost, apocalypse now. We were, he thought, gathered at 'the last chance saloon'. The channel was too heavy, too serious. There were not enough entertaining programmes, particularly at the weekend. There was no understanding of truly complementary programming; what was not required, again particularly at the weekends, was to put serious programmes on C4 against entertainment on ITV – I had *A Week in Politics* in our schedule on a Saturday evening. What *was* wanted, as the alternative to ITV's entertainment, was a different sort of entertainment.

Thames and LWT, alone in ITV, competed with each other for advertising. For years I had listened to and participated in arguments as to how ITV's schedule should be constructed across seven evenings in a way that would satisfy the two rivals. Now, I found this particularly hard to take. I well understood LWT's difficulty in maximizing revenue on the three nights only of their franchise. But was their need, or their perception of it, to shape our schedule? I held my peace and quaked a little. Tesler always made a formidable case.

As Director of Programmes at Thames before me, Brian Tesler had been a ruthlessly skilled scheduler. He could not resist querying what must have seemed to him the deliberate perverseness of our method. We juxtaposed, for example, programmes of utterly disparate nature and appeal. We invited viewers to select one programme only and, unless they were sufficiently tempted by what followed, to switch again, discriminatingly, over or off. Brian Tesler saw this as wantonly throwing away an audience that was there to be held for the asking. More entertainment would do it.

Glyn Tegai Hughes, a former BBC Governor, spoke next. Everything, he thought, was pretty well. The programmes were not as good as they might be, but the mix was about right, though a little more high seriousness and intellectual distinctiveness would not come amiss. More of the same, please, only more so. That evening and next day divisions were clearly evident.

Throughout Saturday the talk went on. The *Sunday Telegraph* had a reporter snooping in the bushes whom Chris Griffin-Beale escorted out of the grounds. But his presence lent a tinge of tension to the proceedings. Would this be reported as a crisis conference, but for real? My impression was of divergence and concern. My task, when I spoke at the end, would be, I thought, to hold things together and make it possible to go forward on our set course, without reneging on our purposes and without rift and division widening.

I thought I had to make the speech of my life, and did my best to make it. I cannot now remember the detail of what I said, and have no note of it to hand. But I was strengthened in holding fast to our intent by the knowledge that there was no alternative; the commissioning process, contracts out to suppliers, had already committed the vast part of next year's funds. It was simply not possible, even if we had wanted to, to halve expenditure in 1983/84 on news, or on documentaries or on the workshops, or on education or on the arts, or even on films, and switch the savings to comedy or drama series. Even were we to plan to do so for the future, it would take more than a year for the results to appear. And by then the channel, thanks to good things already in the pipeline, would either be catching on, would have turned the corner, or it would not. If growth funds were available in 1984/85 that was another matter, though there would be a further time-lag before any change could take effect on screen.

I had always thought we could get by without making too many drama series of our own; we would buy repeats instead. The same went for certain sorts of comedy. We could shift emphasis a little now, and we could commit some additional new resources for the future. I agreed that when we could we would.

But others present, I knew, already felt the channel was too compromised, too conventional, not distinctive enough. They and I drew strength from the bedrock of our purpose, the Act of Parliament. The Act said encourage innovation and experiment, cater for interests ITV does not; provide a distinctive service. It did not say obtain high audiences and entertain the public as others do. If we tried our damnedest to fulfil the purposes set out for us in the Act, and failed to reach high audiences, we would be forgiven. If we made ourselves safe financially but in doing so abandoned the qualitative goals set for us by Parliament, we would have betrayed a trust. That would be to fail unforgivably.

We left Berystede in good heart and good order. There would be more emphasis on how we presented ourselves, on entertainment. 'You gotta accentuate the positive,' the song said. There would be no betrayal of trust.

Some incidents from around that time stick in the memory. After dinner at the German Embassy I spoke to one politician who was sure we were on the wrong lines, Norman Tebbit. 'You've got it all wrong, you know,' he said, 'doing all these programmes for homosexuals and such.' (We'd only done one, actually.) 'Parliament never meant that sort of thing. The different interests you are supposed to cater for are not like that at all. Golf and sailing and fishing. Hobbies. That's what we intended.' He moved on round the room. Francis Pym, then Foreign Secretary, in a speech to diplomatic writers warmly welcomed the additional foreign coverage now provided in *Channel 4 News*. Very pleasantly he commended the channel and wished it well. This was cheering because it came only days after we had broadcast *Ireland, The Silent Voices*, a film whose partly Republican content had provoked another 'Stormover' headline.

I mention these tiny straws in the wind because the tensions at the time were such as to make them seem important. Criticism seemed unremitting, and since we went on doing what was criticized, looked likely to continue. In the end it might take its toll. Some members of the Board were concerned that unless we won over influential voices to our cause shortly, we could be in trouble. Foremost of these, surprisingly, was Tony Smith. We were urged to put ourselves about, appease enemies, cultivate friends.

In March 1983 I accepted an invitation to address the Conservative Back Bench Media Committee in a room in the House of Commons. I explained briefly what we were trying to do; said how I thought we were doing; took questions. From the usual dozen or so attending, one, John Gorst MP, put this to me: 'You talk, Mr Isaacs, of catering for different tastes. I saw a programme the other night in which there was a great deal of bad language, and people were quite openly taking drugs. One chap was interviewed by a film crew sitting on the lavatory. What sort of taste do you call that?'

Thrown somewhat, I racked my brain to determine what particular programme this might be. Then I remembered. It was *The Bad News Tour* in the series *The Comic Strip Presents*, a parody of a film about a louche rock group, Bad News. As I prepared to answer, I spotted sitting next to John Gorst a Tory MP I knew slightly, right-winger Alan Clark, a military historian, Kenneth Clark's son. He, I thought, was something of a man of the world, and a true Tory. I decided to go for broke.

'I've remembered what that programme was,' I said. 'It went out the other evening at eleven o'clock. Actually, it was intended as a parody of bad taste. You thought it revolting. But I do not apologize for it. I must tell you that many viewers of a different age group found that programme very much to their taste. My son, in his early twenties, thinks *The Comic Strip* is the best thing we do. So do others. Our tastes do differ; in a democracy we ought to be free to choose. Is not the whole point of introducing a fourth channel service to cater for differing tastes, allowing viewers to choose what they want to watch for themselves? Is that not what the freedom of the individual means?' A nod. No answer.

As events continue to demonstrate, in the Conservative Party the conflict between individual freedom and the urge to regulate on behalf of nanny state continues unresolved.

I asked to see Willie Whitelaw. He was good enough to offer me lunch at his club, Buck's. Over the gulls' eggs he confided that some of his colleagues did think the channel was a bit left-wing. They accused him of 'letting the loonies on the air'. He hoped things would not get out of hand. I did my best to reassure him. There had been a bit of a splurge of it at first. Some folk had waited years to get off their chest on television what they had not had a chance to say before. But I pledged myself to ensure that in the end, and as soon as we could, we would get the balance right. There would be a fair crack for all.

Had he considered though, I asked, that it was better for people who felt all media were against them to have a chance to put a case on television than, denied all access to a public platform, to take violently to the streets? My advocacy of what Marxist scholars describe as repressive tolerance did not seem fully to convince. Willie looked doubtful. But he assured me of his goodwill. He had welcomed our exchange. He wished to keep in touch.

Actually, from the day when, as an inexperienced speaker in the Conservative interest, he was, by his own account, comprehensively rubbished by an election audience on Red Clydeside, Willie Whitelaw has understood that any society contains hostile elements who must learn, by give and take, to live together. I doubt he had ever seen Channel 4 as contributing in any way to that process. But I do not think he found the notion totally absurd.

His most memorable verdict on Channel 4, though, came back in November on the Saturday after we opened. After a taxing day out of doors in his Cumbrian constituency and a good dinner, he thought it his duty to go to the other room, switch on the television and see how his new creation was getting on. There, twenty minutes later, his wife Celia found him zizzing, peacefully asleep.

Now, in many respects, things were moving our way. But the *Sun* was still running a tagline which, after this time, I found hard to take: 'The Channel That Nobody Watches'. This was patently untrue; from the day we started millions of Britons watched Channel 4, at least for an hour or two every week. This fact was concealed from many because the non-numerate, unskilled in the statistics of audience research, thought that a 4 per cent share of audience meant that only 4 per cent of viewers watched. It did not mean that at all. It meant that 10 per cent, say, of viewers each day, and 40 per cent of viewers each week – over 20 million individuals – watched something of Channel 4. But they did not watch for very long, an hour or so maybe. The aggregate of all that viewing, considered as a proportion of all viewing on all channels, totalled, modestly, 4 per cent.

This was scarcely surprising, given viewers' longstanding and genuine enjoyment of what the other three channels had to offer. Given, too, that they knew when to turn on to find what they knew they liked on BBC or ITV, but did not yet know how to find what they might or might not like on unfamiliar Channel 4. So our share was modest indeed, but not negligible. I wrote to the editor of the *Sun*, Kelvin Mackenzie, to point out that calling us 'The Channel That Nobody Watches' was a whopping untruth. In fact, 23 million individuals watched each week, though briefly. The chances were that many of those watching us were *Sun* readers: 'To tell them no one watches Channel 4 is to tell them what they know to be untrue.' Did he think that was good for him? To my surprise he printed the letter, dropped the catchphrase, and asked me to lunch. At this lunch Rupert Murdoch's then right hand in News International, Bruce Matthews, asked me what I knew about satellite television because, he said, 'we're in it'. 'Not much,' I told him. 'Surely you have expert analysts who can forecast the viability of that sort of massive business venture.' 'Not at all,' he said. 'It's not like that here. When Rupert says "go", we go.'

In March we were to announce our programmes for the spring. By now we'd had *The Irish RM*. We had also seen six weeks of *Treasure Hunt*, in which landscape, the race against the clock and Anneka Rice's bottom bewitched. I had seen *Chasse au Trésor* on a monitor on a landing at the television market, MIP, at Cannes in 1981. Cecil Korer tenaciously wrestled it from the clutch of the BBC; an independent company, Chatsworth, really made it go. Audiences were warming to it. Now came the spring launch. 'Entertainment,' said the blurb, 'springs forth on 4.' On screen, animated graphics answered echo. The mood was jocund; blooms blossomed; birds chirruped; lambs gambolled. Much 'emphasis' was attached, following the Berystede weekend, to entertainment. But we had only one solitary entertainment series, *Father's Day* with John Alderton, to offer. The rest of the mix was very much as before; *Kill or Cure?*, an inquiry into pharmaceuticals; *Alter Image*, modernism in the fringe arts, rather cosy most of it; *Vietnam*, a thirteen-part documentary series. Like lambs, though, the press swallowed the mood and the message.

What the spring schedule did boast was our second season of *Film on Four*, the movies that David Rose had commissioned, and which now began to be available to us. These included *Angel*, a stunning directorial debut by the writer Neil Jordan, commended to us by John Boorman;

Red Monarch, a satire on Stalin; another *First Love*, *Secrets*; Bill Bryden's film on St Kilda, *Ill Fares the Land*; Maurice Hatton's *Nelly's Version* with Eileen Atkins; and, commissioned by the BFI Production Board but salvaged by us when they ran out of funds, Peter Greenaway's stylish *The Draughtsman's Contract* with fine performances by Janet Suzman, Anne Louise Lambert and Anthony Higgins, and music by Michael Nyman. *Film on Four* would follow *Treasure Hunt* on a Thursday evening at 9.30 pm, opposite ITV's *This Week*. ITV, on 7 April, gave a boost to our plans by showcasing an evening of our work on ITV. And they let us have a glossy two-part US piece on Gloria Vanderbilt: *Little Gloria Happy at Last*. The 4 per cents began to turn to 5 per cents. We were on the up, and the press and the public were beginning to know it.

And in spite of the IPA/Equity dispute, time did sell. ITV was beginning to take in revenue. On Friday afternoons I would telephone Ron Miller, the ebullient and energetic Sales Director of LWT, and ask how he was doing. Proudly he would tell me that this weekend he would take £200,000 on Channel 4, then it was £250,000 on Channel 4, then it was £300,000. As the years went on this increased to £500,000 and more.

In any event, a few weeks earlier an unlikely knight on a white charger had ridden to our aid, and was now in the media lists doing battle on our behalf. February 1 saw the launch of TV-am.

In spite of their pleas, the IBA held back TV-am's launch till three months after ours. The delay allowed the BBC to launch *Breakfast Time* in a pre-emptive strike against them. Peter Jay's company boasted a band of talented presenters, Anna Ford, David Frost, Robert Kee, Michael Parkinson and Angela Rippon (who replaced Esther Rantzen when she pulled out). These were now embarked on their famous mission to explain. The BBC's *Breakfast Time*, though, made an effective start. Ron Neil took the programme further down-market than his rivals had anticipated, and before they were on the air. The TV-am team of all the talents, between whom a special chemistry was supposed to exist, were to prove no match for cuddly Frank Bough in his pullover.

When, some weeks after they went on air, I was first shown over TV-am's post-modern building in Hawley Crescent, with the breakfast egg on top, what struck me most were the numbers employed there. 'Those you see now do not include,' my guide explained, 'the night shift who come in to make the morning's programme.' He led me through Terry Farrell's long interior atrium running east to west, with arbours first in the Cambodian style, past a Persian ziggurat, and then, following the sun westward, past Greek colonnades, to, furthest west, a Mexican Indian temple, with spiky cactus on ochre sand. At the ziggurat, a bell rang out, summoning staff to a meeting at which redundancies were to be announced. TV-am was in trouble.

From their first day on air, cruelly, the press turned from us to savage them, and, as changes followed, chemistry crumbled and friends fell out, found plenty to savage them with. I remembered Lucretius:

> Suave mari magno, turbantibus aequora ventis,
> E terra magnum alterius spectare laborem.'

Translated: Safe on land, we all enjoy watching some other poor bugger being buffeted by a stormy sea.

On 2 May Miles Kington in *The Times* laid it down that Channel 4 jokes, which had lasted quite well, would soon be out; TV-am jokes were coming in instead.

> So if you have a good remark about Channel 4, you should make it now. In another week's time it will be totally out of date, because people are now beginning to say nice things about Channel 4. How varied it is, how good the film and book items are, what wonderful repeats and films they have, how refreshing the pop music programmes are, how unusually interesting their news coverage is. . . .
>
> But surely, you may ask, if Channel 4 is now getting praised, it must have been quite good to begin with. Why all the flak and criticism at the start? How can a national joke so soon be accepted as something quite good?
>
> The answer lies in the curious habit the British have, and do not quite understand, of setting up Aunt Sallies in order not to knock them down. Almost every new set-up is pelted with mud, brickbats, custard pies and rotten tomatoes. It may deserve them, it may not, but it gets pelted until the next Aunt Sally comes along, at which point the pelting suddenly gets transferred and the recent target is cleaned up and becomes a much-loved part of the English scene.

But if, outwardly, all seemed set fair, inner tensions threatened.

5

Questions of Leadership

EDMUND Dell, when he was invited by the IBA in May 1980 to chair the panel of consultants that was to become the Board of the Channel 4 Television Company Limited, was full-time Chairman and Chief Executive of the respected City banking firm of Guinness Peat, incorporating the merchant bank Guinness Mahon, one of the choice few houses approved by the Bank of England to operate in this field. Edmund Dell had been a Labour Minister of State at the Board of Trade (1968–69) and Paymaster General (1974–76). He stood down as MP for Birkenhead at the 1979 election. Dell, when still in government, had been lured to Guinness Peat by the previous chairman, and substantial shareholder in the company, Harry (Lord) Kissin. Kissin made the offer in the flat of Arnold Goodman. He thought he was issuing an invitation that would take effect rather later, but James Callaghan, on hearing of the job offer, insisted on Dell's resigning straightaway.

After war service in the Royal Artillery, Dell had lectured on modern history at Queen's College, Oxford. More to the left in those days, he wrote for Marxist historical journals. But his career had been in industry, and in Manchester Labour politics, together with Joel Barnett and his great friend Robert Sheldon. He had been on the right of James Callaghan's Cabinet, seeing no alternative to the harsh measures Denis Healey as Chancellor found himself forced to take in 1976. There were good precedents for the appointment of former politicians to the chairmanship of broadcasting authorities; Charles Hill had been Chairman of both IBA and BBC; Herbert Aylestone succeeded him at the IBA. Interestingly, whether the Home Office was consulted or not, and one must suppose it was, no one then thought it odd that, under a Conservative government, a former Labour minister should be chosen for such a responsibility. It would not happen today. But Dell was not only a politician who might be expected to know his way round Whitehall; he had also, it was thought, experience of business, having worked for years at home and abroad for ICI. Now he was a figure in the City, at the head of a merchant bank. Bridget Plowden, Chairman of the IBA, had been observed stomping the corridors of Brompton Road, muttering 'What we need for the fourth channel is a banker.' In addition to these credentials Dell, a passionate music lover, was educated in the arts. On the Board of the English National Opera, he was Chairman of the Finance Committee there.

To his role at Channel 4 Edmund Dell brought no knowledge of media. But that was not a disadvantage that had hindered others. He was quiet in his manner, tenacious in pursuing his point of view. He was an absolute stickler for financial probity in matters great and small, going to considerable lengths to ensure that proper auditing checks were always in place, and that no scintilla of laxity should attach to any of our multifarious financial wheelings and dealings. He jealously guarded the channel's rights against the pressures of ITV, and the overweening – as he came to see them – claims of the regulatory body which owned us and had appointed him, the IBA. He was staunch always for what he believed to be right. Yet, in some ways, he was an eccentric and difficult chairman.

Edmund Dell is a shy person. His acute mind had never allowed him to make loose play in politics with easy rhetorical answers to complex problems. To some difficulties, he insisted, there were no solutions; we must simply get on with things as they are. The world will be the way it will be. This pessimistic realism – some would call it negativism – had, perhaps, held him back in politics; certainly I doubt whether he had gone as far in it as he hoped.

Now he headed a respected City firm, hobnobbing as of right and station on equal terms with the nobs of that world. But those satisfactions were not to last long either. When in 1981 I first paid my weekly visits to him in Guinness Peat's offices at St Mary at Hill, past the formally dressed waiters on his floor, I was conscious of a coldness and of tensions in the air. But I did not realize that, locked in conflict with some of his colleagues, Edmund Dell was fighting to save his job. His predecessor, who had put him in, Lord Kissin, had turned against him and wanted him out. The company's results were poor. There had been a massive outflow of funds on some venture in California through a loophole in control mechanisms which ought never to have been allowed to obtain. The defect preceded Dell's arrival, but as Chairman and Chief Executive he could not escape ultimate responsibility for what occurred. And there had been other disagreements. He wanted to invest heavily in, even to purchase outright, Telerate, a new business information system in the United States. His wish to make such an investment was overruled. Telerate, he used later to point out as he followed its progress in the financial press, became a huge success, generating vast profits, but not for Guinness Peat. In the end his enemies had him out. In January 1982 he gave way as Chief Executive to Alastair Morton, remaining as non-executive Chairman. In November 1982, just after we went on air, he relinquished the chairmanship also. He was out of a job.

This abrupt change of fortune, its implied censure hard for a proud man to bear, made two significant differences to his relationship with Channel 4; he now had nothing else to do and could spend time and energy, if need arose, on our affairs and on our premises. And it meant also that he could not afford to fail with us. Whatever verdict others had passed on him in politics or in the City, he could not have it said that the new television channel entrusted to his care had also been a failure – that, somehow, he had mucked it up again. The passion with which he now conducted himself in our affairs must have owed much to this realization and reflected, at least in part, the very great strain and tension he had been operating under at Guinness Peat.

Edmund Dell had left the Labour Party and joined the SDP. He allowed his name to be included in a full-page advertisement published in that party's interest in the newspapers in February 1981. This was a slightly odd step for the chairman of a supposedly politically impartial broadcasting channel to take. 'But,' he explained, 'Shirley Williams rang at midnight and begged me. I could not deny her.' The new Chairman of the IBA, George Thomson, Lord Thomson of Monifieth, who had replaced Bridget Plowden, had been a member of an earlier Labour Cabinet before going into the European Community as one of Britain's two Commissioners. He, too, and his wife Grace, had joined the SDP. Sir Richard Attenborough, Deputy Chairman of Channel 4, was a founder member of the party. During the election of June 1983 in which Mrs Thatcher won a handsome victory, when Dickie was in Glasgow publicizing his film

Gandhi, he assured the *Glasgow Herald* that the Mahatma, if he had been living today, would have been an SDP voter.

This was all a bit much, and had one unfortunate consequence. One Board member, Anne Sofer, the most genuinely independent mind on it, was asked to leave in spring 1983 when her three-year term expired. She was SDP too, and had joined us under that flag. With too many others now aboard under the same colours, she was made to walk the plank. In her place were added Anthony Pragnell DFC, a wise old bird who had been Deputy Director General of the IBA, and, at Edmund Dell's particular wish, the Provost of his old college, Queen's, Oxford, the historian Robert Blake, now Lord Blake. Blake, the biographer of Disraeli, was a true blue Conservative. He had the clearest of minds, and was a wholly delightful and admirable colleague.

No relationship could have been more crucial to the channel than that with the IBA. But Edmund Dell and George Thomson, in spite of, perhaps because of, the similarities of their background and outlook, did not get on. There was never, in the early days at any rate, any great dissension between them, any real cause for alarm. But there was a certain acerbity in their dealings. I never felt either held the other in particularly high regard. George would snap his braces, and say, 'Well, Edmund.' Edmund, tapping his fingers on the arm of the settee in George's office, would respond, 'Now, George.' Edmund Dell saw Channel 4 as an independent entity. Thomson saw it as the creature of the IBA.

The IBA already had one representative on the Board of its subsidiary, a newly appointed Finance Director, Peter Rogers, who, in spite of his previous ignorance of all broadcasting matters, did not hesitate to hold forth on contentious issues at considerable length. He was particularly strong on the interpretation of the Broadcasting Act. He had been sent, I presume, to keep an eye on our finances, but since our accounts were always presented with immaculate clarity by the Finance Controller, David Scott, who also now served as Secretary to the Board, he may have felt this did not offer him sufficient opportunity to contribute to our debates. Peter Rogers did, however, deal justly with our annual case to the IBA for the funding we required from ITV.

The ITV companies had chafed under the rule of the previous IBA Chairman, Lady Plowden, and Director-General, Sir Brian Young. Too austere, they moaned, too academic, too otherworldly; no understanding of our problems. They welcomed the incoming Chairman, George

Thomson, a political animal and a man of the world. Thomson passed over as Director-General the leading candidate, Colin Shaw, Director of Television. He appointed instead, to general surprise, the Managing Director of Capital Radio (Chairman, Sir Richard Attenborough), writer, producer, broadcasting entrepreneur John Whitney. Colin Shaw had been perhaps too quiet in his previous role, too much in Brian Young's shadow. But he has stuck to his last, and lasted. Today's Broadcasting Standards Council is fortunate to have him as Director. What satisfaction John Whitney sought in, for him, the new role of regulator, has never been clear, unless perhaps it was a knighthood. The likeliest explanation is that Thomson and he believed they were to preside over a new expansion of commercial public-service broadcasting, with satellite services also coming under the IBA; more media, a looser rein, and everyone off to the races. But, in spite of Thomson's formidable lead, the IBA is a lesser force after their stewardship than once it was. Whitney has left the IBA to become Managing Director of The Really Useful Company, Andrew Lloyd-Webber's business arm.

Channel 4, whose work and progress I regularly reviewed with John Whitney, was beginning to make its mark. In the *Observer* for 3 April 1983, under the banner 'Why the Fourth Channel has Come to Stay', I wrote that the housekeeping sums were beginning to come right, pointing out that ITV in effect had, without markedly reducing profitability, been able to finance a 60 per cent increase in the production of air-time, whose income was theirs, entirely out of revenue, without recourse to the market. Their reward was that they retained and extended their monopoly. And I gave this rationale for our programming:

> Channel 4 is asked to cater for interests not catered for by ITV, and to provide 'a service of a distinctive character'. We have tried to treat viewers as individuals of different tastes who may like, or dislike, part of what we offer. Some tastes are satisfied without provoking dissent. None will complain that the English National Opera's *Rigoletto* or, tonight, Olivier's magnificent *Lear* will be followed by Janet Baker in Glyndebourne's *Orfeo*, Peter Hall's National Theatre *Oresteia*, Peter Brook's *Carmen*. And no one objects to *The Irish RM*, to *Treasure Hunt*, *Upstairs, Downstairs* or *The Munsters*.
>
> But an evening's rock, or an Indian movie, or an hour of reggae, or the Irish angle on politics, or the trade unions' weekly viewpoint, or

an hour for Black Britons or for Britons of Asian heritage, seem to some an affront to the consensus. They want television that appeals to all viewers all the time. Perhaps, risking minimal offence, that is what television has mostly attempted (BBC-2, in its heyday, is the exception). But plainly, that is not the objective Parliament intended Channel 4 to serve. . . .

Should black Britons, should the young, should feminists, should homosexuals see themselves, canvass their ideas, on television? I see no reason why not. They are of this society, not outside it. It is cardinal, surely, to broadcasting in a free, pluralist society, that all sectors of society should be fairly represented on the screen.

Tapping those new sources of energy, letting those voices (within an overall obligation to fairness) come through, is both Channel 4's most challenging task, and the practice that evokes most hostility.

The IBA not only brought Channel 4 into being, and in the form in which we know it, but has been firmly supportive of it at all times. Yet I never looked forward to liaison meetings at Brompton Road. Whatever their public front, in private the IBA exhibited almost constant anxiety. Perhaps it is the role of the regulator, particularly one given by law – ludicrously, in my view – the ultimate reponsibility for what is broadcast, to take for granted what is fine and dandy, and worry ceaselessly over what might go wrong. John Whitney, for example, was concerned about *Brookside*; it was pretty dreadful, he thought. Did I really intend to go on with it? Ought I not to bring it to an end? He never formally so instructed me. He would not, could not, have been obeyed if he had. But, in those days, I thought he would have been jolly pleased to see the back of it.

Brookside, when it started, had technical teething troubles – the sound recording was pretty poor for a start. And it included, at its transmission time at 8 pm, as Phil Redmond had indicated to me it would, language which, although unexceptionable after the 9 pm watershed, the IBA found hard to justify. I could not place it at 9 pm. We cleaned it up accordingly.

But *Brookside* was also, from the word go, a quite remarkable achievement, created from minimal resources by an independent company on a specially constructed location. Phil Redmond's company built and owned the houses in which *Brookside*'s characters 'lived', and the production team worked. It was established in a city, Liverpool, which had never previously contributed to network television. It dealt as faithfully as it could with the stress-and-strain industrial decline and·severe unemployment placed on people's lives. *Brookside* made an immediate impact, particularly on younger viewers. It became their serial, exactly as was intended; one many of them could not miss. And, since we repeated the week's episodes in an omnibus edition at the weekend, a trick the BBC followed with *EastEnders* and belatedly now Granada with *Coronation Street*, its fans had two chances each week to follow the fortunes of their favourite characters. There was strong plotting – Phil Redmond supervised all – and there were good performances. One actor, Ricky Tomlinson playing Bobby Grant, had called some attention to himself in an earlier life. He had been one of the Shrewsbury Five, an early flying picket. Convicted, he had served a sentence for violence and intimidation. As an actor he was not bad. Playing Sheila Grant, Sue Johnston gave week in week out one of the really remarkable television performances of our day. *Brookside*'s audience grew.

So there was no way I could accede to Whitney's persistent hints that *Brookside* should be ended. And no way, had I agreed with him, that I could have brought it about. We had a three-year contract with Redmond's company, Mersey Television. Sixty jobs were at stake. In any event, we had not the resources to whistle up from elsewhere a programme to replace it that could have done a comparable job. As with other of our output – *Channel 4 News* is the obvious example – there was nothing to do, while privately urging particular steps to improvement, but keep cool, keep faith, and wait for it to come right. On the other hand, at this time John Whitney took, to his lasting credit, a decision that was to have important consequences. He authorized for transmission on Channel 4 at 11.30 pm on Friday, 10 June, the day after Margaret Thatcher's election victory, a controversial feature film called *Scum*. There was a fair bit of hoo-ha in the press about its screening; 2.3 million viewed it. It came top of our Top Ten for the week. Pursing her lips and rubbing her hands, Mrs Mary Whitehouse called for a judicial review of the IBA's action in allowing it. On the result of that case, when it came to be decided, much might depend.

The Board of Channel 4 also tended, quite naturally in a way, to take good things for granted, but chivy away unremittingly at anything that worried them. Three programme matters were of concern in the spring and summer of 1983.

IBT, the International Broadcasting Trust, had made *Common Interest*, a low-cost series transmitted in an early evening slot, part of our educational output. It dealt with development – our relationship with the Third World.

IBT were among the first would-be independent producers to make themselves known to us in 1981. They were an unusual grouping; they had no commercial interest. Their interest was to promote studies on the Third World. They pestered the channel for an early commission, or the guarantee of one, to enable them to move on from their other activities – pamphlets, speakers, church meetings and discussion groups – into broadcasting. They saw themselves as exactly the sort of new voice which the channel had been called into being to service. Much discussion preceded the original commission.

Against them, apart from the question of their competence to broadcast, was their apparent proselytizing intention, even though this could be represented as simply a wish to further interest in the Third World and development questions generally rather than to put forward any particular solution to the problems these presented. In their favour was their proposed method. They had funds and would share the cost of production with us, and that helped. More important, on transmission they would, up and down the country, organize discussion groups in schoolrooms, churches, village halls, which would canvass in an open-ended way the issues each programme raised. Here was a pleasant prospect indeed for a channel without an audience. Instead of blushing unseen, wasting our sweetness on a dark and desert air, some at least of our programmes would find a committedly interested audience.

After much humming and hawing, with Edmund Dell expressing the gravest doubts, IBT were commissioned. They hired a reasonably capable production team and went to work. The programmes that resulted were not that bad, but they were not very good. Edmund Dell, who had some expertise in these matters, thought the makers were soft-hearted, soft-headed and the programmes awful. Again and again he came back to it. How could we justify putting on such poor stuff when properly advised, consulting the right authorities, above all facing and answering the right hard questions, the programmes might have been so much better? To this formidable critique there was no ready answer. Of course we could have commissioned journalists of the calibre of those on the *Financial Times* or the *Economist* to make them. But they had not offered. Or we could have invited treatises from Unilever, Nestlé and Hoffman la Roche, though that would certainly have been to go too far in the other direction. But the fact was we had not done so, and must now live with the consequences of the course we had chosen.

The Chairman was not happy; something must be done. Edmund Dell had high expectations of the intellectual quality of television journalism, never having seen anything of it before being appointed to Channel 4. He was gravely disappointed – appalled is probably more accurate – by what he found. He had, he said, no overriding political objection to the work he most despised; it was simply that it was not good enough. Put that right, and any associated political problems would vanish. Not only that, he was of the view that high-quality journalism would be an important means of increasing our audience, though a quick comparison between the circulation figures of the *Financial Times* and of other newspapers might have disabused him of that. In spite of all his qualms, a further modest commission was granted to the International Broadcasting Trust. His concern was not abated.

Ken Loach is one of Britain's most talented and admired film-makers. All his work carries, sometimes worn lightly, and quite unflawed by it, a heavy political charge. *Cathy Come Home* shook the nation; *Family Life* argued that mental illness is caused by the sane; *Days of Hope*, four films on the 1926 General Strike and its aftermath, argued Loach's favourite cause, the betrayal of the working class sold out by its leaders.

Kes, from Barry Hines's story, movingly represented a young boy's hopes of a fulfilled future by his relationship with a kestrel. (When it failed to find cinema distribution, I remember attending a protest screening called by the ACTT's writers' group, at which one stalwart complained that the Yorkshire accents were too much for him, and another, reproachfully, told the film-makers they had made a movie about the wrong sort of bird.)

Ken Loach has the eye and the pulse, that command of framing and timing, that all great film-makers possess. He has an extraordinary ability to work with non-professional actors, and get understatedly natural performances from them. He uses the techniques of realism as a weapon; he makes you believe that the way he portrays it is the way things are. His *Fatherland*, which Channel 4 later paid for and screened, shows an East German musician's search for freedom in West Berlin and in England. The hero arrives at Harwich to be stopped, on the way to Cambridge, by the police. The miners' strike is on; he might be a picket. This is England and this is, obviously, a police state. Yet the film has interest and merit.

79

In 1982 Ken Loach, through an offshoot of Central Television, offered three documentaries on different subjects to Channel 4's commissioning editor for single documentaries, Paul Madden. Madden was charged, as it happens, particularly to look for the work of film-makers of imagination, rather than to find documentaries whose interest was primarily determined by their content. But content came more easily to the fore, and there was never any doubt that the content of what Loach put forward would be of interest, and would be contentious. He proposed two films on party politics, Madden told me, one each on the Conservative and Labour party conferences. He also offered one film on the leadership of the trades union movement. I agreed.

From then on the ground shifted and kept shifting. Each commissioning editor reported directly to me. Paul Madden reported there would not now be two party conference films but one; and not one film on trade unions but first two, then perhaps three, finally four. The besetting failing of all those bursting with a long pent-up urge to utter is to attempt cramming in every single item in the catalogue of, in this case, denunciation. Thus the film-makers, Loach and producer Roger James, allowed their material to stretch to four separate hours, one of which was taken up by a somewhat spuriously cast discussion in which the issues raised previously were canvassed. For Loach and for the rank-and-file trade unionists of a particular persuasion, whose case the films represented, they posed issues which needed answering. They were called *Questions of Leadership*.

Now four films were always going to present a problem to us because, although there was general agreement that any one programme on Channel 4 might purvey any one point of view on basic grounds of liberal pluralism and the comparative ease of mounting, if appropriate, a response, there was no such agreement on series, either at the IBA or from Edmund Dell. Do not, the argument ran, give any one individual or cause the free run of a substantial tranche of air-time, unless you are prepared to allow the opposing view a similarly generous dispensation. To allow one and not the other was wrong and was to risk breaching the Broadcasting Act.

Loach's films ran into trouble. First, some of the 'villains' he wished to film in order to see them safely in the dock jibbed at his method. Frank Chapple of the EEPTU was invited to be interviewed on 'trade union leadership at a time of high unemployment'. When it became apparent to him that the questioning in fact was concentrating on internal democracy in the EEPTU he refused to continue. Alerted, other General Secretaries and members of the TUC threatened injunctions. Given a chance to see the films they threatened writs for defamation. The IBA, while reserving its judgement, suggested that these legal tangles needed sorting out before they could pass the films for showing. In any event there would be a need for balancing material. That autumn the Board of Channel 4 passed them back to Central to clear and complete. After much agonizing, by not putting them forward again to Channel 4 the following year Central eventually killed them off.

None of us, certainly not I, came well out of this saga. The films were long, repetitive, and in their first form defamatory, though legal clearances were later obtained. They held up some odd heroes for working-class admiration, including the laggers on the Isle of Grain who, to keep to themselves their earnings of £1000 a week, denied employment to hundreds, even thousands, of other workers in other trades. They trashed Sir John Boyd of the AEU, Frank Chapple of the EEPTU and others, all of whom were well able to look after themselves. I cannot for the life of me see what harm it would have done to broadcast them. I argued that, but did not prevail.

When Ken Loach's film on the party conferences came in, I saw at once why the two films originally proposed had coalesced into one. Naively, you could say foolishly, I had expected contrasting treatments of two major and opposed political movements. No such thing. What we had, through the eyes of what looked like Militant Tendency activists from Liverpool, was the two conferences seen as one, conspiring together to ignore real issues and to shut out the unemployed. In October 1983 we broadcast *The Red and the Blue*. Later, we paid for and broadcast *Fatherland*. When LWT's *South Bank Show*, which commissioned it, would not, we broadcast *Whose Side Are You On?*, on the art and the politics of the miners' strike, though we had already offered in our treatment of the strike other arguments on that side.

Abroad, Ken Loach puts it about that his work is censored in the UK. No counter-example against his martyrdom counts. In Turkey in April 1988 he spoke at a film festival at which he and others deplored the censorship that ensured that the work of Turkey's greatest film-maker, Yilmaz Güney, was not seen in his native country. 'We have censorship just as bad as this in Britain. I am the victim of it,' said Loach, cheek in tongue. He must need to believe it. How he can honestly so consistently discount the work of his that British television has shown I do not know. But we should have broadcast *Questions of Leadership*.

While the Loach saga dragged on, the more fundamental and conclusive matter before us that summer was the future of *The Friday Alternative*.

When in 1981 Channel 4 declared itself open to proposals for programmes, we emphasized our hope that they would be genuinely fresh and innovative. 'Do not,' I told independent producers and the ITV companies when I spoke at the Royal Institution in January, 'simply reach that old proposal down from the shelf where it has been lying for so long, dust it off and send it in. We want new ideas, please; new forms, new formats.' Of the thousands of proposals we received in the next eighteen months not more than half a dozen contained even a glimmer of originality. One brief document made a contrary impression. It suggested three or four programme ideas. Each was original. It came from a BBC current affairs producer, David Graham.

None of the suggestions he made we, in the end, proceeded with. But it was his company, started by him with graphics artist Peter Donebauer as partner, that was now producing for us *The Friday Alternative*, transmitted each Friday at 7.30 pm, after a shorter *Channel 4 News*.

Liz Forgan, Senior Commissioning Editor for News and Current Affairs, had decided to offer, against two rival submissions, the channel's major news commission to Independent Television News, ITN. We knew there might be a real difficulty for ITN in making what we wanted, which was a different sort of news programme, with a different news agenda from what they already successfully purveyed on ITV. It might require, someone observed, an effort amounting almost to collective schizophrenia on their part to get both right.

We also knew that to give this one major contract to ITN was to risk running counter to the whole pluralistic purpose of the channel. We ought, surely, to be diversifying the sources of news, rather than perpetuating and extending the BBC/ITN duopoly. But ITN, we were agreed, was our best practical hope of a considered, serious news magazine programme. We decided, therefore, to include in the news hour two alien elements over which ITN would have no control; the first four nights of the week, a five-minute *Comment* slot in which someone else might put a view on an issue of his or her choice direct to viewers, just as a contributor might in a newspaper.

Secondly, Liz Forgan and I agreed that ITN's *Channel 4 News*, which

on other week-nights ran almost the full hour, would on Fridays run only
half an hour. In the other half hour we would present an alternative view
of the news of the week. Liz Forgan put this view to the Board:

> I would like to unsettle viewers sufficiently to disturb their notion
> that they know what is going on because they saw one television
> programme. *The Friday Alternative* is designed to make that comfortable
> certainty quiver. This may prove such an uncomfortable feeling that
> viewers will turn away in droves to seek security elsewhere. If we can
> persuade them to stay and understand the process I think we shall
> have rendered a real service to democracy.*

We offered the contract to produce this new programme to David Graham's company Diverse Production. Graham was asked to do two things:
provide a commentary on media, showing how events had been covered;
and second, to involve people who had been on the receiving end of
political decisions that made the news, who had in their own lives been
subject to the pressure of events, so as to be able to give us their
perspective, not the commentators' and not Whitehall's, of the pit closure,
the change in EEC agricultural policy, the IRA explosion, the reduction
in child benefit or whatever. The worm's eye view. There would also be
journalistic reports which offered views in sharp contrast to others more
widely disseminated. Graham set up consultative groups:

> We have the scope to reach a diverse range of people and opinions,
> but we will be putting our professional skills at their disposal to help
> them come over as persuasively as possible – and we will be doing this
> at peak time. The core of the programme will be a series of contributing
> groups who will have a constant relationship with us – for instance,
> trade union groups, blacks, perhaps even small shopkeepers – as well
> as *ad hoc* groups that emerge around particular topical events.*

Graham and Donebauer employed a wide range of consultants. These
included Greg Philo of the Glasgow Media Group, diligent critics of the
pro-establishment news values – as they believed they had demonstrated –
of ITN. This alone meant problems for us, since *The Friday Alternative*
would occupy air-time ITN believed should be theirs and, if it sought to
criticize ITN, would want to 'quote' ITN's material to make its point,

---

*Quoted in Lambert: *Channel Four – Television With a Difference*.

which ITN would be reluctant to allow for such a purpose. I had the impression when I called the producers in for a talk that there might be more look-at-it-this-way journalism in the final magazine format than I had bargained for. But I gave my view of what I wanted, crossed my fingers and left it to Liz Forgan to see to it that we got something worthwhile for our money.

Nothing prepared me for the sheer élan of *The Friday Alternative* on our first Friday on the air. It had spark, it had sparkle. It was presented not by men or women, but by graphics; the first British television programme to be so. It had a visual wit. It caught the attention. Coming only two hours after *The Tube*, our early Friday evening rock show from Tyne Tees which had also made an exhilarating start, it made my weekend. Yet now, six months later, Liz Forgan and I were struggling against the IBA and our own Chairman to keep it in the schedule. And we were losing the fight.

Three things went wrong. The first, and the least important, grated on me in the first edition. The programme was sometimes plain silly; on day one it knocked off an item on the House of Lords, and knocked off the Lords in sixty seconds flat. You can't do that sort of thing for an easy laugh in a programme the rest of whose utterance you hope will be taken seriously.

Second, the groups, in spite of all our hopes and best intentions, did not quite work, at least not for the purposes we had envisaged for them, though they would, by the way, have made an interesting weekly programme entirely on their own. As it was, they were too fixed and unwieldy to provide an effective rapid response to the news of the week, let alone from the perspective of the worm under a topical harrow. Their views covered a wide political spectrum. But, though it was interesting to know what trade unionists in Hull thought of race, or farmers and their wives felt about crime and punishment, this did not necessarily seem urgent or relevant on any particular Friday.

Lastly and crucially, that part of the programme that was journalistically constructed, whether by way of critique of media or of reportage, appeared consistently if not exclusively to present only one alternative viewpoint, that of the left. In the end there was no defending this. The channel had a clear obligation to political impartiality overall, and must fulfil it. Ken Loach would argue for *Questions of Leadership* that the other view, the view to which he was opposed, was always being put, and that it was his turn now. The staff of *The Friday Alternative* equally could take the line that all news had a bias; theirs had a different bias. Surely, at half an hour a week only, that need present no problem. But ITN refused to admit a bias. The IBA would not have it said that ITN showed bias. Anyone might get an emphasis wrong on occasion; nobody is perfect. But ITN and ITN's *Channel 4 News*, like other elements in our output, aspired to objectivity. No other week-in-week-out contributor, whether of the left or of the right, could be licensed to put across only one view of the world. It was an abuse of the Act, and an infringement of the channel's hospitality.

I accepted this argument, but reluctantly. There *is* a subtle centrist, conformist bias in much television output, fact and fiction, whose coded messages convey a reassuring view of the world. A complete broadcasting service ought to carry in itself also regular antidotes to complacency, a touch of vinegar, or anyway of different vinegars, on the chips. But this is a hard argument to maintain in the case of a mainstream, peak-time, current affairs programme, particularly if it always offers the same medicine.

At its best, *The Friday Alternative* made lively and stimulating viewing. Against ceaseless pressure from the IBA, who were sometimes particularly responsive to hurt yelps and cries of foul play from ITN, Liz Forgan and I strove to ensure that Diverse Production's contract to continue *The Friday Alternative* should be renewed, even if the programme format was modified. Edmund Dell, on this issue in agreement with George Thomson, was adamantly against. The Board of Channel 4 determined that *The Friday Alternative* should vanish from the air. At a meeting on 21 July the decision to kill it was taken. At the end of its current run it was not to return. I reserved the right, before the series ended in the autumn, to bring forward proposals for a modified version of it that would meet the objection of political bias, to be provided by the same company. (I did so later, and prevailed; the programme was *Diverse Reports*.) It was not a good day. Liz Forgan's view was that editorial control of the channel had been wrested from the executive, hijacked by the Board.

To many of those, however, who attended the Board meetings of April, May, June and July 1983 (Liz Forgan did not; Paul Bonner, though not yet a member, was in attendance) the principal matter of concern was not political bias in our programmes, real though that concern was, but the behaviour of the Chairman.

Edmund Dell conducted those meetings in the manner of a Grand

Inquisitor consigning heretics to the flames. Sitting on his right, I was not particularly struck by the manner of his speech, except that he began each discussion with a long and passionate harangue from the chair setting out his view and what course he recommended. What I was struck by were the expressions of incredulity on the faces of Board members sitting opposite me. Is he always like this, they seemed to ask. Is he like this when we are not here? Are we to be asked our view? Must we listen to him at such length before we speak? Nowhere else they knew of did chairmen behave in this fashion. Is something wrong with Edmund, they wondered. If he is so violently – on reflection at this remove in time not too strong a word – opposed to some of what we are doing, even if he's in the right on a particular issue, how long can he and Jeremy work together? If he's going to go on like this, how long, even, can we put up with him?

I still do not know what motivated Edmund in those months. I do not doubt that intellectually he thought he was simply putting an unanswerable case. But it was the emotional way he did it that disturbed the Board. Was he simply showing the strain of what had happened at Guinness Peat? Had he been urged by the IBA to be sure to hold the line? Or was it that he had opposed my appointment, was critical of my performance, wanted me out, and thought he saw a chance by forcing these issues to a vote against me, to have his way? At the end of the worst of these explosions, Board members, by the lift of an eyebrow, and a quiet word after, indicated that they sympathized. Some telephoned Dickie Attenborough, Deputy Chairman, to express their concern. They thought there must be a real question mark over whether both Edmund and I could carry on. Attenborough undertook to arrange a meeting between us, at which he would be present, to see if a modus vivendi could be worked out. This was later arranged for September.

After three years of incessant effort, the channel's reach and audience share were growing. Word of mouth and a buzz of critical approval all indicated that Channel 4 was moving ahead, and very much on the right lines. It was plain that some change in structure was needed. Each commissioning editor still reported directly to me. I could not continue that and give a proper strategic lead also. But taxed by the exertions of getting to air, having come through the barrage of critical hostility that had greeted us, I now found hard to take both the IBA's carping and Edmund Dell's consistently negative criticism.

I promised the Board a paper on programme policy for its September meeting, in which I would, nearly a year after going on air, seek to restate and redefine our basic objectives. I would seek their support for that restatement. This intention was generally welcomed. A small relief – there was no Board meeting in August. Instead, after a week or two in Wales, I went to Edinburgh for the Television Festival. Edmund was there also. Ostentatiously, I sat with him in the lounge of the George Hotel to show the world, what some questioned, that we were still on speaking terms. In spite of all, I did not believe that a public explosion of dissension between us was in the channel's interest.

At the discussion session in which I took part, I was asked if it was true that we were now looking out for right-wing programme-makers. I said that I was. With rumour in the air, some were suggesting that all opinionated programming would have to be abandoned by us. I preferred the opposite course, and was now saying so; we would ensure that the opinions we broadcast ran the gamut of right and left. 'You mean you admit that some of your programmes have been left-wing?' 'Certainly.' This brought unsophisticated cries of shock. But it was better, I thought, to be frank about the past and about the future.

In Edinburgh we met Scottish independent producers who were concerned that, from a country whose television was taxed to fund a Welsh language channel in Wales, too little work was being commissioned by us. What to do about it? We refused Scotland a quota, but debated some possible practical measures. In a private room at Prestonfield House, a grand hotel in splendid grounds to the south of the city, we gave a dinner for the Scots. Edmund presided with excessive formality. Some of my fellow Scots had, I regret to say, drunk themselves stotious. There were terrible mutterings across the groaning board of 'Hey Jimmie, what the fuck does this auld fucker think he's on about?' It was not Scotia's finest hour.

I wrote my policy paper for the Board with some care, and at some length, and sent it out. In it I reaffirmed Channel 4's commitment to a mix of programmes from a variety of sources, and sought to show that, seen as a whole, our output had got the mix about right. While claiming credit for our successes in education and fiction, particularly *Film on Four*, I devoted the bulk of my argument to justifying the range and overall balance of our actuality programming, 'dwelling at length upon problems of balance and control because they have been in our minds recently'.

We have firmly established the notion that television programmes from a variety of sources may express explicit opinion, without upset to the body politic. If Channel 4's commitment to innovate is not to be mere lip service, then it must continue. We must continue to search for new forms, and to explore new territory. We must continue to be open to the suggestions of those who have new ideas to offer, and the ability to realize them. And we must understand that to attempt something new is to risk failure. To fail is forgivable. What is unforgivable for a broadcasting institution, charged with the duty to innovate, would be to be content with safe formulae, or to insist that, in homage to quality, all rough edges should be smoothed....

The central dilemma, I wrote, was to allow awkward voices to come through, but still be seen to be fair overall.

If programmes express no opinion, then there is no apparent problem. Broadcasting institutions, television news and documentary departments need only work to eliminate the expression of opinion from any programme passing through the system on its way to the screen. For the broadcasting authority, or the editor-in-chief, no problem.

If, however, it is agreed and admitted that programmes, or even series or strands of programmes, may exhibit a particular view of the world, then immediately a real set of problems is presented. These problems are a necessary consequence of a commitment to pluralism; they need not surprise nor dismay us. What we have to do is to find and agree on ways of maintaining a pluralistic variety in the origin and expression of the channel's programmes while conforming with an obligation, which is wholly accepted, not to allow the channel to be used for the expression of any preponderant view....

The Board needs to agree on both these aims; to represent fairly the spectrum of opinion and to reaffirm that a proper proportion of our output may be reserved for the radical voice. In any case, I argued, our output must be judged as a whole.

Dickie Attenborough arranged for Edmund and me to meet for dinner on Tuesday, 20 September, the night before the Board meeting. We met in a private room in The White House, by Regent's Park, in which a

BMP's advertising for daily newspapers on Channel 4's opening day, 2 November 1982.

Some faces from Channel 4's opening night, 2 November 1982: Ian McKellen as *Walter* in the first *Film on Four* (top); Richard Whiteley, presenting the first programme on air, *Countdown*; Anna Carteret, Sue Jones-Davies and Fanny Viner in *The Raving Beauties' In the Pink* . . .

... and *The Comic Strip Presents – Five Go Mad in Dorset*, an Enid Blyton spoof, with Peter Richardson, Adrian Edmondson, Dawn French, Jennifer Saunders and dog.

How Mel Calman, Alan Parker and Marc (the late Mark Boxer) saw the channel's early days.

Opposite, Channel 4's early headlines – stormover and rentaquote.

TV CHIEF FACES SACK

By STAFFORD HILDRED

ITV chiefs are to call for the resignation of Channel 4 boss Jeremy Isaacs

EXCLUSIVE

VULGAR!

TV director quits in four-letter row

4

The ☒ Mail

ON SUNDAY 30p

...aw urged to ban documentary

Storm over IRA film on Channel 4

By PETER SIMMONDS and SARAH GIBBINGS

HOME SECRETARY William Whitelaw was last night urged to ban a controversial Channel 4 documentary which includes an interview with an IRA terrorist and scenes from a film banned by the BBC and ITV.

It also contains an interview with an Independent Broadcasting Authority official who says the IRA should be given more opportunity to air their views on British TV.

The IBA's Northern Ireland officer Tony Fleck says he believes it is 'quite legitimate' for British television to screen interviews with the IRA.

He says: 'I think that the IRA have got a point of view and I think it is a very good thing that the ordinary viewers and listeners should understand that point of view.'

There is also a six-minute clip from The Patriot Game, a pro-IRA film never shown before in this country which includes an interview with former IRA chief of staff Sean MacStiofan and has been condemned by the Foreign Office as being damaging and highly critical of Her Majesty's Government.

'Traitorous'

Tom MP for

'Provos have a point of view and viewers should understand it'
— IBA official Tony Fleck

sation, which puts no value on life, limb or property should be given TV time.

'Mr Whitelaw should step in and ban it. It's not a question of censorship but one of the national interest'

Mr Donald Rapley 51 of Oxford — whose soldier son Anthony died in an IRA ambush in Ulster last year — said 'It is disgraceful. The IRA are gangsters and it is like Hitler being allowed to go on TV

4

Birth of new TV channel is soured by bitter rows

Party for gays starts new row

BAN TV 4 DEMANDS ANGRY MP

By JOE STEEPLES, TV Editor

Rumpus over

Continued from Page One

Channel 4 losses cannot go on, warns LWT chief

Right turn on Channel 4

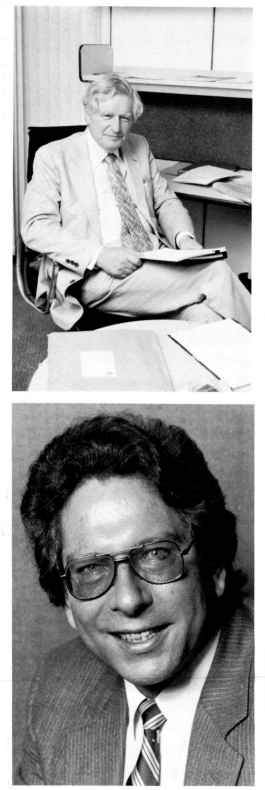

Edmund Dell, Channel 4's Chairman until 1987
(above); Justin Dukes, Managing Director and
Deputy Chief Executive until 1988; Paul Bonner,
Channel Controller and then Programme
Controller until 1987.

Four original senior commissioning editors: above,
Liz Forgan (Actuality), Mike Bolland (initially
editor for Youth Programmes, became Senior
Editor for Entertainment, 1983); below, David
Rose (Fiction), Naomi Sargant (Education).

Faces of 4: Peter Sissons, original presenter of *Channel 4 News*, the computerized *Max Headroom* (Matt Frewer) and the human Jonathan Ross, former C4 researcher who found screen fame at *The Last Resort* (here singingalong with former Bay City Roller Les McKeown and Barry Humphries).

ludicrously lavish cold buffet, enough to feed a platoon, had been laid for three.

We had a drink and began to talk. Where had we got to? What did Edmund think of my programme policy paper? Was he content?

Edmund produced a paper of his own from his pocket, and passed it to us. 'I thought of sending this out in advance to each member of the Board,' he said, 'but have not done so. I propose to table it at the outset of our meeting tomorrow.'

I read what he had written. He had fastened on one sentence in my document. He found that sentence unacceptable, and the whole of my paper, therefore, unacceptable also. He would urge the Board to reject it. We talked a bit of other matters and returned to his paper and mine.

I said: 'Edmund, I suggest to you that you ought not to table your paper, and certainly not at the beginning of the discussion. You are Chairman and must express your view. But you should let others speak and hear what they have to say before you do so.'

He did not directly reply. Instead, a surprise. To Dickie's and to my astonishment, he said he wanted to move the next day to appoint Paul Bonner to the Board. He had the IBA's agreement to proceed. Did I agree?

I have always thought that in a television company it is helpful for the Director of Programmes, or the Chief Executive, not to be the sole programme-maker on the Board. In an argument on programme matters, it must be an advantage to have more than one informed view. Besides, Paul Bonner already attended the Board and reported on scheduling matters to it. And, from now on, the majority of commissioning editors were to report to him. I said I had no objection.

It was late. We broke up. Next morning, I am ashamed to relate, my deputy, Justin Dukes, learned not from the Chairman and not from me, but from our Secretary David Scott who heard from the IBA's Secretary Bryan Rook, that Paul Bonner was to be appointed to the Board and that the IBA was to announce it later that day. Paul Bonner had been summoned by Edmund Dell to his home in Hampstead Garden Suburb the previous afternoon to be made the offer.

There was nothing untoward over the principle of Paul's appointment. That was wholly to be welcomed. But Justin Dukes and I had been apprised in advance of other proposed new Board appointments. The hole-and-corner manner of this one was curious to say the least, and the motivation fishy.

Why the secrecy? Why the haste? Edmund Dell obviously envisaged a showdown between the Board and me, or between himself and me. He might force me out, or perhaps I would walk out – as I had of my volition once left the BBC, and left Thames. It would be prudent in that case to have Paul Bonner on the Board, ready to assume my responsibilities.

Next morning the Board meeting began with the discussion of my policy paper. Edmund Dell behaved with perfect propriety. What did the Board think of it? He wished to hear their views. These were given, and at length. They had enjoyed it. They thought it admirable. Various points were taken, some critical. But overall, unanimously, they warmly welcomed it.

We passed on. Edmund's paper, which he had proposed to table with its rejection of my stated policy now agreed, never appeared.

What I could have said the previous evening was: 'Very well, Edmund. Put your paper and mine to the Board. Let them choose between us.' But I did not say it. So, with Paul Bonner now on the Board, and with Edmund Dell still Chairman, on we went.

6

Sianel Pedwar

In April 1981, after speaking at an educational conference at York, I drove to Harlech in North Wales to speak at a festival of Celtic film and television. En route I passed through Ruthin, birthplace of Owain Glyndwr, more familiar to the English as Owen Glendower, the last great Welsh warrior prince to fight on against them. And then on past Bala and Trawsfynydd to Harlech. There I would greet the newly appointed chief executive of Sianel Pedwar Cymru, S4C, the Welsh language fourth channel, Owen Edwards. He and I were to speak on the responsibilities television owed to the cultural minorities we were to serve. It would be an occasion to affirm, in the face of sceptics, our faith in our respective missions. There would be pledges and toasts.

The case for a separate television channel for Wales, broadcasting in the Welsh language, was a purely cultural one. The language, and the culture it enshrined, was one of the oldest in Europe. But its survival was now threatened; fewer Welsh men and women spoke it each year. Pembrokeshire, where we went each summer to the second home we owned, was known as the Little England beyond Wales. But our neighbours, Idwal Jones, his wife Lil, his daughters Rhian and Janet spoke Welsh to each other, though, courteously, English to us. In the hill farms behind and in the villages, the language was Welsh. At the Eistedfodd, the great annual festival of Welsh language and music, only Welsh may be spoken. But Wales was part of a unitary United Kingdom. Economic interaction with England, the cultural pressures of the twentieth century, jobs and travel and newspapers and radio and television all conspired to favour English against Welsh. Offa's Dyke was no protection. The language was in decline. In industrial South Wales it was hardly spoken; in accessible North Wales it was dying also. In the hills of Merioneth, on the Llyn peninsula, there were communities that spoke no English, but these were few. A new influx of English posed a further threat in rural Wales; they purchased holiday homes, as we had done, driving up prices, so that it was more difficult for Welsh people to find somewhere to live – if, that is, they could find a job there in the first place.

The language was still spoken in the home and taught in school. Indeed it was the language in Welsh-language schools in which English and other lessons were taught. There was a BBC Welsh-language radio service, Radio Cymru. There were a few hours a week of television programmes in Welsh on both BBC and ITV. These pleased no one; to the Welsh speaker who wanted more they were a sop; to the non-Welsh speaker a nuisance. The belief grew that only a television channel wholly in Welsh could save the language or arrest its decline.

Welsh nationalism was not an overwhelming political force. Plaid Cymru won some famous victories at the polls. It was hard for anyone who saw him to forget the Police Inspector leading the crowd in singing Welsh hymns as they waited for the declaration that would return Gwynfor Evans for Carmarthen in 1974. But Plaid Cymru's fortunes fluctuated. In the devolution referendum of 1979 Wales, in spite of having a language as the cultural fuel and focus of the nationalist cause, as Scotland did not, voted categorically against. And yet the language had a life-force in it that would not be denied.

The Conservatives had accepted the argument for a separate television service for Wales, and pledged themselves in their 1979 election manifesto to bringing it about. Later, the impracticality of doing that and of giving the non-Welsh speaking majority the United Kingdom fourth channel also struck home. The government changed its mind. Wales would have Channel 4, the UK Channel 4; but Welsh-language programmes would continue, somehow, on two of the four channels. The Principality, enraged, breathed dragon's fire. Welsh nationalism had a violent arm; the Welsh Language Society campaigned for its use by knocking down signposts in English and insisting on official forms and notices being printed in Welsh. Fanatics set fire to English-owned cottages. In the hills wilder men yet were rumoured to be in training and in arms. There had been incidents in 1969 when Prince Charles was invested at Caernarfon as

Prince of Wales. Since then there had been an explosion or two in pillar boxes and at a television mast. Ireland was just across the sea, the crossing shown in the atlas, typically, as St George's Channel. Things might get worse. A faint but wholly undesirable possibility of terror loomed.

At this juncture Gwynfor Evans, MP for Carmarthen, announced that, unless the government kept its word that Wales should have a Welsh-language television channel, he was prepared to fast to death. A delegation of elders, four wise men of stature, visited the Home Secretary, Willie Whitelaw, to warn him of the risk of civil disturbance, to plead Wales' cultural cause, to remind him of his promise. Whitelaw gave in. A separate and independent authority would be set up to bring the channel into being. Like Channel 4, it would be funded by a levy on the revenues of ITV. The IBA would ensure that adequate funds were made available. The ITV companies would be allowed a modest tranche of profits, post corporation tax, free of levy, to alleviate this new burden on them. Wales was to have Sianel Pedwar, not Channel 4, bringing it, at fixed hours in the mid-part of the evening, twenty-two hours a week of general popular programming in Welsh. There were perhaps 500,000 Welsh speakers in Wales. It was hoped the new channel would help sustain that number, and even, in time, enlarge it. Non-Welsh speakers, except those in South Wales, or on the Marches, or on the borders to the North who could tune their aerials to other transmitters, would have to forgo Channel 4 and the delights it proffered, at least in peak time. But then, in 1981, no one knew, or much cared, what they might be missing. And there was a bonus for the non-Welsh speaker; on BBC and ITV there would no longer be any Welsh-language programmes at all to interrupt the even flow of Anglo-Saxon.

At sunset I came, with jagged Snowdonia above me, to the sea. In a quiet hotel below Harlech I found Owen Edwards hard at work on his speech. He had written it in English, unaware that simultaneous translation would be available at the Festival. Now he could and must turn it into Welsh. Gwyn Erfyl, the IBA's man in North Wales, assisted. Gwyn Erfyl had once been a minister of religion at Trawsfynydd where, twenty-five years before, I and countless others as officer cadets on national service had gone to battle camp. We had a glass or two and debated serious matters, in particular how could the funding of S4C for audiences of Welsh speakers only, numbered in thousands not millions, be justified. Gwyn Erfyl cited an old Welsh saying: so long as there is a gem in the royal jewel casket, a horse in the royal stables, or a goat unmilked on the mountainside, the money can be found. Indeed, he volunteered, there is a tune to those words. What is more, there is a choir of young women here from Aberystwyth. They could sing it tomorrow. We agreed that in my speech next day I would argue that finance was not a problem, and would cite this most apposite and authoritative proverb in support. In the spirit of the occasion the choir would then rise in its place and, as if spontaneously, affirm this evident truth in all its historic force and power. We shook hands on it. I went to bed. Next door Owen's typewriter clattered through the night.

Next day I rose to bring the good wishes of a United Kingdom broadcaster to my Celtic colleagues. Channel 4 and S4C could easily have been at loggerheads from the word go. They, after all, prevented our reaching into all Wales. They laid claim to funds which would otherwise be ours, and of which we might yet stand in need. Yet it seemed to me then, and seems to me still, that in our different obligations to service special needs and fulfil distinctive cultural goals there was much, much more to unite us than to divide us. Before I spoke Gwyn Erfyl, in the cold light of the morning after, approached me pale and hesitant. 'You were not serious about the singing, were you?' 'Oh yes I was,' I said, cheered on by the silent presence of Gwynfor Evans in the hall. Piling on the rhetoric, in the excitement that I sensed was in the air, I pointed to Gwynfor Evans and quoted *Henry IV, Part One*:

GLENDOWER: I can call spirits from the vasty deep.
HOTSPUR: Why, so can I, or so can any man;
            But will they come when you do call for them?

'Gwynfor called,' I jabbed it out, 'and they came!' And I cited, as if I had known it of old, the goat unmilked on the mountainside. At Gwyn Erfyl's nod, the choir rose in the gallery and sang. It was a bright, confident morning. Owen Edwards' speech was moving, serious and practical.

Glyn Tegai Hughes was a member both of the Welsh Fourth Channel Authority and of the Channel 4 Board. At Harlech he walked with us up the path into the fields behind our hotel, talking of how we could co-operate. There was never any problem between us. Channel 4 made all its progammes available to S4C free of charge. They were free to schedule them as they wished. At peak time they broadcast, by statute, only in Welsh, so our programmes of necessity – even the finest of them – went late or early. And there was not room in their schedule for all of our stuff. But I was always content to respect Owen's sovereignty over what was his, and leave scheduling decisions to him and his colleagues, Euryn Ogwen-Williams and Chris Grace, a Welsh-speaking Englishman. I urged only that, in their discretion, they should not leave out altogether what we were proudest of. To our lasting regret, *Channel 4 News* placed at 7 pm in our schedule, has never been seen in Wales except on the fringes. But it could not have been. The statute prevented it. The rest of our output went straight to Sophia Close in Cardiff. There, having made their selection, S4C transmitted it in a schedule of their own. On rare occasions Owen Edwards could decide not to show something Channel 4 had put on if he regarded it as too offensive to the spirit of Welsh Nonconformity. I left that to him.

We provided our programmes free of charge. BBC Wales undertook to provide without payment, purpose-made in Welsh, programmes worth upwards of £10 million a year. In addition S4C was to get 20 per cent of the special fourth channel levy on the revenues of ITV. Only if this exceeded their demonstrable need would they receive a lesser proportion. This was acceptable. Helped by the continuing buoyancy in ITV's revenues, we got by without difficulty on 80 per cent, though we were at pains, annually, to insist that we should not have less. What was continually irksome was that ITV, in calculating the cost to them of funding us, consistently represented us at Channel 4 as receiving the entire proceeds of the levy, rather than only four-fifths of it. But we could live with that.

S4C made a splendid start. In a series of village concerts, *Noson Llawen*, they drew on the country tradition of communities providing their own entertainment. (The Scots Gaelic equivalent is the ceilidh.) The James family, our butchers in Cardigan, Dewi James and Son, provided a programme in themselves. They included Eirian, the very promising operatic soprano. Her sister was thought by some to be just as good. In news and current affairs, in entertainment and in fiction, S4C made programmes that appealed to audiences. They even made a corner in animated film. *Superted*, a cuddly Welsh-speaking bear, but easily dubbed into speaking other languages also, was sold around the world. Cardiff became an important centre of film animation. And Welsh-language feature films were seen at international markets such as Cannes, and, with subtitles, on Channel 4.

Superted was made by a Welsh independent production company in association with an international marketing agency. S4C's most remarkable achievement was to bring into being in Wales an independent production sector of programme-makers working on film and video, and in Welsh. In doing so it overcame the scepticism of all those who doubted that that there could ever be an alternative to the conventional broadcasting institution as a purveyor of programming. Like Channel 4, S4C was a publisher, not a production house. The work it publishes is strong evidence of the vitality of Welsh culture in this age.

S4C's function was quite different from ours. We had to cater for interests the mainstream channels ignored. They were to *be* a mainstream channel, but in Welsh. At first the figures suggested their share of audience was higher in Welsh Wales than was ours in the United Kingdom. Later, as our audience grew, it became evident that the advertising revenue earned on Channel 4 alone could fund us. We could pay our way. This would never be the case for S4C. But good relations between us were never ruffled. It is still early to judge whether S4C has in fact sustained the Welsh language, whether more children learn Welsh and more men and women speak Welsh than before, whether, at least, the decline in Welsh speaking has been halted. The next census will show.

What is clear is that S4C has demonstrated, as have television in Catalonia and in the Basque country, and radio in the Gaeltacht, that broadcasting has a vital role in the cultural life of a people, and particularly of a people whose nationhood is not evinced in a self-governing autonomous state. Gaeldom in Scotland, confined to the Western Highlands, has little succour.

S4C, speaking confidently in Welsh to Welsh-speaking Wales, is one of the more remarkable living cultural phenomena of our time. It is a mark of generosity in the political practice of the United Kingdom that there should be a general will to preserve and sustain it for the future.

7

Terms of Trade

'IF you try that, there will be blood in the streets.' Jack O'Connor, the booze-battered Scot who was ACTT's national television organizer, was informing me in the nicest possible way that his members, whose fingers were firmly on the button that controlled all ITV transmissions, would want to exercise the same power over Channel 4's output also. There was a problem. We recognised ACTT, the principal union in film and television. We did not want to be subject to its veto. The problem was that the design of the transmission system which the IBA's engineers had drawn threatened to risk just that. Channel 4 provided a unitary signal feeding the nation; there were to be no regional opt-outs. Our signal was to go by line from Charlotte Street to the Post Office Tower, conveniently close, thence by line again to the main transmitters in each ITV region then on by broadcast diffusion either direct to the domestic receiver, or by microwave booster and relay links to remoter parts. ITV had no right to interfere with our signal, only to insert commercials in it.

The design called, however, for our signal on its way to the transmitter, to pass through each ITV control room, where ACTT personnel would manually insert the commercials before sending the signal onwards. We were not so much concerned that there might be disagreements between them and us, as we feared being caught up in industrial disputes between them and their ITV employers.

The switch which would determine whether the signal went on to the transmitter or stopped at the ITV station was on ITV premises. It was physically vulnerable to industrial action in that company, which, had it been situated elsewhere, it need not have been. That was the weak link. We designed a switching mechanism, a black box which could be remotely controlled by us from Charlotte Street. Activating it, we could send the signal directly to the transmitter if that was necessary. Or the IBA could order British Telecom to achieve the same effect. ACTT in dispute with ITV could not prevent the transmission of our signal. But they could refuse to insert commercials, thus denying revenue to the employer. This disfigured our output – commercials are a necessary part of it – but did not kill it.

Channel 4's transmission system in Charlotte Street was computer-driven; Computerized Automatic Transmission System (CATS), cued every videotape machine to run, delivering an on-air signal of programme, presentation announcement or station ident as required. Six people only in videotape, presentation and transmission control could put and keep the station on the air. In fact, the channel went to air before the computer was ready. In the early months our presentation editors kept us on air manually, using the normal procedures in which they were trained. CATS hiccuped along, alongside. When the bugs were ironed out and the computer was ready to play its part it was not easy to persuade them to trust it, to take their hands off and let the computer get on with it. Gradually they came to do so. Channel 4, thanks to Ellis Griffiths' determination and thanks to the skills of his colleagues, notably software expert John Haselwood, was able to broadcast more hours employing far fewer people than other television stations in the UK.

Ironically, the biggest dividend our system promised was never achieved. Channel 4's signal contained a pulse which could itself have activated ITV's videotape machines to inject the commercials. Each ITV company had negotiated separate agreements with ACTT which determined the level of manning in the purpose-built control rooms that handled the Channel 4 signal. Those numbers varied widely. All but the barest minimum, a supervisor or two maybe to keep an eye open for malfunction, were unnecessary. C4's signal alone could have triggered the action required. (Recently, late, late at night it has begun to do so.)

In the event, industrial disputes in ITV did not keep Channel 4 off the air. The companies involved lost commercials; our signal, with the IBA's blessing, went straight to the transmitters.

Channel 4 recognized ACTT. We were able to negotiate staff agreements suitable to our needs. The rates we paid were related to the annual increases negotiated by ACTT nationally, though formally we were not party to the ACTT-ITV agreement. Our difficulty was in recruitment. We could not match the wages paid by other employers to ACTT staff in Central London. Our staff tended mostly, therefore, to be beginners or to be ex-BBC. Rarely did we manage to lure anyone of experience from the well-paid ranks of LWT or Thames.

The performing unions, Equity and the Musicians Union (MU), welcomed our arrival; we represented the hope of more employment for their members. We needed Equity's annual and specific agreement in each case to use repeats. Since we did provide more work we got what we needed. Their one anxiety stemmed from the new breed of independent producers, called into existence only by commissions from us. Their representative trade association, the Independent Programme Producers' Association (IPPA), was chary of getting involved in industrial relations. Equity and the Musicians Union were concerned over the secure payment of their members' fees, and of the residuals they would expect to earn on exploitation of their performances. John Morton, General Secretary of the Musicians Union, was certain that the companies we commissioned programmes from would be fly-by-night cowboys, intent on salting away monies due to his members in Montevideo, Uruguay, and that, unless we stood behind the independents, the exploited musician would have no redress.

We were not willing to be a party to agreements between producers and the unions. We did agree to require suppliers to recognize the appropriate union, and to negotiate and abide by agreements with them. And we undertook to allay fears about Fly by Night Television Ltd, Montevideo. We would notify the union of all commissions, from which they could deduce payments properly due. In the case of bankruptcy we would stand surety ourselves for their members' fees. Apart from that, we left it to the producers and to ITV. The end result was that a tiny proportion of management time at Channel 4, minimal as compared with other broadcasters, was taken up in industrial disputes. We got on with our job of putting programmes on air.

The industrial dispute that did us most harm was none of our making; it was that between Equity and the Institute of Practitioners in Advertising (IPA). Equity members received residual payments for the re-use of their work in commercials, which were shown many, many times. The advertising agencies, with the advertisers who actually paid the bills standing behind them, believed that the scale on which these residual payments were made was too high. Though they did not seek to negotiate it down for usage on ITV, they were determined to agree different terms for the lower audiences they anticipated on Channel 4, and for the future on other far-flung media. Equity, which reckoned that its members' fees consumed a low proportion of the advertisers' total expenditure, held firm to what it believed to be an important principle; payment ought not to be related to the size of audiences. You could not agree to pay the players £90 a week, say, and then negotiate that down because the house was only half-full. Advertisers responded that this was nonsense; fees were bound to be related to audience. In spite of months of negotiation, the dispute was not resolved before Channel 4 went on air. Agencies could not use Equity members in commercials for screening in our air-space. Commercials without actors could still be made and screened. Each ITV company sells its own air-time. Some ITV companies might have sold time on which they could insert these commercials; others had not. Channel 4's was a unitary signal. To close the commercial breaks would be to deprive the companies that had sold the time of revenue. The result was an endless succession of disfiguring gaps in our output.

The ITV companies suffered little or nothing. The absence of air-time to sell on Channel 4 simply hardened the price they could charge on ITV. And, since they were paying to fund us, they successfully made a case to the IBA to be allowed, while the dispute lasted, to sell two additional minutes of peak air-time a night on ITV. That brought them in £50 million over two years. It was not until late 1984 that Equity and IPA settled and normal service could be commenced.

ITV paid the piper, but it did not call the tune. This alone meant that their relationship with us would be an uncomfortable one. I was determined that any tensions between us, the inevitable consequence of the fundamentals of our relationship, would not impair our performance or our partnership. Channel 4 jealously guarded its independence from ITV, though as a subsidiary of the IBA it was certainly not a wholly independent entity. But Channel 4 was ITV's sister channel: like them it was governed by the IBA, was part of Independent Television in the fullest sense, was, indeed, expected to provide a service that was complementary to theirs. Independent Television, from our arrival, would confront the BBC with a rival service on two television channels. ITV, which preceded us, which was taxed to pay our bills, saw us first and foremost as an adjunct and an ally in that struggle. We had a part to play in that, but were eager to play it in our own way.

The first bugbear was complementary scheduling. At the BBC two channel controllers collaborated, at least when compatibility of temperament allowed. In the case of disagreement as to who would schedule what, opposite what, when, the matter could presumably be resolved inhouse, if not by neighbouring planners sitting down to talk the problem through then by Managing Director, Television, banging the heads of Controllers BBC-1 and BBC-2 together. But ITV was not like that. In the first place its schedule was not decisively set forth by a Channel Controller given full responsibility for it. Instead, like a jigsaw without a precise pattern, it was laboriously eased and argued into place by a Committee of Programme Controllers, none of whom need agree with another, each of whom represented the separate interest of his company, and two of whom represented companies with conflicting interests in attracting revenue to London in the weekday (Thames) and at the weekend (LWT). What one took the other feared it lost. This was direct competition: the only internal instance of it in the ITV system. Over this the IBA presided. It stood ready to perform the same function between ITV and Channel 4. The IBA in the end approved the two schedules. It had to satisfy itself that they were complementary and, if necessary, would have to act to reconcile them. But it was clear to me that the two schedules could not easily be compiled together, or even in parallel, though that was the theory of it. For one thing, ITV took so long always to make up its collective mind. Paul Bonner and I, on the other hand, had a pretty clear idea of what we wanted to do, and very few options as to how to do it. Our suppliers were out of the building; they were not represented round the scheduling table. I tend to swither a bit in scheduling, but there was little real cause for agonising indecision. We found we were always ready with next season's schedule ahead of ITV and that it satisfied our notion, at least, of 'complementarity'.

We set out to commission and then to broadcast programmes which met our varying qualitative obligations rather than to meet the needs of a putative ideal schedule. The schedule had needs which must be met, but it must also include, whatever the harm to ratings, the elements needed to characterize our output. I never saw 'complementarity', except when it suited us, as the careful matching of one programme against the other. I saw it as colouring stretches of the evening in contrasting tones and textures; we would be challenging when ITV was popular, serious when they were gay. So *Channel 4 News* would find its own audience against ITV's *Coronation Street*, and our documentaries against their drama series. We placed our potentially most popular programme, *Film on Four*, against their current affairs, against their documentaries – if we could find any – and against *News at Ten*. ITV would be at its most popular mid-evening. We would be most appealing in the afternoons, as with *Countdown*, or in the late evenings, with our movies. What was pointless was to waste the strength of our most entertaining offerings when ITV and BBC also were both at their competitive best. Our output would include hours of programming weekly that attracted audiences numbered not in millions but in thousands. Some of these – *Voices*, *The Eleventh Hour* – would normally go late in the evening. Others – *A Week in Politics* or *People to People* – would go in peak time. This was a disappointment to some in ITV who would have preferred us to maximize revenue only by aggregating numbers viewing.

Much play was made in discussion with the need to meet common junctions, to help cross-promotion, as on BBC-1 for BBC-2, and with it to move the audience from one channel to the other. It was easy enough to arrive at common junctions between 7 pm and 10 pm on a week-night when our schedule and theirs included items of comparable length. It was much more difficult to achieve this in the late evening when I favoured films and programmes of varying duration, or at the weekend when ITV's pattern was irregular.

This refusal to tailor our schedule to a precise fit with theirs was a constant source of grumbles on their part. We in turn complained that our willingness to promote their programmes at junctions in our unitary schedule was never matched by reciprocity in their various parts. Each of the fifteen companies determined its own local promotional output, and was on its honour, individually, to do the same by us as we did by them. But we thought their performances in this consistently spotty.

At the end of the third volume of the official history of Independent Television, the author, Jeremy Potter, laments that, in ceding Channel 4 too much independence and denying ITV ultimate ownership and control, the IBA wantonly threw away the opportunity to deploy the weapon of complementarity to the full, so that Independent Television was the poorer for it. This judgement is characteristic of an attitude on ITV's part which, had it been given free rein, would have cribbed and confined Channel 4's development in an intolerable fashion. Whatever the imperfections and occasional mismatches of the two schedules, viewers gained far more from a Channel 4 pressing on according to its own lights than they ever would have done from the inhibited formalism of a Channel 4 schedule agreed on in committee or under arbitration.

ITV took time also to agree among themselves on what terms they would trade with us. And this delay may have cost them dear. We went on air in November 1982, which meant that the programmes we would screen in the succeeding twelve months would, many of them, have to be commissioned by the end of 1981, terms agreed by Easter 1982 at the very latest, if they were to have any hope of being ready in time. But in 1981 ITV was still recovering from the franchise round which was determined at the end of 1980. The ITV companies spent most of that year negotiating with the IBA the precise terms of the contracts to which they would operate from 1982 onwards, including the terms on which they would agree to fund Channel 4 and, in Wales, S4C. We wanted to buy programmes from them, but not at any price they might care to charge, pointing out that they would be making for us on spare marginal capacity, that it would pay them to make full productive use of their staff and studios, that they could supply us at below cost but retain rights to a run on ITV or overseas, that they were rich and we were poor, and so on.

We were, besides, pretty choosy in what we were prepared to take from them, bearing in mind always our duty to provide a distinctive service. And we wanted our commissioning editors to deal directly with programme producers, not through directors of programmes or even heads of department, and so down hierarchically, but face to face. Some managing directors did not wish to entrust their company's fortunes to the persuasive powers or business acumen of their subordinates. Did a commissioning editor, perhaps new to television, really know enough about it to deal with a programme producer direct? Surely Managing Director should deal with Chief Executive? And so we did, to agree terms. But commissioning editors resented even this and wanted very much to make the choice themselves, and, operating within their own budgets, to fix a price they could afford.

Some ITV companies knew what they would want to sell to us. Some did not. They decided that until terms were agreed formally between themselves, and then between the Independent Television Companies Association (ITCA) and us, no one ITV company was to enter into a contract with Channel 4. This left a vacuum into which independent producers, busily hawking their wares, keen for a sale, wanting to deal at the earliest moment, eagerly rushed.

Thames and LWT, planning ahead and perhaps with more spare capacity than the rest, broke ranks and were ready to deal ahead of the others. But ITV as a whole held back. For us there could be no delay. Every planner's nightmare is a blank screen. I could not afford to leave the channel short of programmes. I bought abroad. At home I commissioned from independents. Of the commissioned programmes in the schedule in our first year, excluding purchased film, independent producers supplied, by volume and by value, more than half. This was more than they had ever expected. They never looked back.

ITV sold no programmes to Channel 4 as of right. But I was keen that each ITV company should have some stake in what we screened, some opportunity to recoup something of the funds it supplied to our upkeep. The big boys could look after themselves; it was not the intention that the ITV majors should extend their relative dominance on Channel 4. They would have more popular repeats to sell to us than would the others. LWT's *Upstairs, Downstairs* and Thames's *Man About the House* were always on my shopping list. The smaller ITV regional companies I particularly cultivated, going out of my way to ensure that we purchased something from Grampian; from TSW; from Border, from whom we got lovely things; from Ulster Television, which suited well my interest in Ireland; even from Channel Television by way of co-production. Gerald Durrell, the animal film man, was based on Jersey.

The ITV companies which expected to contribute most to Channel 4 were the five medium-sized companies: Anglia, HTV, STV, Tyne Tees, and TVS, this last an aspirant major. We took programmes from each. But there was a difficulty. These companies had for years matched their programme ambition against the achievements of the ITV majors; their object was to sell programmes to the ITV schedule. They were not well equipped to cater for the more idiosyncratic needs of Channel 4. The smallest ITV company, without a sizeable production staff, might take on people specially to make something for us. The biggest might well harbour talents eager to work on something out of the mainstream. The middle five were puzzled as to how to proceed. I urged them to try to identify something viewers wanted and could not find, and then provide it. The real answer, perhaps, was that a more receptive, looser ITV was the natural home for their output. All the same, each made substantial contributions to our schedule.

It was Tyne Tees Television which, initially under an old colleague of mine, Andy Allan, saw an opportunity to make a name for itself and some revenue by gearing up to meet a specific, defined audience need. They offered a live music show for younger viewers, *The Tube*. Not just their main studio but the whole station, it seemed, and every camera on it, was turned over on Friday evenings to *The Tube*. Each week *The Tube* generated a buzz and an excitement in Newcastle. It was a valuable contract. But *The Tube* was, particularly in terms of staff and resources, a costly programme to make. It ran five seasons. After Andy Allan left to go to Central, when Channel 4 decided not to commission a further series, a new Managing Director, David Reay, took steps to restore the company's profitability on a lower cost base. The horns of Tyne Tees' programme ambition were retracted.

Three ITV Managing Directors sat on the Board of Channel 4. Brian Tesler of LWT was accompanied by William Brown, Managing Director of Scottish Television, and David McCall, another Scot, Chief Executive of Anglia. They were not supposed merely to represent ITV's interest; but what else then were they there to do? ITV had objected, but been overruled, when the IBA insisted on appointing not half the Board from ITV ranks but four directors only. Of those four one was not to be a managing director at all but an unrepresentative programme executive; Joy Whitby, Head of Children's Programmes at Yorkshire Television was the first such choice. The MDs wore Channel Four hats, they said, when they sat round our Board table, and also, presumably, when their colleagues at ITCA got at them at Knighton House. They were calm and supportive in the most difficult days. Brian Tesler was particularly scrupulous never, by a single syllable, to represent his own company's direct interest in any commercial transaction between us – and these ran to millions of pounds. But they did, of course, convey an ITV view to us.

ITV funded Channel 4 and S4C by a formula agreed with the IBA. The IBA, by a happy and determining coincidence, throughout 1980 and 1981 held the ITV companies over a barrel. They were allocating franchises throughout the system. Companies awarded or re-awarded franchises would be expected to contribute to the costs of the two new television channels; those that were not prepared to do so need not bother to apply.

The franchises once awarded, and contracts to be settled, the companies pointed out that they could not be expected to enter into open-ended commitments. How much were they to pay?

It was agreed that the IBA should levy on the ITV companies' actual revenue of the preceding year an impost fixed at between 14 per cent and 18 per cent. The arrangement, provided there was no cataclysmic change in the economic climate or the industry's fortunes, was to hold for three years before being reviewed. The sum thus provided the IBA then split 80 per cent to Channel 4, 20 per cent to S4C. So the companies knew, roughly, what they were in for, and had the comfort also of knowing that it was only monies earned that could be taxed; they were not to provide for us from income not yet in the bank. To build the transmitter system, the IBA borrowed £49 million on the companies' behalf and asked them to repay it. To cover our start and first five months on air the IBA provided £84 million. The subscription for fiscal 1983/84, levied on the income of 1982, was set at 17.9 per cent, virtually at the upper limit. This gave £131 million, of which Channel 4 received £105 million. In the subsequent year the IBA was subjected to the most ferocious lobbying by the companies for a reduction, and tempered the wind to ITV accordingly, charging only 16.2 per cent. In January 1985 ITV prepared to put it to the IBA that, in difficult times, a lower charge would again be appropriate. On the very day they were due formally to meet the full Authority to plead their case, however, their plea of straitened circumstance and the consequent need for economies at Channel 4 was somewhat spoiled by Thames Television's unilateral deal to purchase *Dallas* from its American supplier, taking it away from the BBC at twice the price the BBC had been paying for it. We, too, made our case in terms of a programme budget for the year ahead. The IBA determined that the proper level of subscription that year was 17.6 per cent of ITV's growing revenue, providing £129.1 million to C4, 16.3 per cent up on the previous year.

The Authority, caught between pleas of need from us and cautions on ability to pay from ITV, found performing this judgement of Solomon wearisome and taxing. Justin Dukes and I undertook to agree with ITV on a fixed annual percentage which would end this annual squabble. We thought we could afford to fix a percentage below the maximum because we took a bullish view of their revenue prospects. Justin Dukes took the initiative in this. After patient negotiation, he found that ITV were willing to reach an accommodation. They welcomed the certainty a fixed percentage would bring to their budgeting. They offered 16 per cent annually. We were clear that this, split between ourselves and S4C, was not enough; 17 per cent, we calculated, would do it. ITV swallowed and agreed, and we settled on that. Deducting S4C's share, this would leave us with 13.6 per cent of revenues which were expected in 1987 to top £1 billion. From now on we rode with ITV's fortunes, receiving in the next year an increase in funding of 19 per cent. It was agreed the arrangement should last until the current ITV franchises end in 1993. Of these lush pastures the world of the arts, of theatre, of opera and ballet, in which I now find myself, knows nothing.

In our early years, particularly, our calm was occasionally pricked by the remarks of ITV company chairmen explaining away last year's figures and next year's prospects to their shareholders in terms solely of the depredation wrought by the Channel 4 subscription. It would be necessary, said one, to retrieve control of the fourth channel to ITV. Another worried that the lifeblood of the ITV system might be drained away. In fact, so far as I could see, ITV profits kept up nicely. In the end, the revenues earned each year on Channel 4 came to match, and then to surpass the level of subscription paid. The ITV companies argued that they would never fully recoup their investment in us, or be able to wipe out the deficits of our early years. But in fact those costs, which paid for a vast expansion of their business, were written off against revenue, and still left them a level of profit and a return on capital which provoked envy in others. ITV, after seven years of Channel 4, is as profitable as ever. With whatever reluctance, ITV footed the bill for C4. I am ever grateful to them for it.

'Stand up for free enterprise, Mr Isaacs, won't you?' the Prime Minister called to me at a reception in Downing Street in the summer of 1982, some months before we began transmissions. Tamara and I had waited in line to be received at the top of the stairs. She greeted us. I passed on, only to be summoned back. 'The channel will not stand up for free enterprise,' I said. 'But some of our programmes will.' In fact, in an important sense the channel did what she asked. It brought into being, pursuant to the Act, a modest new productive sector of British industry; television producers who make a living by selling programmes in a domestic market.

As MPs debated the precise wording of the Broadcasting Bill, some producers made their case to them in straight economic theory terms: we are denied access to a market. Do something about it. They found a response on the Conservative benches; the Bill provided that the new channel be required to take its programmes from a diversity of sources, and that these should include independent producers.

The independent producers who soon bombarded Channel 4 with their offers were a disparate lot. Some were individuals, natural freelances, touting a particular one-off idea that interested them to work on. Others were would-be entrepreneurs, looking to make substantial numbers of programmes, to build on that, to see their business grow.

The channel held to one principle, which was not music to the entrepreneur's ear; we saw independent producers as a source of diversity, as a help towards the fulfilment of our pluralist purpose rather than primarily as businesses. We saw our needs for programmes being best supplied from a multiplicity of sources. Faced with a hall full of independent producers, or with a pile of submissions on one's desk, that seemed a natural attitude to take.

There was an alternative. That would have been to evaluate as businesses, paying due regard to the quality of product they were likely to create, all possible suppliers in the field; pick the half dozen seemingly most competent; apportion our programme requirement among the six selected; deal only with them. On this scenario, we would watch large turnovers justify amply resourced business bases; see them achieve economy of scale; note that manufacture in bulk led to profit, and that profit led to further growth. That did not happen, because it was not in our nature to bring it about, and because it seemed the wrong way forward for a channel with our particular cultural remit. We were charged to provide a distinctive service first and foremost, not principally to sustain a viable business sector.

In the end we did both. The channel commissioned programmes from a thousand different sources. But even though our commissions were parcelled out so widely among them, the independents made programmes whose high quality and low cost were impressive. By doing so, they made a case to government to enlarge their market further. Instead of being dependent on the judgement of a monopoly purchaser, Channel 4, they now have access to the markets previously closed to them. BBC and ITV are required to take 25 per cent of their output from the independents. There is now a guaranteed and expanding market for them. Channel 4 can justly claim to have shown the way to that. Independent production is still at the cottage-industry stage. Few companies are viable and secure. All the same, with hindsight, I see I made the wrong response to the Prime Minister. 'Stand up for free enterprise' we certainly did.

In the early days all was to play for. Negotiations with IPPA to agree on terms of trade were protracted. Colin Leventhal, Head of Programme Acquisition, David Scott, Finance Controller, and Justin Dukes spent hours locked in discussion with IPPA's negotiators, headed by Michael Peacock. In the end, pages of fine print set out agreed terms of trade. In the case of fully financed programmes, the channel would meet the entire costs of production and post production, including fees to the programme-makers. It would also, on completion, on time and on budget, pay a production fee or profit calculated as a percentage of the budget, ranging normally from 10 per cent to 15 per cent, over and above the total programme cost. For this the channel would obtain the right to UK transmissions and would divide residual exploitation of other rights with the supplier 70 per cent to us, 30 per cent to them. IPPA thought this too harsh a division. Later it was modified in some cases to 60 per cent/40 per cent.

These terms were sometimes said by IPPA to be unfair; no outside observer ever found them so. Anyone who puts up 100 per cent of the total cost, and a profit on top, is surely entitled to a share of distribution proceeds. At first these proceeds were modest. Net profit from overseas sales of programmes – films were another matter – amounted for some years to a small percentage only of the channel's revenues. Today the picture is different. In fiscal 1988/89, Channel 4 earned £10 million gross in film and programme sales and remitted £3 million of that to independent producers.

The most profitable contracts with Channel 4 were not to sell us an expensive film or entertainment programme, but to supply a long-run series. Produce a soap opera, *Brookside*, two episodes a week, fifty-two weeks a year, for six years, and there's guaranteed economy of scale, low unit production cost, and real money in it. The same goes for *Countdown*, knocked off by Yorkshire Television at six or more in a day's recording session. But those are the exceptions.

Channel 4 entered into thousands of contracts each year with hundreds of suppliers to make hundreds of individual programmes. Most were offered to us because their makers believed in their worth and point and interest, and wanted to make them. Most were commissioned because the channel's commissioning editors saw a spark in them and wanted to put them on. Producers have to make a living but, in the case of most of our suppliers, the purpose was not merely to make money; it was to say something that mattered, describe something that might move us or might give pause for thought or just make us laugh.

To their great credit, 99 per cent of independent producers did deliver on time and on budget. Some made poorish programmes, some good, some marvellous. Few made fortunes. All, in a sense, did well; a decade previously no one believed they could do it at all.

8

Scum, Sebastiane, and the Case of the Raspberry Condom

In September 1981 I spoke at the Royal Television Society Biennial Convention at Cambridge – two years after the Convention at which the Home Secretary, Willie Whitelaw, had given a green light to Channel 4, and just over a year before we were to go on air. Mrs Mary Whitehouse was there. She asked me if Channel 4 would broadcast pornography. I had never paid great heed to her view of broadcasting or to the views of those she claimed to represent, since an incident during my time as editor of *Panorama* at the BBC in 1965. In tribute to Richard Dimbleby, whose death we mourned, I included in a profile of the year a report he gave as a war correspondent, his account of what he saw when he entered Belsen. We used his radio commentary over images of the heaped corpses and huddled, emaciated survivors of the death camp. Mrs Whitehouse wrote to commend the programme generally, but she deplored and condemned the use on it of sights which, she said, were not fit to be seen on television. They must offend. This notion that viewers need to be protected from harsh realities has never appealed to me. Her espousal of it has ever since coloured my response to her strictures.

Facing her now in Cambridge, I saw that I must put Channel 4's policy on these matters on the record. We will not, I said, show pornography ever, either hard-core or soft-core. It would be quite improper for a public-service broadcasting system to do anything of the kind. But in work of merit, which we shall screen properly signposted and at an appropriate hour of the night, we will not shrink from allowing language which may offend some, or even the explicit depiction of sexual behaviour if it is necessary or germane to the narrative or to the texture of the piece.

Mrs Whitehouse took note of what I said, but did not comment further at the time. Later she accused me of intending to do precisely what I had said I would not do; Channel 4 would, she asserted, be showing blue movies, and should be prevented from doing so. Later still, when we were on air, she would claim that that was exactly what we were doing.

On the issues on which Mrs Whitehouse's Viewers and Listeners Association campaigns, my position is clear. I agree with their view that too much violence is regularly represented on the television screen. I am against their view that violence should not be shown if it might offend, and that sexual relations outside marriage should not be depicted. I am for discretion in the use of violence in news and documentary and current affairs; you cannot report war or terrorism and not show the effect of it. Though as squeamish as they come, I would not ban the depiction of violence in fiction, though again there must be justification for it, and discretion in its use. This is an aesthetic as well as a social argument. In the theatre, we imagine rather than actually see Gloucester's eyes put out. The rule of Greek classical drama is: tell us horrors, but keep them out of sight.

> 'Ne pueros coram populo Medea trucidet.'
> (Medea should kill her children off-stage.)

Film-makers are wrong if they think that the medium itself demands a vivid, lingering imagery of violence or of its effects. Because a camera can show horror in close-up, it does not mean it has to do so. Film directors have other means to convey the horror of violence than closely observed gory detail. But that argument is to be gone through in terms of a particular script, as it arises, always in a marginally different form than before, on each separate occasion.

What I find unacceptable is the head count of killing in entertainment series, particularly those purchased in the United States. Cops and robbers, cowboys and Indians, agents of domestic good and foreign evil take part in weekly sagas in which issues are resolved and happy endings achieved by casual and routine mayhem. Channel 4, I decided, would not purchase American series in which killing was the motor of the plot. We bought comedies: *Cheers*, *The Golden Girls*, *The Cosby Show*. And we bought *St Elsewhere*; and we bought *Hill Street Blues*. *Hill Street Blues* had violence in it, was the exception. But it deserved to be. In it, character was brought to life, and the texture of life in the streets. Episodes of *Hill Street* without killings still worked. *Miami Vice* without the shootout and its victims would not have been feasible. Our rule, which we faithfully followed, was that far fewer fictional characters would die on Channel 4's screen each week than elsewhere.

The sex act is, in humans, a private act; there can be no good reason for its indiscriminate display in public, or on stage, or on film, or on television. Whether to show it or not is not a frequent issue, but it does arise. I remember Trevor Griffiths' peak time series *Bill Brand*, dealing with the politics of the left, in which a radical young MP tangles with the compromises and conformities of Westminster. Before he wrote a word of it Trevor Griffiths was in my office arguing that sexual politics were as important to his theme as party politics; I must agree there and then to the graphic depiction of the sex act, and of a certain wearisome performance of it, as a vital part of the tale he had to tell. Of course, I could not agree to give him the licence he sought. Verity Lambert and I undertook when we had a script and came to record to give every consideration to the intention and context of his scene, and allow what we thought feasible and proper. In the event we cut ten seconds. Trevor Griffiths complains still that the effect he was after was damaged. There was no help for this in peak time on ITV. Nor was there any way a similar argument could be avoided over what might and might not be shown on Channel 4. The Broadcasting Act lays down that no matter may be shown which is offensive to public feeling. To show sex simply for the sake of doing so was obviously, to no sane person's regret, out. To show it, even in exceptional circumstances, would require good reason and reasoned argument.

Specific examples could wait; I had very few in mind, though movies like *Last Tango in Paris* or *WR: Mysteries of the Organism* would perhaps one day turn out to be test cases. But there was a principle I wished to put forward, challenging this central diktat of the Broadcasting Act, which I believed was reasonable and right. The Act says: 'Nothing shall be broadcast which is offensive to public feeling.' But what is public feeling? Is it unitary and monolithic? Or do we all, members of that public, feel and think differently on different issues? Some values command so general an assent that a public-service broadcast channel cannot and ought not gratuitously to decry them. I would not countenance, for example, a programme which cruelly or flagrantly insulted the Queen. But I would not seek to veto or to censor a programme which put the case for a

Republic. Had Channel 4 been on the air during the Falklands War, we would have conveyed the feelings of British people for our soldiers and sailors at risk there. We should also, I think properly, have wanted to hear and display the opinions of those opposed to our actions.

Society is not a slab of solid feeling on these or on any other issues; it is composed of different strands of people with differing views and varied tastes. It was a pluralist Britain in which Channel 4 was called on to broadcast. In our appeal to different audiences we needed to cater for that diversity of taste, reflect that plurality of view. What was offensive, in short, to some of us might not be so at all to others.

In every utterance I made before Channel 4 went on air, I took pains to spell this out. In regulating Channel 4 under the Act, the IBA would need to interpret its provisions liberally if the channel's purposes were to come to fruition. Whether they would or not remained to be seen.

The simple notion that public feeling was unitary suited both the regulator and the purveyor to mass taste. It suited both to suppress matter that risked offence; the former because it made the Act simpler to administer, the latter because it maximized the audience. Offend no one and, in theory, all might watch. Risk offending anyone, and you risk losing them from your audience; some themselves offended, and some who, although themselves not offended, might nevertheless be embarrassed in the presence of others who were. This bogey looms large for all broadcasters who aim only at a mass market. In the United States network executives of rare intellectual distinction, graduates *summa cum laude* of Harvard and Berkeley and Yale, never take decisions as to what may or may not be shown on grounds of taste. Instead they submit to lobotomy; all decisions are passed to acceptance officers who ruthlessly exclude anything which, in their view, offends. Their word is law, enforced for a supposed majority, against all exception.

In Britain, the innate conservatism of the commercial television executive had been reinforced for years by the notion that they were addressing not an audience of individuals, but a family audience, whose various generations, watching together, mum and dad and children and gran might each, if offence were offered, compound each other's embarrassment. (I always rather doubted this, feeling pretty sure that whenever a warning announcement that something potentially offensive might be broadcast granny would want to watch too.) But Channel 4's very existence queried the prevalence of that unitary, family audience. We served audiences of differing composition at different times. We catered for the interests of individuals who could make viewing choices on their own, and for themselves. We would show matter that pleased some, even if it risked offending others.

What most offended British viewers, repeated surveys show, was not violence and not sex, but language. Language which dad might use unthinkingly at work he did not want to hear in his own home when watching *Coronation Street* or *Brookside*. I broadly accept this argument; televison should have a care in its output for the common feelings of its viewers. What I cannot accept is that on a growing multiplicity of channels it should be so constrained all of the time. Channel 4 would treat viewers, who would make the choice to turn to it, as adults at all times. Specifically, from late evening onwards, when most, but not all, children have gone to bed, we would not be constrained from using, in work of merit, language or imagery which was salty or sexy. ITV's Programme Controllers Group met on Mondays. For years I heard my colleagues tell each other how much, over the weekend, they had enjoyed such and such a movie, and add, 'Pity we could never show it.' This was said of *The Last Detail* for its language, and of *Shampoo*, for the same, sexier, reason. I thought then this was nonsense; if the movies were as good as they said they ought one day to be shown on television.

Throughout 1981 and 1982 Derek Hill and Leslie Halliwell recommended to me movies for purchase. We bought several thousand. Halliwell bought in Hollywood; very few of the films he purchased would cause problems for us. I asked him to obtain the original, not the emasculated-for-television version, of certain films. In the case of Martin Scorsese's *Raging Bull* we slipped up. The wrong, bowdlerized, version was screened first time round.

For Derek Hill the world was his oyster. He acquired for us a library of films for the cinema rather than for television, which reflected the creative judgement of writers and directors whose eye and feel was not confined by the limits of the small, domestic screen. All the films we purchased had been licensed and certificated for screening in the cinema, and admired there. None had been made by television's lights. There would certainly be problems in bringing some of them to the screen.

On the run-up to our launch, I warned the then Director-General, Sir Brian Young, of difficulties I foresaw, for us and for the IBA, in reconciling a duty to disparate publics with the unitary provision of the Act. He accepted that there could be a dilemma. He urged me not to be precipitate in seeking confrontation over it. I promised not to. On another question, the freedom to broadcast polemic, I threw down a gauntlet on our third night by scheduling *The Animals Film*. But on taste and decency I held my fire.

The hoo-ha over language in our first weeks was unintentionally provoked; we knew about *Network* and *Sitting Ducks*. We were caught out by *Semi-Tough*. We should probably have shown it later at night when it would haved been more acceptable, and with a word of warning. But all the time I knew that we owned and would, at a time of our choosing, screen films which would pose more serious problems, yet which, if we were to be true to our purpose, must be shown. I waited.

The Television Division of the IBA employs liaison officers to watch over the programme executives of ITV companies and the commissioning editors of Channel 4. Sometimes a matter in dispute could be sorted out at that level. Sometimes Paul Bonner was brought in; he had regular meetings with David Glencross, the Director of Television. If Paul lost an argument, I took a hand. David Glencross had either to make the decision himself and stand by it or, on a really contentious issue, take it up to the Director-General. Thence – but this was rare – it might go to the Chairman and, rarer still, to the full Authority. The officers' arguments with us, and their rulings in them, were reported to the Authority at its regular meetings in an Intervention Report. Sometimes, at the end of year, the Authority's displeasure is recorded in its Annual Report to the Home Secretary and to Parliament, retailing, along with praise, reproof. The list of interventions in regard to Channel 4's output is not long, given the hours we broadcast. It does convey the flavour of our wearying but inevitable disagreements.

Channel 4 was owned and regulated by the IBA. The first real crux was *Scum*. *Scum* began as a film commissioned by Margaret Matheson for a BBC television series of plays in 1978. Written by Roy Minton, it portrayed life in a Borstal institution. Directed by Alan Clarke, it had a cold steely beauty. The life it depicted was harsh, with scenes of unremitting cruelty and brutality. The whole institution conspired against the good in humanity, except for one inmate and one warder. The moral seemed to be: treat people like scum, and they will behave like scum.

Scum gave concern to some at the BBC; it was referred to the then Managing Director of BBC Television, Alasdair Milne. He ordered that it not be shown, explaining that its realism carried such verisimilitude that it might be believed that Borstal institutions were in fact as bad as this. Although he did not doubt that all that was portrayed in the film could have happened, and even, as the author testified, had happened at some time or other, yet all could not have happened within the time-scale of the film. This insistence on the Aristotelian unities did not seem appropriate, even as enunciated by a Wykehamist, for the film medium, in which time and place can be altered at will by a single cut. To insist in fiction on journalistic literalism seemed harsh on the makers of a tough but particularly well-made, and even moral, movie. I viewed *Scum* on a borrowed VHS cassette and admired it. Years later came the chance to do something about it.

The screen rights in *Scum* were bought by producers Clive Parsons and Davina Belling. They remade it for the cinema. Alan Clarke again directed. Not surprisingly it was broader, coarser, not quite so elegantly controlled the second time around. *Scum* received an 'X' certificate and did reasonable business. Parsons offered to sell it to Channel 4. I viewed it, and found it held up well. The moral, if anything, helped by one or two different performances, came across even more strongly. But some of it was pretty hard to stomach. Parsons offered to discuss cuts with the director. I asked for two, one of a homosexual rape, the other in a long hold on blood seeping through the sheet that covered a suicide. These cuts were made. I put the film forward for transmission, calling the IBA's particular attention to its history.

The programming officers of the Authority, including Director of Television Colin Shaw, recommended that *Scum* should not be shown. John Whitney, the Director-General, decided to view the film and take his own decision. John Whitney is a Quaker and a prison visitor. He viewed *Scum* at home with his wife. He decided Channel 4 could show it. *Scum* was broadcast on 10 June 1983, at 11.30 pm. More than two million watched it. Mrs Whitehouse charged the IBA with dereliction of duty, and lost.

When in 1984 it came to trial, the High Court found that John Whitney had followed a wrong procedure in arriving at his decision; the members of the Authority ought to have been consulted. On the matter of more substance, they found that he was right; it was within the Authority's prerogative to rule that *Scum* be shown. The film might be harsh or even distasteful; it was not offensive to public feeling. In April 1985 the Court of Appeal ruled that the lower court's criticism of Whitney's procedure was equally misplaced. Given the importance Mrs Whitehouse attached to her action, and in view of the likely consequences of her success in it, this was a famous victory. Had it lost, the Authority might never have stuck its neck out again. The two million who had watched the film on our screen had rights also, and these were vindicated.

To mark our first anniversary on the air, we broadcast late at night *Richard Pryor Live in Concert*, in which the comedian enthralled a Los Angeles theatre audience. Richard Pryor's favourite noun is the revolting Americanism, 'motherfucker'. Nevertheless his is a manically, inventively funny act, and *Live in Concert* was a very funny film. Viewers enjoyed it. The IBA was not amused.

It took even less kindly to another such film, *The Complete Millie Jackson*, broadcast in January 1985. In this Millie sang one song whose lyrical refrain, constantly repeated, and to the tune of 'Amazing Grace', was simply 'Fuck You'. Paul Bonner did ask me if even at 1 am this was all right; I thought it was. The IBA, after the event, disagreed. The heavens, though, did not fall in.

The Tube was broadcast live at 5.30 pm on Fridays; from time to time spontaneous ruderies were uttered on it. Some of these were accidental, and some accidentally deliberate. Knowing Jools Holland and Paula Yates, its presenters, I never found it surprising that such mishaps should occur; but at that hour of the evening there was no defending them. *Come Dancing with Jools Holland* erred also. Wrists were duly slapped. Live transmission proved too tricky, too, for our very effective comedy satire show *Who Dares Wins*. *Who Dares Wins* specialized in scripted and crafted sketches, pre-recorded. One sketch of, almost, indefensibly bad taste showed Christ on the Cross accepting a Hamlet cigar. That called for apologies; and tighter editorial control. There were more hits than misses, though, on that front. We took precautions, read the riot act, and kept the programme on.

In the aftermath of censorship the channel came between supplier and the IBA, and could end up falling out with both. One of the wryest cases concerned a film in our *Visions* series on world cinema, *Brazil-Cinema: Sex and the Generals*. Political repression in Brazil had led to severe censorship of cinema film. Brazilian film-makers got round this by portraying politics metaphorically; the metaphor was sexual. Clips from these serious, imaginative but very sexy films would, our colleagues at *Visions* hoped, make the point. What followed was all too probable; the sex scenes, pregnant with political meaning, were too sexy for the IBA. *Brazil-Cinema: Sex and the Generals* in its turn was censored. Patiently Paul Bonner tried to put the pieces together again, trading a cut here for a sequence there. To no avail; it proved impossible to agree on a version that *Visions*, C4 and the IBA were happy with. Cries of betrayal and dismay.

It is always difficult on television to make a serious political point through sexual imagery. However austere one's motive, the image soon takes over from the argument, leading to oohing and ahing, and 'look what's going on there'. In this case *Visions*, regrettably, was dimmed.

It is not easy to keep a straight face when solemnly discussing the justification for this four-letter word, this glimpse of naked flesh, this gesture, that embrace. The most ridiculous of such incidents may have occurred after I left Channel 4. A fight for market share in the rubber trade was the subject of an edition of *Diverse Reports*. That eternal vigilance which is the price of liberty was once again called into play. Liz Forgan conducted the argument with the IBA on the channel's behalf. This was over whether we could allow a condom manufacturer to say, 'I've got banana-flavoured condoms. I've got strawberry-flavoured condoms. I've got liquorice-flavoured condoms. But you should taste the raspberry.' The IBA wanted all that cut. After a heroic defence of free speech, Liz managed to keep all of it in except, 'But you should taste the raspberry.' Ten years earlier I lost the argument when a similarly well-intentioned series I authorized for Thames was comprehensively stopped. In a programme on sex aids, a shopkeeper demonstrated a vibrator by rapping it on a table. 'But doesn't it interfere,' the interviewer asked, 'with the television reception?' No, it did not. All too often, though, sex on television does just that.

More serious in retrospect than it appeared at the time was the rumpus that followed our transmission in February 1983 of *Blood of Hussain*, a striking film by a self-exiled Pakistani film-maker, Jamil Dehlavi. Dehlavi's film contained at least one remarkable sequence: from beneath the desert, a great white stallion symbolizing revolt rose in a swirl of sand, which had appeared to cover it, shook itself free and galloped off. *Blood of Hussain* portrayed Muslim womanhood offensively – that is, it showed a female character naked, about to make love outside marriage; it contained language disrespectful to the prophet Mahomet; it was equally disrespectful to the military dictatorship of General Zia ul-Haq. Channel 4 was going out of its way to provide matter of particular interest to the Muslims of Britain. But the Muslims of Britain were hugely offended by this movie, or by what they heard of it. In Bradford, in Birmingham, they met to express their displeasure. They wished dreadful things might happen to its perpetrator, Dehlavi. In Leicester 365 members of the assembled Muslim community voted unanimously to recommend to the government of Pakistan that they should take steps to apprehend Dehlavi and, when caught, should convey him back to Pakistan and publicly execute him. Years later the full force of the reaction called down on the head of Salman Rushdie, after he published *The Satanic Verses*, still came as a surprise.

In the spring of 1985, thinking about the schedule for the autumn and about an ample stock of movies waiting to be broadcast, I decided that the time had come to show some of our more difficult pictures. I was determined that in considering them the officers of the IBA should think of the films as a whole and not be allowed to narrow discussion down to contentious sequences in them. It was only if the films were any good, were of some genuine merit, however subjectively determined, that the case for them was made out. It was no good allowing the censor to nick out the 'naughty bit' and ask – can we justify this sequence? The movies ought to stand or fall as entities.

I thought it might also help if these films formed a season, if each was considered not on its own, but as part of a pattern. And I thought my life would be easier if the Authority, instead of being invited to test its judgement against mine, was confronted instead with someone whose views would command respect. I invited David Robinson, film critic of *The Times*, to make a selection of films from our catalogue, write a pamphlet introducing his choice, and speak to the reasons for it in a brief introduction to each film. *Robinson's Choice* would go on the air in the autumn. David Robinson, the biographer of Chaplin, is indisputably one of Britain's and Europe's most admired and respected critics. He had the free run of our library, and chose twenty films. They included Ozu's *Tokyo Story* and Kurosawa's *Living*; Bresson's *L'Argent* and Truffaut's *Vivement dimanche!*; Fassbinder's *Fox and his Friends* and Sándor's *Daniel Takes a Train*; Güney's *Yol* and Visconti's *Ludwig*. They also included Derek Jarman's *The Tempest*, *Sebastiane* and *Jubilee*. And Ron Peck's *Nighthawks*.

In his written text, Robinson remarked on how difficult the choosing had been. 'Of course, you can't please all the people all the time; but it would be nice to please as many people as possible ... and for sure no

As a TV presenter, erstwhile faker Tom Keating proved the genuine article, revealing the old masters' techniques in *Tom Keating on Painters*. Below, cinematic controversy and classic: Derek Jarman's *Sebastiane* provoked serious debate about censorship; Kevin Brownlow's painstaking reconstruction of Abel Gance's *Napoleon* (with Albert Dieudonné) proved a major TV event – even without the climactic triptych!

Some of Channel 4's women of substance: Sue Johnston (top left) as Sheila Grant in *Brookside* – 'one of the really remarkable television performances of our day'; former MI5 employee Cathy Massiter, whose allegations prompted Channel 4's most controversial current affairs programme, *MI5's Official Secrets;* and below, Anneka Rice, the original skyrunner for *Treasure Hunt*.

The Golden Girls (above: Rue McClanahan, Bea Arthur, Betty White) proved among the channel's most successful imports; Hélène Delavault was one of three Carmens in three parallel films of Peter Brook's production of *The Tragedy of Carmen*.

Above, some of the cast and crew of *Brookside* with the series' creator Phil Redmond (foreground, left) on the Liverpool close that serves as location, studio and offices in a unique TV production centre.

Below, Roger Rees (as Nicholas) and David Threlfall (Smike) in Channel 4's television version of the RSC's *Nicholas Nickleby*.

Daniel Day-Lewis and Gordon Warnecke in perhaps the quintessential *Film on Four, My Beautiful Laundrette*.

Above, seven guests and a host late at night in a darkened studio: the innovative live open-ended discussion programme, *After Dark*. Below, Saeed Jaffrey and Zohra Segal in Farrukh Dhondy's *Tandoori Nights*, a comedy set against the rivalry of two tandoori restaurants, 'The Jewel in the Crown' and 'The Far Pavilions'.

Channel 4's youngest and smallest cameraman – during filming of Phil Agland's award-winning study of the diminutive Cameroon tribe, *Baka – People of the Rainforest*.

Right to Reply offers viewers a genuine opportunity to talk back through the Video Box. In a special edition on 2 January 1988, the departed Chief Executive Jeremy Isaacs faced the programme's departing presenter Gus MacDonald.

one else in the world is going to go along with my personal choice of twenty films. But then, the world at large would be a good deal less entertaining if we all shared the same tastes.'

It was obvious, he pointed out, that his choice was limited by what was in our repertory. It did not by any means represent his own once-for-all Top Twenty. Only two of them, the Ozu and the Kurosawa, would make it to that. He commended the four British films in his list, the three Jarmans and Ron Peck's *Nighthawks*, because

'they and their directors represent an important area of our native cinema that is unjustly and unwisely ignored by the commercial mainstream of production promoted by the current 'British Film Year'. All four films exemplify the possibility to find means for individual creative work without dependence on the conventional and restrictive resources of film finance. The season provides an opportunity to screen the entire feature film work of Derek Jarman, who came to direction from painting and art direction. It seems to me that Jarman's work offers British cinema an object lesson of the first importance. Each of his films has been made on derisory budgets, but each shows that true film spectacle is not bought with millions of dollars, but comes from the eye and creative genius of the artist.'

Earlier he had noted, playfully, that he expected to have to defend *Sebastiane* against protestors at its Latin dialogue. Now he stated,

'Looking over the season I am struck that besides *Nighthawks*, three others of the twenty films – *Sebastiane*, *Ludwig* and *Fox and his Friends* – have homosexual heroes.... Each of the four is a film of exceptional and distinctive quality. Apart from that, I can offer no particular explanation of the grouping, unless it is that in treating a hero belonging to an uncomfortable minority among the population, the film-maker is more than usually challenged to achieve what the great Japanese director Akira Kurosawa once stated as his aim in making films: 'to give people strength to live and to face life; to help them live more powerfully and happily'.

That apart, he finished, 'The choice is, I admit, idiosyncratic.' He hoped some would share his pleasure, and that the selection would succeed in pleasing a lot of people a lot of the time. It did too, exactly as Channel 4 was set up to do.

David Robinson made better than I could the case for showing both these movies. But *Robinson's Choice* also annoyed some: *Sebastiane* for its explicit portrayal of physical affection between men, and *Jubilee* for its jagged and ferocious imagery of a punk Britain. *Sebastiane* was scripted demurely in Latin, and preceded by a long roller text placing these goings on firmly in the time of the Emperor Diocletian. Though there was much visual iconography of the martyrdom of Saint Sebastian it was essentially a romp; there was much play with joke phalluses. The IBA's consent was purchased by an electronic elision of the only erect fleshy member on display. *Jubilee*, and one scene of violence against the police in it – prophetic enough in all conscience – caused most stir. Derek Jarman's work since has only confirmed his unique talent as a film-maker. *Caravaggio*, in particular, is another sumptuous visual feast conjured out of minimal resource. And his version of Britten's *War Requiem* won him new admirers. His *Last of England* has not yet been screened by Channel 4.

Defending the decision to transmit *Sebastiane* and *Jubilee* on *Right to Reply*, I was brought up against the one argument I found difficult to answer; a most articulate aggrieved father complained that the children he and his wife had left at home had recorded *Jubilee* on the cassette player and were found next day re-running the bits they found most interesting. This was his problem; he argued it was our fault. The BBC, in the cheery person of Michael Grade, hastened to point out that they would never have shown either movie; I had singlehandedly, they thought, brought on the day when broadcasting, already regulated, would be made subject to the Obscene Publications Act. This never worried me; no film Channel 4 ever showed would be successfully prosecuted under the Act, even, in my view, as amended by this government.

Robinson's Choice was a clear success. The question a year later was how to screen more of the films on our list, which millions of viewers might want to see, without falling foul of the objection that some who ought not to see them or did not want to see them might inadvertently bump into them. I came up with the notion of the red triangle.

Any potentially tricky film we would place fairly late at night. Many viewers in need of protection would be in bed anyway. How to warn those who were still up and might be flicking the channel selector switch? How to help parents advise their kids – this one is not for you? What we needed was signposting. A red triangle, I decided after not all that much thought, would be printed in the *TV Times*, in the newspapers and shown on screen before and during any film that required particular care in its selection. This symbol would help viewers make informed choices, as does certification in the cinema. It would signify 'Special Discretion Required'. The IBA's officers agreed the rationale and methodology of it. In the autumn of 1986 we made the experiment. We would use the red triangle on half a dozen out of twenty-odd late-night films in the coming season.

Things did not turn out as I had hoped or expected. The red triangle was an early warning system that proved explosive. When it appeared in the *TV Times*, newspapers were alerted in advance, and those that wished to vent alarm and indignation in their headlines duly did so. Viewers who would otherwise not have known or cared about the movies thus learned about them, and may have watched them in search of a quick thrill, though few would have been likely to find one in *Themroc*, the fable which opened the series. Out of curiosity, perhaps prurient curiosity, 2,373,000 viewers did watch.

Mrs Whitehouse was sure my sole motivation was to increase the audience. Others, who never saw the films, learned about them from the press and waxed indignant. But no great harm was done. We kept the red triangle, but next time round decided to give no advance warning of its use. No one would now be misled into watching some earnest disappointment. On the other hand, now that the red triangle was known and recognized, it could be usefully attached to any film without warning if it was needed to alert the unwary. So far were we prepared to go to protect viewers who, of course, could always protect themselves by switching off. Behind all this lay a considered purpose; Channel 4 put itself out to ensure that adult viewers who wanted to see films of merit which they could previously only find in the cinema, could now see them on television also. In the West End of London, this was an advantage. In Inverness, where there was no cinema showing such films at all, it was a lifeline. Viewers starved of such work in the cinema wrote to say so. Theirs were among the interests not catered for by ITV that Channel 4 was set up to serve.

It is not the films that Channel 4 has shown that I regret, but the films I was not allowed to show. I could never persuade David Glencross to share my enthusiasm, on air at least, for Dušan Makaveyev's masterpiece, *WR: Mysteries of the Organism*, though we did show his *Montenegro*, and nearly three million enjoyed it. In the mainstream, I regret never having been allowed to show *The Exorcist*, even in the version shown to tens of millions on the American networks. The nannies that govern BBC and ITV have always prevented this popular blockbuster being seen on our screens. Never having seen it, I am not quite sure what the fuss is about; something to do with possession and green ectoplasm. But I do know millions would have enjoyed it, and come to no harm. The same certainly goes for Bertolucci's *Last Tango in Paris*, which I much admire. Both will turn up on satellite shortly no doubt, and do good business.

The film I fought hardest for, and lost every round over, was Monty Python's *Life of Brian*. This was held by the IBA to be blasphemous – though the courts have never found it so – and offensive, therefore, to public feeling in a Christian country. I saw *Life of Brian* in a packed cinema in central Manhattan. It has been seen and hugely enjoyed by millions. I found a majority on the Board of Channel 4 in favour of screening it, though one Director, a practising Roman Catholic, would have resigned if we had gone ahead. But we did not, because the IBA forbade it.

One beacon of light and victory over the Philistine shines out. On 4 November 1987 at 11 pm Channel 4 screened Richard Eyre's film of Tony Harrison's poem 'V'. It was Michael Kustow's idea to commission a film on this text when the poem appeared in the *London Review of Books*. Harrison tells how, visiting his father's grave in a Leeds cemetery, he finds gravestones defaced by the graffiti of Leeds United supporters making their way home from Elland Road. Meditating on the lives that lead young men to vent frustrated anger in empty obscenities, 'V' rises to a panoramic view of division, antagonism, aspiration in British society, and within the poet himself. In the film Harrison is seen reading the poem to a Yorkshire audience, who hear him out with avidity and quiet. The word 'fuck', often in the mouths of the kids the poem is about, occurs often in the poem. Poem and film have a compelling seriousness.

Concerned there might be a problem, though knowing in my bones that work of such quality must get through, I asked the Board of Channel 4 to view it. Unanimously they were for showing it. We put it forward to the Authority. They too viewed it. They too were all for showing it.

The yobbish press were up in arms, as they too often were, unthinkingly, and hypocritically. MPs called, on cue, for the film to be suppressed, and the Channel reprimanded. The *Independent* printed the text. The *Sun* reported the *Independent* to the Press Council. When we showed 'V', a rich duty log of viewers' comments variously blamed us for corroding the moral fibre of the nation, and thanked us for giving them the chance to see something so moving, so thoughtful, so unusual.

23.25 'V' Mr Badder, regular viewer of C4 who was astounded by this having been shown. It's disgusting.

23.42 'V' Mrs Richardson, congratulations on this marvellous programme. It's wonderful; one of the most wonderful programmes I've ever seen.

Both testified that the channel was doing its job.

9

News and Views

IN November 1981 we agreed with ITN the deal that would bring us *Channel 4 News*. From the beginning I had argued that Channel 4 should have a different news programme, more reflective than reflexive, placing emphasis on context and exposition rather than on colour and incident. Nothing in my work used to upset me more than the argument that television was inevitably a trivializing medium, whose product could never be taken seriously. True, an hour of television narrative might contain only two thousand words, less than appeared on a single page of a serious newspaper. True, too, that a documentary might lack the critical apparatus of a scholarly book. True, even, that TV was primarily a visual medium in which journalists might exercise judgement in favour of the striking image against the cool text. But none of this was inherent in the medium. It was owed to the thoughts and actions of those who used it. What was needed was that television journalists should take different decisions, work to a different set of priorities. Why not provide a framework in which different choices were possible, and promulgate a brief for a programme instructing that difference choices would be made? *Channel 4 News* would have twice the running time of other British news programmes, and would follow a different agenda.

Until recently the idea that there could be different news agendas came as news to hidebound journalists, whether on newspapers or in television. 'What do you mean?' they would splutter. 'The news is the news. All we do is report it.' To refute this all one need to do is consider the front and inside pages of papers as disparate as the *Sun*, the *Daily Mirror*, the *Guardian* and the *Financial Times*. Of course if you put a journalist in charge of a ten-minute news bulletin, or a half-hour news programme, and tell him to come up with bright and watchable viewing, to keep an eye on the rival show on the other channel, to make sure he never misses a big story, and to see that the viewing figures keep up, it is not hard to predict the outcome. British television news is a considered attempt, within severe constraints of space, to reflect something of reality; it is also an artificial, highly compressed, rigorously selective artefact, following its own rules of grammar, order, mix, pace and rhythm of narrative. The running time which limits range and forces selection is, in some cases, so tight that it does not seem unfair to call such programmes tabloid. Their makers prefer to see their products as the equivalents of a middle range of newspapers – the *Daily Express*, say, or the *Daily Mail*. The distinguished early editor of ITN, Sir Geoffrey Cox, said that his bulletins aspired to the tone of the old *News Chronicle*. *Channel 4 News* would be upmarket of that.

In public utterance, and in meetings with ITN, I stressed that we wanted a news that not only did not rely on but actively eschewed violent incident for its own sake. If such incident were portrayed it must be justified, whether in Ireland or in Israel, by the political context. We did not want stories of individual crime, or of minor natural disaster. We did not want coverage of the daily diaries of the Royal Family. *Channel 4 News* would deal with politics and with the economy. It would bring coverage of the City, and of industry. It was to report on developments in science and technology, and in the arts. It was to cover the politics of other countries and to supplement that reporting with the output and insights of foreign television news programmes.

The buzz word was 'analytical'; news analysis. In fact, no one ever worked out what that might really mean. The programme's principal virtue was its length. ITN told us not many weeks before transmissions began that they had conducted a briefing in Whitehall for government information officers. One fact about the new programme made an instant impression. *Channel 4 News* would last an hour, twice as long as any other television news; their Minister, if he or she accepted an invitation to appear on it, would have twice as long as on other programmes to deal with the complexities of the issue of that day. Every pencil made a note. I knew then that we were on to a winner. Whatever attention our brasher utterance might call to itself, at the heart of the channel's factual output would be a sober, journalistic vehicle which would be better placed than others to tackle large subjects, and, as important, would give a fair hearing to opposed viewpoints on them.

Liz Forgan hammered out the brief to this effect with ITN. Jealously ITN's editor, David Nicholas, reserved to himself the right to appoint the programme's editor. We insisted on prior consultation. I asked that he go outside ITN to find the right person. I put forward as my preferred choice the late David Watt, former political editor of the *Financial Times*, then chafing slightly as Director of the Royal Institute of International Affairs at Chatham House. David Watt could have been, but never had become, an able editor of the *Observer*, or the *Economist* or *The Times*. He knew little of television, and did not care very much for what he did know. But he had the command of subject matter and the judgement I looked for. Put an experienced technician beside him and something remarkable might have resulted. David Nicholas, well aware of the rough-and-tumble of ITN House, shied away from so academic a figure. He hired instead Derrik Mercer, a managing editor (news) of the *Sunday Times*, who convinced him, and half convinced me, that he had the combination of editorial drive and intellectual clout that was needed. Mercer set about learning about television, finding his way – not easy – around ITN, recruiting a team of editors and presenters. David Nicholas told me quietly one day that, if I was interested, it was just possible that Alastair Burnet, who had after all edited the *Economist*, might be prepared to give up presenting *News at Ten* to front the new programme. I dismissed the idea. Though no one doubted his abilities, it seemed to me wrong that we should rest our appeal on Burnet's familiar image. The hint was never dropped again. In all the years *Channel 4 News* has been on the air bringing credit and distinction to ITN, of which he is a Director as well as an employee, Sir Alastair Burnet has never uttered a syllable of commendation of it to Liz Forgan or to myself.

Channel 4 News was presented instead by Peter Sissons. And an excellent job he made of it, growing in stature and command each year. Derrik Mercer took on presenting editors: Sarah Hogg, economics; Godfrey Hodgson, foreign affairs; Ian Ross, industry. Ross was an experienced BBC industrial reporter; Hodgson, too, though on screen he gave off a soporific quality which belied his acute and informed mind, had considerable experience as a broadcaster; Sarah Hogg, former economics editor of *The Times*, had no experience of television. Gallantly, she took on the task not just of determining the content of chunks of the nightly programme but of presenting them herself. She even read out 'the rest of the news'. Sarah Hogg was lucid and authoritative, but never quite at ease. The dual role, behind the screen and on it, was too much first for Godfrey Hodgson, then for her. The team was strengthened by the foreign reports of Trevor MacDonald. Laurence McGinty did well as a science reporter. So did Stephen Phillips on the arts. Jane Corbyn made her mark as a reporter at home and abroad. But Mercer never found his way round ITN. The programme's brave ambitions were not underpinned by an adroit use of technical facilities or by a grasp of presentational techniques. There was too much uncomfortable narration to camera. The first months showed inadequate progress.

The Channel 4 Board was concerned. Edmund Dell had conversations with his fellow chairmen at ITN and at the IBA. Partly our concern was justified; the programme was not good enough. But we also had set an unrealistically high audience target of 1.5 million viewers, which even today is, except on rare occasions, well out of the programme's reach. Harried by Liz Forgan and by myself, David Nicholas, in the summer of 1983, removed Derrik Mercer and, after an interim in which Paul McKee more than competently held the fort, suggested an editor from inside ITN, Stewart Purvis. Forgan and I met him and agreed.

The Channel 4 Board, part of whose apprehension was that ITN simply did not understand what we wanted, were not so sure. At The White Tower – not all eating in Charlotte Street is out of doors – Edmund Dell and I, joined by Dickie Attenborough, had lunch with Stewart Purvis. Over the pâtés, the fish salad, the duck, Edmund quizzed Purvis on his views on the IMF, Third World debt, the EMS and other such topics. Purvis manfully responded. At the end of it, Dickie Attenborough leaned forward and put a hand on his arm. 'Darling,' he said, 'we are all, you know, in show business; never forget that, will you?' Out on the pavement Purvis was understandably bemused. He got the job, though, and moved the programme steadily on, using ITN's facilities and his own packaging skills to the maximum effect. With Peter Sissons at the helm, the programme began to realize its full potential. On our, and its, first anniversary, 2 November 1983, I stood on a desk in the newsroom at eight o'clock and told the team that they were pioneers of a new form of television news, and successful at it; they had shown up other news programmes for the skimpy, inadequate things they were. This may have been good for *Channel 4 News* morale. It did not carry well to other floors in ITN. But it was true, and recognition from their peers duly followed.

1984 brought the miners' strike. *Channel 4 News*, with space to play in, rose to the challenge. Only the ablest journalists working together – I think of John Lloyd and his colleagues at the *Financial Times* – could hope to do justice to the seriousness of the issues, the strength of emotion, the particularity of local incident, the complexities of statistics bandied about by both sides, the tactics, argument, recrimination of both protagonists, the rights and wrongs of police behaviour. *Channel 4 News* made a better fist of reporting the course of events and examining both cases than did others. Stewart Purvis, brightly, invited Arthur Scargill and Ian MacGregor each to make a separate report putting the argument. These were broadcast on successive days. A debate between them, on Wednesday, 22 August 1984, was a major off-again on-again coup. It brought *Channel 4 News* its highest audience to that point. Now under a new editor, Richard Tait, *Channel 4 News* goes on from strength to strength. Its presenter, Peter Sissons, much wooed, is off to the BBC.

Placed too early for some – City businessmen and London professional people tend not to get back to their homes in the South-East in time for its start – *Channel 4 News* now has a loyal following. Many relish its calmer tone and statelier pace. It never 'analysed' the news. It reports serious matters, though, at appropriate length and in context, and it probes impartially the relevant issue of the day. Though Peter Sissons interviewed them tenaciously, ministers kept on coming on. They valued the opportunity to put a point at greater length. So did their opponents. We valued the opportunity to put another question or to ask the same one again. *Channel 4 News* won the channel influential friends.

There had not been a regular programme on parliamentary politics since the demise of the BBC's *Gallery* more than twenty years before. *A Week in Politics* would remedy that. Never easy to place in the schedule, denounced by some as stuffy, praised by others for its impartiality, *A Week in Politics* survived because it filled a perceived political need. Channel 4 long wanted to cover the House of Commons, and particularly the work of its committees. Since the Commons still dithered on this brink we reported the Lords' debates instead.

Under constant fire in the press and under pressure from government, trade unionists, through their leaders, wanted to know why there was no space for them in media on which their affairs might be untendentiously reported. They hoped we would cover Congress, and for some regular reporting of their affairs in which, perhaps, they could be involved. We did, for a year or two, carry live reports on the annual Congress. We refused the notion that the TUC should provide programmes. *Union World* was presented from Liverpool by Gus MacDonald for Granada TV. But just as we came along trade union power and influence were in decline; our coverage reflected that decline.

The Business Programme and *Business Daily* are contributions in a growth field. In this Channel 4 has reflected trends, not bucked them. *Business Daily* appears to be there to stay. Advertisers welcome such programmes and the chance to place their messages around them. *Face the Press* and *What the Papers Say* were old favourites. My colleagues could see no place for such ancient relics in our output. They pointed to my personal prejudices, and with reason. *Papers*, though not easy to schedule, survived so long because it was the first regular programme I produced. I could not bring myself to chop it.

The IBA asked that Channel 4 should cater for Britain's ethnic minorities, but not in their own languages, for that might involve us in separate programmes in Hindi, Gujerati, Bengali, Punjabi and several others. Our programmes would be in English; they would be of special interest to particular segments of this multi-cultural society; they would deal with matters that affected their lives and their children's lives here, and also with the cultural and political climate of their places of origin. In a country in which Britons still encountered discrimination and racist hostility, they would fulfil a rallying function. You matter; this is your show.

Sue Woodford, commissioning editor for multi-cultural programmes, could not entrust her first commissions to black production teams acting on their own; there were none experienced enough to be capable of it. Instead she asked a unit at LWT, which undertook to employ editorial personnel from within those communities, to give us two alternating fortnightly magazines, *Black on Black* for Afro-Caribbean Britons, and *Eastern Eye* for Britons of Asian origins. Each had merit though, as magazines will, each combined items of hard reportage with entertaining chit-chat that did not always sit easily together. Each found a following. Each provoked violent hostility from those few viewers who objected to any space at all on a British television screen for black Britons. These were vociferous but easily discounted. They were joined in their hostility by a writer on broadcasting of high ability and repute. This was Christopher Dunkley, television critic of the *Financial Times* who, on this issue, exhibited a blind spot of such perversity as to stand out on the arts pages of the *FT* as does Nelson's Column among the pigeons of Trafalgar Square.

According to Dunkley, all programmes edited by and aimed particularly at any one segment of society were an abomination which threatened not only to perpetuate and reinforce divisions in society, but even provoke some that did not yet exist. To show programmes edited by women or aimed at blacks was 'crypto-fascist'; it was to practise a form of 'apartheid'. In fact, apartheid denies political rights to the majority of a population and insists on separation on racial grounds. Our multi-cultural programmes were mere islands of blackness in a white sea. No one was confined to them; no one forced to use them. All were free to sample as they chose. I could never see the force of Dunkley's repeated objection. All right, one might hope to live one day in a society where race or cultural origin was not an issue. That day was not yet. Blacks need role models. Trevor MacDonald on *Channel 4 News* or *ITN News* will do more for a young black journalist's confidence and self-esteem than the presenter of *Black on Black* ever could. But the latter does something, too. Asian Britons enjoy Indian popular movies. They are keener to see the stars of those movies or of Asian popular music than others who have never heard of them can possibly be. People appropriate cultural emblems to themselves. Irish schoolchildren in Coventry, I was told, talked of the series Robert Kee and I did on Ireland, *Ireland – A Television History*, as 'our series'. I would not myself want to live in a society whose plural parts did not have their own concerns or distinctive causes for celebration.

Such concerns ought certainly to be reflected in mainstream coverage. Those who train on programmes of specific scope in the first instance do, indeed, go on to work in the mainstream. But they have to start somewhere. It is a matter of pride at Channel 4 that some started with us. Trevor Phillips has moved on from *Black on Black*. Samir Shah, editor of *Eastern Eye*, is now a deputy to John Birt in the controlled revolution at the BBC. (It was Samir Shah, incidentally, who employed as the presenter of *Eastern Eye* the Dr Aziz Kurtha who later figured so comically in the case of Jeffrey Archer and the prostitute.) Farrukh Dhondy, who succeeded Sue Woodford as commissioning editor for multi-cultural programmes, has replaced both *Eastern Eye* and *Black on Black*. *The Bandung File*, a lively current affairs programme which keeps a particular eye on the Caribbean and the Asian subcontinent, is produced by Tariq Ali and by Darcus Howe (though in our early days a junior government minister once specifically warned me against him). A variety of fictions, comedies and documentaries of clear cultural identity but of no fixed category now grace Channel 4's screen. One, *Salaam Bombay!*, was nominated for an Oscar.

'Programmes,' I had stipulated for Edinburgh in 1979 'by women, for women, which the rest of us will watch.' Liz Forgan shared my wish to see what the world looked like through women's editorial eyes. Not very different, one would have to report on the evidence of what we were actually able to achieve. Our first stab at the genre, *Broadside*, made a mixed start, and then aborted, torn apart by internal dissensions on the production team. *20/20 Vision* did better and lasted longer. Later, more overtly proselytizing series such as *Watch the Woman*, inventively edited by Carol Sarler, came on too strong for some viewers and were never quite persuasive enough to win out in the competition for budgets. The producers ought, ideally, to have been granted a longer licence to fail. If Channel 4 had done less, as perhaps it should from the outset, in the mainstream of current affairs, there might have been air-time free and resource to spare for such problematic ventures.

These would certainly have included programmes for gays. The problem there, though, was to persuade the Board of Channel 4 to give the go-ahead. Nobody on the Board of Channel 4, or I imagine on the IBA, objected in principle to programmes *about* homosexuals, though there might have been objections to the content of any one report. We broadcast several such, including widely admired accounts of lesbians by Melanie Chait, *Veronica 4 Rose* and *Breaking the Silence*. What was objected to was the idea of any programme specifically *for* homosexuals. The objection was not merely that this was, à la Dunkley, to divide the audience, but that it might proselytize for gays and even convert some to be of that disposition, as if that was possible. In every case, when such a proposal was put forward, it was the occasion of debate, demeaned once by an ITV Board colleague arguing that we should absolutely not show programmes about the activity that had led to the fall of the Roman Empire.

I had been concerned over the representation of homosexuals on television since my days as editor of *This Week* in the early Sixties. Amidst some apprehension – in the event unjustified – we devoted two editions of the programme to interviews by Bryan Magee with male homosexuals and lesbians. The interviews were conducted in silhouette. There was concern that voices were not adequately disguised. It seemed wrong then that anyone should be unable to make public so overwhelmingly important a truth about the self, or even to acknowledge that it was a truth. One film showed men dancing with each other in a shadowy club in Amsterdam. There was some hesitation over whether we could show something so shocking. A single viewer telephoned, in high indignation, to say that we had described Amsterdam as the capital of The Netherlands. That was incorrect; it was The Hague. No one else complained.

The serious point is that homosexuals, particularly covert homosexuals, are helped to self-awareness and self-confidence, can become therefore happier beings and more effective citizens by seeing that others, in all their individuality, share their nature, enjoy the same pursuits and aspirations, face common difficulties. Television has an obvious role to play in this. We did bring to air one lively series of gay portraits, *Six of Hearts*, but I only succeeded in partially preparing the ground for a more journalistic magazine format. *Out on Tuesday* was eventually broadcast, well after my departure, under the stewardship of Caroline Spry. It is, I think, a mark of progress that these useful programmes should have passed without adverse criticism or hoo-ha.

Comment is the three minutes at the end of *Channel 4 News*, once contained within it, in which an individual puts a point for our attention. Memorably launched on our opening night by David Watt, who argued that nothing useful could be said in that space, *Comment* was made worthwhile by its founder editor, Fiona Maddocks, who refused to be coaxed by me into settling for second best. I suggested that after a few weeks she would surely have found a core of contributors who could then take turns to appear and utter. It was a case of 'a word from me, and they do as they like'. Fiona would have none of this; it had to be somebody new every evening. This was pluralism with a vengeance. But, sure enough, two hundred different contributors a year have appeared on *Comment*, stretching out almost to the crack of doom. We gave an annual party for them which grew and grew. It may be, the point well and truly made by now, that the time has come to end *Comment*, and to try a new method of adding the spice of nightly opinion to the news.

The Friday Alternative, as I have told earlier, was ended at the IBA's wish, and on the Board's *obstat*. The motorbike bearing the videotape of the last recording to Charlotte Street memorably failed to arrive. The result was a symbolic hole, inappositely plugged. The bike went, we later found, to the BBC instead. The tape was broadcast by us the following evening. But *The Friday Alternative* did spawn, as I had urged that it should, a more than adequate successor from the same company of origin, Diverse Production. This was *Diverse Reports*.

Gradually, and at times stumblingly but in the end successfully, this programme embodied my notion of screening committed or opinionated journalism. *Opinions* – argument or polemic straight to camera – was the other regular example. This is not my favourite sort of journalism; I would rather read the observation of the reporter than the message of the propagandist. But I would not expect a reporter in any medium to be precluded from giving me his view. Yet, on television, a reporter might well be prohibited from doing just that, except on the condition that someone offering a contrary view was given equal time. I wanted to take this veto head-on by inventing series whose *raison d'être* would be to provoke thought in the viewer by making a case. Such programmes, and this was the lesson of *The Friday Alternative*'s debacle, would have to come from every point of the political spectrum. *Diverse Reports* succeeded in giving us just that.

David Graham, at the company's head, devised an effective editorial structure. He hired producers of contrasting political viewpoints. He hired contributors of different political views, some leaning more to observation, some to argument. Between them they made watchable viewing and kept to a political balance of cause and provocation. When, at the outset, I had stated Channel 4's intention to offer opinionated journalism, Aubrey Singer, then Managing Director of BBC-TV, turned his nose up. It would prove disastrous, Singer asserted, to allow such stuff to coexist in a broadcasting service with objective news and current affairs; the one would contaminate the other and 'poison the wells of truth'. But news and opinion co-exist, of course, in any decent newspaper. Why not on a television channel? *Diverse Reports* gave us some marvellously provocative reporting, along with the usual bumpy ride provoked by pieces that did not quite hit their target. Peter Clarke argued well and provokingly for the privatization of coal, for example; Christine Chapman on apartheid and Beatrix Campbell on women in Northern Ireland also come to mind. Alongside them, unperturbed, *Channel 4 News* went its fair-minded way.

David Graham and *Diverse Reports* needed to find right-wingers schooled or schoolable in television's journalistic techniques. They did. This led on to series, worthwhile in their own right, but also serving as a counterbalance to other stuff we put on, that advanced a right-wing cause. Most notable of these was an account of the ideology of the new right here and in the United States, *The New Enlightenment*.

Right to Reply is the viewer's chance to answer back. It is, in a way, the quintessential Channel 4 programme. Although as broadcast hours have expanded everybody now has their version of it, when we started *Right to Reply* was unique. The BBC had the chirpy, trivializing *Points of View*; ITV nothing. *Right to Reply* – then ably presented by Gus MacDonald – is the only programme that Channel 4 makes itself; everything else is bought in. The idea was simply that *Right to Reply* would give whoever felt maligned by what we had broadcast, or even was simply critical of it, a chance to have his or her say in rejoinder, no holds barred. In our early weeks, I was confronted by a letter of complaint from South Africa House at something we had shown. The letter, as was usual from that source, ran to several pages, itemized more than twenty points, and was copied, of course, to the Chairman of the IBA. At Thames, my previous employ, the drill to be followed in this circumstance would have been clear. A note from me to the Head of Current Affairs: How should I reply? Head of Current Affairs would have asked that question in turn of the programme's producer, who would have put it to the reporter and researcher concerned. Eventually, when these last had been retrieved from Accrington or Armagh or Afghanistan or wherever they had gone next, a point-by-point rebuttal (or admission of error) would have been prepared, laboriously typed in draft, and submitted as the basis of a possible reply. Approved, retyped, signed, posted, it might well have drawn an equally lengthy rejoinder. Here at Channel 4 all was to be different. I rang *Right to Reply*. 'Please offer the South African Ambassador the opportunity to appear in *Right to Reply* and rebut, if he can, what was put in the other programme.' We did. H. E. Marais Steyn was delighted to accept, and had his say, taking the opportunity to lambast, in passing, much else of our output. A viewer telephoned. 'This is a democracy; you have no right to put the South African Ambassador on television.'

It was the labour-saving element that most appealed to me; not even a letter needed to be written. I never succeeded in persuading the IBA, though, that *Right to Reply* was a safety valve which would justify the depiction of one side of a case only elsewhere in our schedule. That is one of the functions of a newspaper 'Letters to the Editor' column; I do not yet understand why our equivalent might not serve the same purpose, and be counted to us for virtue. I also failed to persuade my colleagues to let the programme act simply as the complainants' mouthpiece and platform. They insisted that justice was better served and better television made by requiring the producer or commissioning editor who had committed the enormity and was now under attack to confront his or her critic, and plead in self-defence. This had the effect of allowing the perpetrator a second innings. I argued against the practice, but could not prevail.

Right to Reply also exhibited one marvellous device that moved television on a bit. It brought viewers' letters to life for the first time by allowing them to speak to the camera in the Video Box. This was Liz Forgan's idea; walk in, sit down in the sort of booth you could have a passport photo taken in, push a button, look at the lens and speak. The first Video Box was in Charlotte Street, the second in Glasgow. I thought we might get drunks and weirdos. In fact we got articulate viewers passionately, pithily telling us where we got off. Their use will widen; airline and rail passengers, I guess, might also welcome an opportunity to criticize the service they have received, in person. Enlightened service companies will provide the facility to do so. I used the Video Box myself on one occasion to tell a viewer who was miserable at having missed it, the happy ending to our Brazilian soap opera *Isaura, The Slave Girl;* the heroine was freed, married and lived happily ever after.

Given the freedom we sought to allow programme makers who contributed to our screen, it was inevitable that we should find ourselves in disagreement both with them and with the custodians of the Broadcasting Act. Law and order, police conduct during the miners strike or in confrontation with black youth in Brixton or Tottenham, all threw up occasions on which it was hard to agree on what might, within the law, be said. So did Northern Ireland.

I continue to believe that it is the Loyalist, Protestant case that is under-represented on British television, but I do not regret finding space for the Republican sentiments we broadcast, on any occasion. Nor do I regret insisting on occasion on cuts. *Turn It Up*, from a youth collective in Birmingham started off as a legitimate critique of the use by the security forces of plastic bullets. I ordered the deletion from it of an incitement to 'get the RUC'. Channel 4 did its best to put across to British viewers something of the feel of the politics of Ireland, but had as much trouble as anyone else when it came to contentious detail.

But there were happier Irish encounters. There are millions in Britain who are Irish. I decided to cater for them. We showed the Gaelic Games Cup Finals, hurling and Gaelic football from Croke Park in Dublin. It was when a manager in The White Tower asked me if it was true one of these was on our screen that weekend that I first knew we were catching on. Britain's political life and the Republic's impinge on each other. Wanting also to offer something of Irish politics, I decided on a weekly window on events each side of the border. *Irish Angle* was an opportunity to show – unedited and unmediated – from Belfast an edition of Ulster Television's *Counterpoint*, or from Dublin RTE's *Today, Tonight*. This was in the charge of John Ranelagh, who knows about Ireland, once spotting in the nick of time after an election that the Taoiseach Garret Fitzgerald's victory statement and press conference which RTE had sent over had something fishy about it. They had sent the material from a previous election. Frantic telephone calls to RTE that weekend went unanswered. Eventually, it took a call to the pub to dig out the technicians who could remedy the matter.

Irish Angle made a slow start; a debate on Dublin housing was a particular downer. Then one week Ranelagh came to see me with a gleam in his eye; RTE promised a really lively programme the following Sunday. The Minister of Justice, Sean Doherty TD, had been interfering in Gardai affairs in County Roscommon, warning station officers that if they persisted in prosecuting a local pub that was rather too openly open after hours, he would have them transferred to Kerry or Donegal. It was a Fianna Fáil pub and they ought to know better. The evidence for this and other goings-on was on video, and the charges were backed by a sworn affidavit at every material point. A lively *Irish Angle* would certainly result.

Next day Ranelagh had bad news; we could not have the RTE programme because, on reflection, they did not think its subject matter was fit to be seen this side of the Irish Sea. Go back, I told him, and say that, on the contrary, this is exactly the sort of stuff that is of interest. They have a contract with us; let them honour it.

Next day, another long face. RTE were now saying that they would like to let us have the programme, but legal obstacles stood in the way; the allegations in it were defamatory; Channel 4 might be sued for libel if we broadcast. 'But surely,' I asked in some astonishment, 'they told us earlier that they had reliable witnesses and sworn testimony to every allegation in it?' 'Ah yes,' said John, 'but they are saying that those witnesses would testify in an Irish court, but might not in an English court.' We told RTE we would take that risk, and went ahead.

After the miners' strike we broadcast three separate programmes, *Battle for Orgreave*, *Whose Side are You On?* and *May the Force Be with You*, which dwelt on bitter feelings in the mining communities and vigorously attacked police behaviour. The film-makers who collected these angry voices showed more police response to provocation than provocation itself. Sometimes, illegitimately in our view, they egged the pudding by technical tricks, adding, for example, a soundtrack to the picture of a batoning, or rerunning the video to show it happening again and again. Both these devices were unacceptable. Nevertheless the programmes did perform a service. They put in front of us acts committed in our name. The IBA decreed that they called for programmes that put the police case in reply. These always turned out easier to summon up than to make, given the reluctance of the police to participate.

My Britain was a useful occasional device for an illustrated informal tract for our times. Various political figures made films giving a personal picture of this society. Of the IBA's various interventions the dottiest was the suggestion, issued as an edict by a junior officer in the Television division, that 'David Steel's Britain' could not be broadcast on grounds of 'balance'. A weekend telephone call to the Director-General's home succeeded in reversing this patently overprotective nonsense.

Down on the Farm by Ceddo, a black film and video workshop, was an aggrieved tirade against police behaviour triggered by events at Broadwater Farm, where PC Keith Blakelock was brutally murdered in a riot. The film spoiled its effect, I felt, by trying to cram in too much. It included Mrs Thatcher's reception here of South Africa's President P. W. Botha, and the death, killing, murder – take your choice – of Mrs Cynthia Jarrett in Brixton. It insisted, absurdly, on talking about black 'uprisings'. But it did represent a ferocious point of view it would have done good rather than harm to expose. Unfortunately the workshop could not agree with Channel 4, nor Channel 4 with the IBA, on a version that could be transmitted. After months of stalled argument, *Down on the Farm* simply faded away.

The row over *Greece: The Hidden War* was the product of a series of mistakes that cost us dear. The three programmes were put forward to us by TVS, just about the most solidly conservative of ITV companies, as an account of resistance activity in Greece under German rule in the Second World War, and of the Greek Civil War that followed it. It would stress the point of view of the defeated left, many of whom had exiled themselves after it to Communist Eastern Europe, and had only now returned to Greece. I instructed our commissioning editor Carol Haslam that the views and experience of both parties to the civil war must be included. They were not. But included in the first episode were accounts by British participants in the resistance, who had an unshakable view of the rights and wrongs of those bitter conflicts and who plainly thought, and claimed they were led to believe, that they were taking part in a balanced account of these still-controversial events, as indeed their own participation in the films must have indicated to them was the case. The film-maker, Jane Gabriel, denied she had misled them in any particular, and I accept that she did not deliberately do so. But the British believed they had been hoodwinked. They were appalled to find themselves in such leftist company, and made an almighty row. They insisted the only true version of events was theirs. The fallout followed me to the BBC. When, in early 1987, I applied for the Director-Generalship of the BBC, I found the Governors much exercised as to how to prevent programme cock-ups regularly occurring. I muttered a suggested procedure. One Governor, Daphne Park, then Principal of Somerville College, Oxford, previously of MI6, was scornful. 'How can we believe that you could prevent such things?' she asked. 'You broadcast those lies on Greece.' *Greece: The Hidden War* did not lie, but I did not know enough to debate it with her and feebly, which I now regret, let her barbed challenge pass.

Public arguments about what may or may not be shown are inevitable when the law treats the regulatory body as the responsible broadcaster and allows it to have the last word. This denies responsibility to the broadcaster, an anomaly that will be altered for the future. The ITC that is to replace the IBA will cede all such responsibility to those it enfranchises, and ride them on a looser rein. It will, or says it will, abandon the power to view a programme and second-guess the broadcaster, before transmission. From that day on, the broadcaster will take responsibility for what he publishes. He will take his chances, under the law. I have been arguing for this change for more than twenty years. It will mean less argument and quicker decisions. It will not necessarily mean braver ones. The Authority and its officers on occasion display more mettle than some commercial broadcasters may yet prove to be capable of. My hope is that some day those who do take these decisions will agree with Milton that no harm is done by allowing to be published, under the law, truths that someone or other passionately wants to utter. And I would hope that regulators, if they still exist, will understand that a serious defence of free speech involves not just standing up for what is brave and well said, but also for what is ugly and unskilfully argued. The right to free speech is everyone's.

During the trial of Clive Ponting on charges of breaching the Official Secrets Act, a bright independent, Dennis Woolf, suggested to us that we report the court proceedings nightly, using actors to speak extracts from an edited daily transcript. Apprised of this intention in the press, the trial judge, Mr Justice McCowan, without hearing argument, instructed that this was not to be. There was a risk these midnight reports might prejudice the jury. There was no appeal; no recourse open to us against his ruling. Rapidly taking further legal opinion, and strong in the belief that what was possible for newspapers ought to be allowed to television also, we decided to use newscasters instead of actors to read out the edited report, and went ahead. Geoffrey Robertson advised throughout. Godfrey Hodgson held all, very ably, together. The judge indicated he was content with the revised method we had adopted. Later we reconstructed, this time with actors, the *Spycatcher* hearings in Australia, in which Robert Armstrong gave evidence for Her Majesty's Government, and Malcolm Turnbull appeared for author Peter Wright and publisher Heinemann. These were small steps forward for a much-regulated medium. Channel 4, the NUJ and others later took Her Majesty's Government to the European Court over the Ponting trial, arguing that the judge ought not to have ruled against us without hearing argument, and that it was wrong that complainants against rulings of contempt of court should have no recourse of appeal. On this latter point the court found that HMG had a case to answer.

Cathy Massiter, a former officer of MI5, was the star witness in a programme made by Claudia Milne's company 20/20 Vision called *MI5's Official Secrets*. Miss Massiter had left the service after complaining to her superiors that actions she knew were going on, and had herself been asked to commit, were illegal. She was unwilling to go on. She now came forward to say publicly what these were. They included the unauthorized, or perhaps authorized – but, if authorized, why authorized? – tapping of the telephones of trade unionists during industrial disputes, of CND members, and of the legitimate left, including two Labour MPs. No one doubted the importance of these statements; they were not a surprise perhaps to the cynical, but they came as a shock to others. They seemed to indicate what later revelations bore out, that MI5 could act outside the bounds of its due authority, and not be held to account for those actions. Liz Forgan warned me, and I warned the Chairman, that this programme was in the pipeline. Exceptional care was taken to corroborate every detail of its text, and to state each charge accurately, moderately and with precision. Hugo Young spoke the commentary. The programme was sober, factual, persuasive. Yet there was an obvious difficulty.

Every word Cathy Massiter spoke was in plain breach of the Official Secrets Act. Bravely she was prepared to utter in public, and in the public interest. So were the programme-makers. So might Channel 4 be. But would the IBA? We did not publicize in advance our intention to screen *MI5's Official Secrets* because of the obvious risk, indeed virtual certainty, of an injunction by Government to prevent transmission. We did, however, have to warn the IBA and, if they asked as they certainly would, submit it to them for scrutiny and approval. Our lawyers advised us that there was a risk of prosecution both of Miss Massiter and of ourselves, but it was for her and for us to say whether that risk was worth running. On that basis, the programme could be shown.

The IBA's lawyers were less sanguine. It was wrong, they counselled, for a statutory body to break the law. The full Authority, meeting on 20 February 1985 – on the evening of which, had they permitted it, we would have broadcast the programme – refused us permission to screen *MI5's Official Secrets*. They issued a press statement:

20/20 Vision

The IBA received proposals from Channel 4 for a programme on MI5 and the Special Branch. This programme was seen by members of the Authority this morning.

The IBA has been advised by counsel that it would be deliberately committing a criminal offence under the Official Secrets Act if the programme were shown. The IBA is a statutory body responsible to Parliament and should not deliberately break the law.

The IBA recognizes that a number of serious allegations are made in the programme about the surveillance methods operated by the security services and that surveillance is an area of public and parliamentary concern.

The IBA considers that these allegations should be brought to the attention of the proper authorities for consideration and investigation.

The IBA has decided that it cannot accept the programme for transmission.

So did we:

20/20 Vision

Channel 4 had intended to interrupt its published programme schedule tonight at 8.00 pm to broadcast a *20/20 Vision* programme entitled *MI5's Official Secrets*. The Independent Broadcasting Authority at its meeting today decided that it would not be broadcast.

Channel 4, after taking opinion from leading counsel, put the programme forward for transmission as an important report on a matter of considerable public interest, and regrets that the IBA has decided that it may not be broadcast.

Channel 4 has therefore returned the programme to the makers of *20/20 Vision*.

In releasing the programme back to its makers, we were mindful of the *Guardian*'s misfortune when the documents leaked to them by Sara Tisdall were kept, and later subpoenaed by the courts. We thought the tape might be physically safer with the makers. We also knew that they would let journalists and MPs see the programme on video-cassette, in order to ensure that the allegations were made public and followed up. This they did, and a fair stir followed.

The Board of Channel 4, till then not involved, viewed the programme at its next meeting. Unanimously they approved and reaffirmed our willingness to screen it, and urged the IBA to think again. Edmund Dell and I went over to represent this to Lord Thomson. But the IBA was adamant, and the following day the Director-General, John Whitney, restated their position in a public speech. The explanation of their refusal, he said, lay in the constitutional position of the Authority itself. The Authority would be committing a criminal offence if it were to be shown. Others might risk such a course. The Authority could not. They had the last word. So that was that. This was precisely the constitutional absurdity of letting the regulatory body assume the publisher's responsibility which I had been attacking for twenty years.

A week later, when so many others had now seen the programme, the Attorney General let it be known that he did not propose to prosecute anyone in respect of it. Principally, obviously, this came as a relief to Cathy Massiter and to the programme-makers. It came also as a relief to the IBA. On Wednesday, 6 March, the Authority, its members now absolved in advance from the risk of prosecution – after all, why should any of them have gone to jail? – performed a graceful U-turn and allowed the programme to be shown. On the Friday we put it out. Viewers had an opportunity to see and hear for themselves a sane and honourable woman bearing witness to MI5's murky goings-on.

As a result of this programme's making and showing, MI5 did have to re-examine its procedures. Parliament tried to take a tighter grip of MI5. Government, on the other hand, took sterner measures to prevent others speaking out as Massiter had done. *MI5's Official Secrets*, thanks largely to Cathy Massiter's brave witness, became that rare exception in television's current affairs output, a programme which actually made a difference.

10

Film on 4

TELEVISION is heavily dependent on cinema, even, you could say, parasitical upon it. It buys movie libraries, shows dozens of films a week, hundreds each year. In spite of high prices paid for popular films, the film industry has always argued that television gets its products on the cheap. As television in the UK has prospered, the British film industry has declined. 'You take so much out,' was the charge, 'you put nothing back.' British film-makers could not raise the cash to make British films. Yet the television industry was rich enough to contemplate another channel, which might add to home viewing and would increase the use of feature films on TV.

The film industry argued for higher prices for its product, with a tax on usage to be put to film production. BBC and ITV united in their joint self-interest and fairly easily fended this off. Cinema exhibitors insisted on rules to protect cinema exhibition; no film was to be shown on television until three years after its first UK cinema screening. Distributors would sell films in advance to television, but the film was not available for transmission till the embargo expired. The best of television drama was made on film, and at virtual feature length. But – sometimes to its makers' chagrin – the work always went straight on to the domestic screen. The agreements under which it was made did not allow the film to be put first into the cinema. If it was, this ensured a delay of years before it could be screened on television. No TV drama department had sufficient spare funds to wait that long. So the two industries, instead of co-operating, pulled against each other. Film had to be sold to television in the end.

Television had little incentive to invest in film-making.

They ordered things differently elsewhere. In Germany and in Italy television, acknowledging a symbiotic relationship with the film industry, put money into films which played first in the cinema and then, shortly after, on television. Films were not made exclusively either for cinema or for television but for both. And good films too. In Italy RAI had funded the work of Fellini, Bertolucci and the Taviani brothers. In Germany ARD and ZDF helped underpin the careers of Herzog, Wenders and Fassbinder. That was why, the argument went, those countries had film-makers and film industries to be proud of, and we had not. Surely a new television channel could find a modus vivendi, attempt a new partnership with cinema, put back into film-making something of what it was bound to take out. Channel 4 would try.

In my letter of application for the job of chief executive, I said I would make it a priority to put money into 'films of feature length for television here, for the cinema abroad'. I was proposing help for a British film industry, but acknowledging that, because of the way exhibition was organized, it was difficult – in 1980 impossible – to make films for both outlets. This state of things had to be changed, and in time was.

Once appointed, I put Channel 4 into film-making. David Rose was not hired as Head of Drama (his present title) but as Senior Commissioning Editor, Fiction. We had no electronic studios. He and I agreed we would do most of our work on film, not video – in itself an odd decision for an innovative channel. Video was, after all, the newer medium. He would provide the schedule with a twice-weekly soap opera, *Brookside*. But series, which some credibly argue is the characteristic television art form, I would buy abroad. Or I would acquire repeats from ITV. We would make few of our own. (Later we found resources to add drama series and serials to our programme mix, and hired a separate commissioning editor under David to look after them.) For the rest, we would make movies.

The playwright and screenwriter Stephen Poliakoff came to lunch with the Channel 4 Board. In a backroom upstairs at Bertorelli's he urged us to commit to feature film-making; it was galling for film-makers, writers and directors, to see their work flicker briefly, one showing only, on the television screen and not reappear. A film for the cinema could be seen by its author with an audience, more than once. It gave a sense of achievement to those who had laboured to realize the dream, the passage from idea to script to celluloid reality that was film-making. This was useful corroboration of our purpose. The Board, though it asked for reassurance that making feature films would, somehow, be worth our while, consistently approved the necessary budgets. Dickie Attenborough, himself a film-maker of renown, equally consistently supported our modest investment in the British film industry, or what there was of it.

David Rose set out to make low-budget films. He had £6 million earmarked; with it he proposed to attempt to get twenty movies made, at £300,000 each. Some we hoped, in those earliest days, to make entirely for that sum. Some would be made in partnership with others, our £300,000 a contribution to the budget. In all of them we would own television rights. For all of them we would try, hurdles overcome, to secure some cinema showing.

The first batch were ready for television transmission in our first weeks on the air. They had been among David Rose's earliest commissions. One or two had some minimal cinema exposure, were not yet available and had to be withdrawn from the first schedule.

David Rose, and his colleagues Walter Donohue and Karin Bamborough, preferred contemporary Britain as subject-matter in the treatments or scripts offered to them, but there was no hard and fast rule. The past was not debarred as period. Fantasy was not disallowed, though realism was the prevailing mode. Locations could be abroad, though budgets mostly determined otherwise. Here co-finance could help. Channel 4 has nearly 150 *Films on Four* now to its credit, 130 British, 20 from abroad. The first batch or two must stand for others. Not a particularly spectacular offering, nor yet revealing our full ambition, but of some substance all the same.

On our first night on air we showed *Walter*, directed by Stephen Frears for Central TV. Ian McKellen's moving performance as the mentally retarded boy took the eye. Pigeons filling the bedroom in which a mother lay dead, their feathers fluttering over the corpse, stick in the memory.

David Puttnam had sold me a series, *First Love*, in which he would offer opportunities to British talent. Jack Rosenthal's and Michael Apted's *P'Tang Yang Kipperbang* I thought too soft for our first night. Viewers loved it. A few weeks later, June Roberts' hilarious tale of life backstairs in a seaside hotel, and a virginity lost in it, *Experience Preferred, But Not Essential*, directed by Peter Duffell, capped the earlier success.

Colin Gregg added to the swearword count with *Remembrance*, a shipload of tars ashore in Pompey the night before the fleet sailed, rowdy, salty, violent. Jack Gold, to whom at Thames I owed *The Naked Civil Servant*, gave us a glossy French thriller, spread over two evenings, *Praying Mantis*. The delectable Cherie Lunghi held the eye. Karl Francis persuaded Glenda Jackson and Jon Finch to star in *Giro City* as a TV director and investigative journalist on the trail of graft and municipal corruption in South Wales, with a diversion to cover a major Irish story. Joseph Despins' *The Disappearance of Harry* had Annette Crosbie in a fanciful political mystery set in Nottingham during Goose Fair. Philip French, seeing it at the Edinburgh Film Festival, described it as an 'irresistible paranoid thriller'. *Bad Hats* starred and was co-written by Mick Ford. Two soldiers, one English one French, desert from the Western Front in the First World War; they meet and love a young woman before the war reclaims them.

Hero was the first new film for years by Barney Platts-Mills. He had *Bronco Bullfrog* and others to his name, thus entering the then fabled ranks of young British directors who had actually made a film. *Hero* was a recreation of the ancient Gaelic legend of Dermid, Grania and the great warrior Finn McCool. It was seen as one of Isaacs' follies. Barney Platts-Mills was living and working in Scotland and wanted to make *Hero* with a group of boys from a Glasgow community project he was associated with. They would recreate an ancient mud and wattle village in Argyll. They would also act all the parts. The lads were great over the moor and up the mountains and in the battle scenes. They were not, according to Barney, at home with the dialogue; their accents jarred. Halfway through the location came the message; he was shooting in Gaelic. We could not stop him. *Hero* thus became the world's first Gaelic-language feature film, and was shown with subtitles. Other *Films on Four* in our first season got very substantial audiences. *Hero* did not. The Gaels were not pleased either; the Glasgow lads' Gaelic was not correct enough to impress the true Gaelic speaker.

In April 1983 a second season of *Film on Four* included Jerzy Sko-limowski's *Moonlighting*. Michael White agreed with Skolimowski to put up half the budget over a game of tennis. We did the rest. Maurice Hatton made *Nelly's Version*. Earlier, when Maurice's work was retrospectively shown at the National Film Theatre, he had complained that it went from production to retrospection, without distribution or exhibition inter-vening. This at least was seen. Bill Bryden gave us *Ill Fares the Land*; STV put up the money. Peter Wollen's and Laura Mulvey's *The Bad Sister* was shot on video and exploited electronic effects to lend a disorienting, hallucinatory quality to Emma Tennant's tale of witchcraft and wild women. Peter Greenaway's *The Draughtsman's Contract* was being made for the BFI Production Board when they ran out of cash. In funding its completion, we obtained the right to screen this deft and dazzling puzzle picture, as good to look at as any English movie ever. More good Greenaway was to follow. Both *Moonlighting* and *The Draughtsman's Contract* had had runs in cinemas. So had *Angel*, the directorial debut of the Irish writer Neil Jordan. Jordan had become known to the film-maker John Boorman when he was making *Excalibur*. Boorman recommended him to us, and himself produced *Angel*, which Chriş Menges shot. Stephen Rea gave his usual fine performance as Danny, a saxophonist in an Irish band who witnesses the killing of a young girl and is drawn further into violence. I saw it, before the show print, in a Soho viewing theatre and staggered across the street into The Intrepid Fox, sure that I had seen the first work of a screen master. Jordan went on to direct *The Company of Wolves* and *Mona Lisa*. There was much more to come from *Film on Four*; and we were only six months on the air.

Films do not exist in limbo; they depend for a useful life on cinemas, run by exhibitors. Exhibitors are themselves dependent for their supply on distributors. As important as getting a film made is to get it shown. Derek Hill bought foreign-language films for us. He also consistently represented to me the needs of exhibitors and distributors, on one occasion publicly advocating that we should pay them higher prices. Given our need to make the pennies go round, I had to tell him to shut up. Nevertheless, in the privacy of our meetings Derek pressed his point. It was a real one.

British exhibitors could only afford to bring a film to Britain if they got a decent price for the television rights. For such a film to do well on television it was helpful for it to have had a run in the cinema first, benefiting from the reviews and word of mouth that would follow. So it could suit us to pay enough to guarantee the cinema showing that would raise our audience's expectation when we put the film on our screen. We ought, therefore, Hill argued, in our own ultimate self-interest, to pay prices that would keep Romaine Hart at the Screen on the Hill or Andi Engel at the Lumière thrivingly in business. We did not pay over the odds. But we did have some regard for the needs of our suppliers and for their continued existence. These exhibitors in their turn recognized our need to see films we funded on our screen at a date of our choosing, as soon as their cinema life was exhausted, rather than having to wait for the three years from first exhibition that the Cinema Exhibitors' Association (CEA), insisted on. We were entitled to use them on television when we needed them, otherwise they would not get made at all. This prevailed in the end. With the aid of allies in the industry, Justin Dukes successfully negotiated a ruling that for films costing less than £1.25 million, which safely covered most of ours, the three-year embargo need no longer apply.

Leslie Halliwell bought in Hollywood for Channel 4, lovingly combing the libraries for the neglected masterworks for the period he cared for most, the Thirties and Forties. He resurrected the B-movie; *Mister Moto* sleuthed again. He arranged his favourite black and white, stylish classics in attractive packages, and added prints of rarities never seen before on television in Britain. We called his black and white pictures 'golden oldies'. Leslie Halliwell, who died early in 1989, was himself a 'golden oldie', making an unsurpassed contribution to our success.

The enjoyment of film suffused many of the channel's activities. As Director of Programmes at Thames I had given the go-ahead to make *Hollywood*, a series on the early years of the industry. Halfway through making *The World at War*, at a party for the sixty or so people who worked on it, I gave each of them a paperback copy of *The Parade's Gone By*, Kevin Brownlow's book of interviews with the Hollywood pioneers. Our next project together, I meant to tell them, after the hells of Warsaw and Nagasaki, would be fun. Later, my colleague at Thames John Edwards introduced Kevin Brownlow to David Gill, and a fruitful partnership was born. They interviewed on film the witnesses to the growth of film-making in California. Then, when Mike Wooller's strenuous negotiation over rights succeeded, they were able to add footage of the great 'silent' masterpieces of the period. Carl Davis wrote the music.

When I left Thames, they asked me to work with them on the commentary and the fine-cuts of the thirteen episodes, which, creeping a little sheepishly back to Teddington, I gladly did. *Hollywood* gave great pleasure when shown by Thames. But there was no room on ITV for the films the series celebrated. Carl Davis' music triumphantly restored these films to us as living cinema, no longer 'silent' but accompanied, rendered whole, and transmuted back to greatness by music specially composed and performed by orchestras of symphonic size, just as when they were first seen in the fantasy picture palaces of those days. Thames Television now agreed, at Brownlow's and Gill's urging, to prepare the films for live performance: *The Thames Silents*. Channel 4 paid for the commissioned score; and, later, for the recording of these scores, very expensive since MU agreements ensure, not unreasonably if perfection is the goal, that no more than twenty minutes of music can be recorded in any three-hour session. Exciting presentations could now be given in cinemas, and, after the recording, the films could be seen on TV. Gill and Brownlow supervised the marriage of celluloid to music sound: Lillian Gish in *The Wind*, Greta Garbo in *Flesh and the Devil*, King Vidor's *The Crowd*, Douglas Fairbanks in *The Thief of Bagdad*, the full splendours of *Ben-Hur* and *Intolerance*. Most remarkable and the first of the series was the five-hour version of Abel Gance's 1927 *Napoleon*, the first part of a projected much longer film dealing with the Emperor's whole life. Gance's film, lost and in pieces for years, was, from reels retrieved from all over Europe and America, magically restored to pristine glory by Brownlow, who had nearly all his life dreamed of seeing *Napoleon* whole again. Carl Davis pillaged the Emperor's contemporaries for thematic material – his favourite composing partner, he says, is Borrowed-In. From Haydn, Beethoven, Cherubini, he wrought a rich score, writing a great romantic theme for the eagle that symbolized the young Bonaparte's destiny. *Napoleon* was given triumphantly at the Empire, Leicester Square.

Bowled over on the day by Gance's virtuosic mastery, I knew that Channel 4 must screen it also. There was a slight difficulty in doing it full justice. At the film's climax, as Napoleon takes over the Army of Italy and gazes down with them, set for conquest, on the plains of Lombardy, the image expands, refusing to be confined to one screen. Instead, three projectors set beside each other fill three cinema screens; first a panorama; then, in vast close-up, the eagle of destiny, head and beak in the centre, one wing to either side. It may be the greatest single moment in silent cinema. How could we show *Napoleon* without reproducing it? But how could we achieve it on TV?

I thought I must find a way of doing so. If when Channel 4 showed *Napoleon*, I could persuade ITV to join us for the last reel that would give us two out of the three screens necessary. For the third, how about BBC-2? I rang its Controller, Brian Wenham, and put the point to him. Would his channel co-operate? Brian Wenham was sympathetic. But his senses had not deserted him. He would like to help, but, without actually saying that I was off my rocker, asked how many people I knew who had, in one room, lined up alongside each other, three television sets on which the triptych might, at this climactic moment, be displayed? Squelch! We showed *Napoleon* in a modified version with the end printed on one roll of film.

Channel 4 showed the best and *The Worst of Hollywood*. Mesmerized over a jolly lunch by Michael Medved, author of *The Golden Turkey Awards* and *The Fifty Worst Movies of All Time*, I agreed, for the autumn of 1983, to a season of the worst films Medved could disinter from the industry's 'not wanted this century' vaults. Our press release claimed he looked at 2000 third-rate films to find those bad enough for inclusion in this unusual Top Ten. As Medved said, 'We have plumbed the depths of bad movies: it's tough, punishing work, but someone has to do it.' His introductions were filmed in front of audiences willing to be initiated into the cult. The season included *They Saved Hitler's Brain*, *Plan 9 from Outer Space*, *Wild Women of Wongo*, my personal favourite, and, appropriately scheduled on Christmas Eve, *Santa Claus Conquers the Martians*. The turkeys gave some mild amusement; the cult did not catch on.

Channel 4 funded the ambitious, but parsimoniously run, Children's Film Unit. Colin Finbow, its director, came to see me and explained that each year a group of schoolchildren came together to make a feature film, which they themselves had scripted. They played all the parts behind the screen as well as on, acting as director, camera operator, sparks and editor. But they had no money. I agreed to fund the first year's film, *Captain Stirrick*. We showed it at the Christmas holiday period, and a Children's Film Unit Christmas film became a happy annual event.

Film culture demanded that we have a serious regular programme about cinema. But *Visions*, the channel's film magazine, though it ran various excellent items, never quite caught on. Mamoun Hassan came to me with the inventive but simple programme idea that best took further an interest in film. This was *Movie Masterclass*, in which three teachers – he, Jack Gold and Lindsay Anderson – each analysed their favourite movies shot by shot on a Steenbeck before a class at the National Film School. After each *Masterclass* the film itself followed.

At the Academy in Oxford Street audiences had queued to see *Pather Panchali* and its successors, a resonant, subtle body of work by the Bengali film-maker Satyajit Ray, one of the world's great directors. Indian in every particular, these were, however, art-house films for the connoisseur of cinema worldwide. At the Odeon, Southall, or in Whitechapel by the mosque, crowds assembled on Sunday mornings to view another sort of movie, the products of the great film factory of Bombay, making popular entertainment on a lavish scale for a market of hundreds of millions, not yet pre-empted by television. Channel 4 was bidden to cater specifically for Britain's ethnic minorities. There were certainly well over a million Britons from the Indian sub-continent who might welcome on television the movies they most enjoyed. Shashi Kapoor and the other great stars of Indian cinema were interviewed along with pop stars, cricketers and other celebrities on *Eastern Eye*. On Sunday afternoons we showed a careful selection by Munni Kabir of the best of the movies which had made them famous. In *Sholay*, which first persuaded me what pleasure such a series could give, sheer *joie de vivre* lent such energy to a rumbustious narrative that wider audiences, it seemed to me, might unresistingly be captured. *Sholay* had romance, thrills, spectacle. True, you could have lopped twenty minutes of serenading out of it, or of look-at-me stuff on bicycles, without holding up the plot. But the scene in which the bandit chieftain in his hilltop retreat forces the heroine to dance on broken glass to save her lover's life, before rescue, embrace and happiness ever after, is pure cinematic pleasure.

Indian movies tend to run long, claiming more air-time than we could easily afford; yet there were so many to choose from. This dilemma was resolved by *Movie Mahal*, a fan magazine for addicts, whose lollipop content was delectable enough to claim, briefly, peak-time screening. Indian cinema on Channel 4 triumphed in new forms, not through David Rose when he funded Mrinal Sen's Cannes entry *Genesis* but, most appropriately, through Farrukh Dhondy, commissioning editor for multi-cultural programmes. He backed Indian film-makers of talent. *Dabbawallahs* was an account of the life of tea-boys in Bombay, which showed much else. After that came *India Cabaret*, a quiet film about a bar girl's life in the city, contrasting that with the village in which her family still lived. Its director, Mira Nair, went on to make *Salaam Bombay!*. This won the Camera d'Or at Cannes and was nominated for an Oscar. To the envy of his colleagues, Farrukh, with the director, took his place at the Oscar ceremony in Hollywood, sporting beneath his elegant tailored white silk top coat a T-shirt blazoned 'Watch the Bandung File'.

The Comic Strip worked on film. They soon harboured feature film ambitions. *Supergrass*, directed by Peter Richardson, made it to the market at Cannes, and to a profitable run in cinemas in Britain and abroad. And it was with a skilled parody of Hollywood, *The Strike*, that the Comic

Strip won the Golden Rose at Montreux. *Baka – People of the Rain Forest* was almost a feature film. Phil Agland and Lisa Silcock, commissioned by Carol Haslam, lived for much of two years in a village in the Cameroon, to take us into the private world of the pygmy, and a family scandal – a documentary portrait of a vanishing present. We funded Russ Karel to make a feature-length history of a vanished past, the story of Yiddish cinema, *Almonds and Raisins*. *Max Headroom The Movie* prophesied a future. Annabel Jankel and Rocky Morton made a stylish account of the birth of television's first robot presenter. Commissioned by Andy Park, this was as good a movie as we ever made. *Max Headroom*, so called because in ignoring a sign setting a height limit for safe passage he lost his human head, gave birth to a cult show with a cult following.

Naomi Sargant got into the act by several commissions to the talented Scottish animator Lesley Keen. *Taking a Line for a Walk*, her tribute to Paul Klee, stood out in good company. I have a 'cel' of it on my wall. Spurred on by Paul Madden in Charlotte Street and by Antoinette Moses, who prevailed on us to help fund the Cambridge, and then the Bristol, Festivals of Animation, we took an interest in animated film. The youngest single contributor to the channel's film offering was Mole Hill, a 16-year-old animator who went on to direct for the cinema. We drew on the imaginations of the Brothers Quay for films on Janáček and Stravinsky and for *Street of Crocodiles*, an extraordinary piece based on the work of the Polish writer Bruno Schulz. In Prague we put money into the work of Jan Švankmajer, author of feature-length animations; we helped commission *Alice*. We commissioned work in Bristol, where a network of animators has made a base. *Animated Conversations* used a natural soundtrack of overheard dialogue to depict scenes in the pub, the theatre box office, the dosshouse. *Sweet Disaster* was an opportunity for various talents, including David Hopkins of Occam, to embroider variations on a nuclear theme.

John Coates, with Dianne Jackson as director, gave us *The Snowman* based on Raymond Briggs's picture book. This instantly became a children's favourite, as it deserved to be. Howard Blake wrote the very appealing music. We followed that vision of impermanence with, on a grander scale, a full-length feature version of Briggs's vision of the nuclear holocaust visited on the people next door, *When the Wind Blows*. John Mills and Peggy Ashcroft voiced the old couple who are not quite sure what has hit them, but carry out the government's first-aid- save-yourself-from-the-bomb instructions to the letter. The instructions do not work. Neither, quite, did the film.

Some of the more remarkable films the channel showed or funded came from the independent sector. Till we came along film and video workshops had been virtually unwaged and unfunded. We offered them some continuity in funding, on condition that the work they produced was of interest and identifiable quality. They did not let us down. From Frontroom came *Acceptable Levels*, showing a TV crew covering events in Northern Ireland and its experience of censorship and auto-censorship. *Acceptable Levels* tackled instances unlikely to be faced so frankly in conventional broadcasting institutions. *Seacoal*, from Amber in Newcastle, married research deep in a community with a poet's eye in its photography. *Seacoal* showed a new poor hauling a meagre living, with pony and cart, from the open-cast coal thrown up by the North Sea on Tyneside. In 1986 at Munich, *Seacoal* was named by its cinematic peers best European film. *Zina*, Ken McMullen's stab at the life of Trotsky's daughter with its volcanic Prinkipo landscapes, and Cinema Action's *Rocinante* with John Hurt and Ian Dury both won notice in Europe.

Two supreme independent talents found their way to our screen. From the BFI we purchased a triptych of compressed personal film-making by Terence Davies. Three films, their making eked out over the years, now coalesced into one. Terence Davies' account of a Liverpool Catholic childhood is unlike any other film you have seen, a very personal, powerful piece. We agreed to fund Davies's next film for the BFI, *Distant Voices*. When David Rose and I saw it we thought it extraordinarily fine. Davies revealed it was only half completed. Could he have the money to make the other half? We coughed up. He made *Still Lives* and joined the two together. With it he won the International Critics prize at Cannes and was short-listed for best European film at Berlin. Davies is an original eye and ear and voice in British cinema. In that year dear old BAFTA, the British Academy of Film and Television Arts, which muddles British and American films each year and sometimes does not do timely justice to either, never even tipped the brim of its hat to Terence Davies.

Channel 4 purchased from the BFI the autobiographical masterwork of another British independent whose images are carved in granite, Bill Douglas. We showed the Bill Douglas trilogy. We also agreed to fund his long-awaited feature film, a history of The Tolpuddle Martyrs, *Comrades*. Bill's script was, mostly, diamond sharp. David Rose and I found much in it to admire. Douglas wrote in visuals, and wove a history of image-making from peepshow to camera into the tale of Dorset agricultural labourers convicted of combination for a living wage, transported to Australia, pardoned and made heroes. We put up £1 million, the most we had put into any movie, half the budget. Viewing rushes on location I thought this the work of a poet of British cinema, every frame a Samuel Palmer. The pace was stately. Months later, assembled as a whole, *Comrades* seemed to me, to David Rose, to the editor Mick Audsley, to the producer Simon Relph, too long. Nothing any of us could say could affect Bill Douglas' passionate commitment to every syllable of text, every frame of film. The film ran three long hours. *Comrades*, if it is a masterpiece, is a flawed masterpiece; but I would rather have funded it than a hundred whizz-bang thrillers that start at a cracking pace and never let up.

An award which gave Channel 4 special pleasure came to us in New York in 1986. The lump of metal this time was an Indie. The award is given by independent film-makers. The United States is the richest country in the world with a powerful film culture; millions of dollars pour each year into film-making for the cinema and for network television. The American independent sector, bursting with creative vitality, is woefully neglected. American independents have everything going for them except finance; they have know-how, skills, a feel for film as a medium they learn in childhood. But they have no money. They raise the funds they need one tranche at a time, pausing sometimes for years between research and script, script and shoot, shoot and edit, edit and dub, until another round of calls and begging letters brings the next cheque. When American independent film-makers hear about Channel 4, their eyes pop slightly and they reach for the telephone. Now they recognized the example we set, and thanked us for drawing on their talents.

I bought American independent films early. Not only did they tell their stories forcibly and well but they did so in English, giving us the singularity of a particular voice and accessibility also. We bought the documentary oeuvre of De Antonio, of Fred Wiseman and of Les Blank, including *Werner Herzog Eats His Shoe* and *Garlic is Better than Ten Mothers*. And we funded Greg Nava and Anna Thomas to complete *El Norte*.

The American public broadcasting system, PBS, will show anything in a British accent and in crinolines – many Americans think life here is like *Upstairs, Downstairs* or *The Pallisers*. Some American independent features, eagerly picked up by us, were never shown on US television. In front of the Carlton in Cannes one year, Henry Jaglom and Jonathan Demme advanced on me from either side to shake my hand for buying and screening their movies.

There was an argument that Channel 4 should confine its investment to British film. But I had stipulated always that we would be the least insular of Britain's TV channels. We bought film abroad; why could we not help it happen there, to our taste? Film is expensive; international partnerships which share costs are an obvious attraction to film-makers everywhere. At the watering holes of the film world minds meet and partnership begins. Few were funding adventurous feature film-making. Channel 4 was. Inevitably our help was sought by others.

David Rose listened sympathetically always, and recommended on occasion that rather than purchase on completion we should assist completion by investing up front. *Film on Four*, therefore, not only made films itself but helped cause all sorts of other films to be made. Sometimes we made a modest contribution only; delighted with Istvan Szabó's masterly *Mephisto*, shown in our first week, we pre-purchased an interest in *Colonel Redl*. We had bought Theo Angelopoulos' *The Travelling Players* and *Alexander the Great*. We were glad to help with his next, *Voyage to Cythera*. Nearer home, we made a substantial contribution to the budget of Merchant Ivory's *Heat and Dust* and *A Room with a View*. Maddeningly, we had no profit share in the latter.

The first substantial investment we made in a foreign film was in Wim Wenders' *Paris, Texas*, the German director's first movie set in the United States. Nastassja Kinski starred. Ry Cooder wrote the music. *Paris, Texas* won the Palme d'Or at Cannes. We preened. Anna-Lena Wibom at the Swedish Film Institute asked us to join them in financing Andrei Tarkovsky's *The Sacrifice*. The script was luminous, mysterious, reaching for the sublime. We agreed to come in. Later, Tarkovsky rang me from Stockholm to ask me to increase our contribution. We could agree that too. *The Sacrifice* was in competition in Cannes, and highly fancied. We assembled in black tie, were picked up by the Festival limousines, escorted to the Palais, mounted the steps to the screening to the sound of trumpets. As his last testament unfolded on the screen, Tarkovsky was succumbing in Paris to the cancer that killed him. *The Sacrifice* was just pipped for the first prize that year by David Puttnam's and Roland Joffe's *The Mission*, winning plaudits not just from the gala audience, some of whom had walked out from our Russian austerities, but from the jury also. Next year we were back in competition with Peter Greenaway's *Belly of an Architect*, set in Rome and co-produced with Italy. That didn't win either; Brian Dennehy's large-bodied performance never seemed to me quite to match the cool stylized look of the rest of it. But 1987 was a sort of annus mirabilis for Channel 4 at Cannes; twenty films we had funded, or helped fund, were on display there in the Competition, in the Directors' Fortnight, in selected screening, in the market. David Leland's directorial debut, *Wish You Were Here*, wowed the audience and went on to do so around the world.

At the end of the Festival David Rose accepted the Rossellini award to us from our peers for the contribution Channel 4 had made to film-making and to cinema. 'Why Doesn't TV Do Something For Cinema?'; the plea that greeted us at our birth had been answered.

Scholars from France, Scandinavia and the United States, writing theses on what is happening in the British film industry, file into Charlotte Street, and have pursued me to Covent Garden, asking David Rose or myself to define what we were up to or what we achieved. I do not know that any of them ever received a very coherent answer. Some talk, though we do not, of a 'renaissance' of British film. In my view, reports of that birth are somewhat exaggerated. Film-making in Britain remains a chancy business. There is no conceptual framework to which I can point that defines a body of work. Yet something of substance has been done.

When we started, we set out to make not less than twenty films a year, putting not more than £300,000 into each. We ended up making rather fewer and putting much larger sums, up to £1 million in some few cases, into some of them. Yet the numbers have kept up remarkably well; to date – I write in early 1989 – the channel has caused to be made or helped make around 130 British features for *Film on Four*. We would distinguish in our budgeting; £250,000, say, for UK TV rights, the rest an investment. Periodically the Channel 4 Board queried whether the term 'investment' is, in any way, justified; do any of these films show a return on capital? Not a lot, is the answer. But that is the channel's great strength, being able to make fictions on film, in which we and the authors believe, irrespective of whether we also believe in their success at the box office. Looking at it in another way, *Film on Four* paid its way on the channel's television screen. Each of these films would find an audience on television not once but thrice and, in the end, more often. Three million viewers each time – and some reached very many more – add up to nearly ten million in all. At a cost of £1 million, that was 10p per viewer. Cheap entertainment, by any standard.

David Puttnam, urging the British industry to stop talking and get on with it, and seeking always an opportunity for new talent to learn its trade, used to say that the important thing was to have film running through the camera. I asked a good critic what he thought of our achievement; what did it add up to? He paused, and then said rather the same thing: what mattered was that we'd made possible a continuity, an expectation that next year, too, films would get made. In later years we were aided in this by the British Screen Finance Consortium which government persuaded us and others to join and fund. Under Simon Relph it has proved a creative and valuable partner.

I think myself that David Rose's *Film on Four* is one of the channel's proudest achievements. I took, and take, great pleasure in it. He helped good films get made; *Another Country*, *Insignificance*, *The Company of Wolves*, *A Private Function*, *Dance with a Stranger*, *The Good Father*, *A Month in the Country*. I am glad that in Scotland we made *Ill Fares the Land*, *Heavenly Pursuits*, *Living Apart Together* and, on the Black Isle, Mike Radford's *Another Time, Another Place* – I think his best film – with Phyllis Logan's touching performance, and Italians as the prisoners of war; and glad that in Ireland we filmed *Country Girls*, *Reflections* and *Eat the Peach*. I was proud to fund Richard Eyre's *The Ploughman's Lunch* and *Singleton's Pluck*, David Hare's *Wetherby*, Mike Leigh's *Meantime* – try telling the Board sometime that there is not and will not be a script for the film whose budget they are now to approve. I was proud we managed to co-produce with ZDF *A Song for Europe*, a fictionalized version of Stanley Adams' treatment by the multinational whose villainy he shopped, now recompensed by the European Court. John Goldschmidt got a fine performance from David Suchet in that. He also directed our for long most popular home-grown movie, *She'll Be Wearing Pink Pyjamas*, women on an Outward Bound course in the Lake District. I care most of all about the first films of promising talent; Mike Figgis in *The House*, Neil Jordan in *Angel*, Barbara Rennie in *Sacred Hearts*, Beeban Kidron in *Vroom*.

From Liverpool came *Letter to Brezhnev*. Frank Clarke and Chris Bernard started out on this themselves, and ran out of money. Karin Bamborough went up to take a look at what had been done. She thought it remarkable, and recommended we bail them out and take it over. *Letter to Brezhnev*, a brief love affair between a Scouse girl and a Russian sailor, tingled with

Merseyside life. The city was broke; people kept cheerful. Bedsprings bounced. The Russian ship sailed away. The lovers reached out across the sea. Audiences cheered.

But the archetypal *Film on Four* was *My Beautiful Laundrette*. When David Rose asked me to read Hanif Kureishi's script he said he needed my view on it because some of the subject-matter was a bit sensitive. And he needed an answer, please, by the day after tomorrow. Stephen Frears was available to direct, was very keen to do it, but only if we started straightaway. It would cost £650,000. There was no chance of anyone else putting a penny into it, so we would have to find the whole of that. I did as I was asked, read it fast, liked it a lot and agreed we should make it. When I saw a fine cut in Preview One, tucked away behind the smelliest refuse bins in London in Falconberg Court at the top of Charing Cross Road, I liked its pace, deftness, vitality, assurance. When I saw it at the opening of the Edinburgh Film Festival in August 1985 I was delighted at how much the audience enjoyed it. I knew then that we had a hit. In February 1987 when I saw *My Beautiful Laundrette* on air on our screen at 9 pm on a Thursday I felt that, in a way, with this transmission Channel 4 itself had come of age.

The duty log recorded the predictable angry telephone callers. Here was this film of much vaunted merit, and what did they find? Saeed Jaffrey and a white mistress at it in the opening reel; National Front bovver boys; an old dying man mourning lost idealism; a young Asian girl temptingly showing her breasts; the young protagonists, one of them Asian, gay; an Asian middle class sitting around counting its winnings under Thatcher, singing her praise. Hanif Kureishi's script provided continuous surprises (not least when it was nominated for an Oscar for Best Original Screenplay). Gordon Warnecke and Daniel Day-Lewis gave performances to remember. Mick Audsley cut it. Sarah Radclyffe and Tim Bevan brought it in on budget. Stephen Frears, with a light touch, made making it look easy, which it never was. *My Beautiful Laundrette* captured a moment in Britain, which is one of the things film-making is for. And it gave audiences in the cinema and on television great pleasure, which is the other. To see it on our screen and to know that we had put it there and that millions were now enjoying it was rather satisfying.

I I

People and Programmes

At 6.28 pm on our first day on air a telephone caller rang the duty office to inquire:

> 'Does the fact that you have no commercial breaks mean that no one has booked air time?'
> 'But we do have commercial breaks. . . .'
> 'Oh bloody hell, I have been watching BBC.'

First thing every morning I read the duty log recording the views of callers of the night before. Those who telephone television stations to praise or blame are not typical viewers; they are self-selecting, self-import-ant, vituperative, concerned, appreciative, enthusiastic, angry, drunk, mad, lonely. But a new broadcaster needs to know if there is anyone out there watching. In our early days, when the viewing figures were low and some of the press was hostile, it mattered to me to know that anyone at all was looking in, and to learn what he or she thought of what we did. So I read every letter addressed to me, and replied to those I could. And I read the duty log.

Duty Officer's Report – Monday, 8 November 1982
9.40 *Opinions*. Mr Patrick Martin, London W2:
'This programme has completely cut the bullshit. Admire C4's courage and conviction. If I was not bald already would take my toupee off to Channel 4. May I say, madam, your programme has balls.'

9.47 *Opinions*. Mike & Kate Westbrook 'were bowled over by the programme and thought that Channel 4 has earned its place in heaven'.

9.55 *Opinions*. Mrs K. Miller rang from Oxford to say 'Thank you – it's great to be treated as adults at last.'

E. P. Thompson, whose *Opinions* programme garnered these compliments for us, would, I think, have been pleased to know that what he had to say had struck home both on those infuriated by his views and by those who supported them. I was just delighted that these one-to-one connections had been made.

Channel 4 needed sizeable audiences to survive, but our programmes invited individual viewers to make choices as to whether to watch anything we had to offer or not. Most television was aimed at family audiences, the generations viewing together. But, in the Eighties, nearly a quarter of all Britons lived on their own. Our viewers could choose what they wanted to see, without necessarily consulting anyone else's taste in making their choice. The trick, of course, would be to try to persuade enough of them to turn to us.

We did not make too bad a start. In *The Times* for 14 December 1982 Torin Douglas reported:

> In terms of what advertisers have been used to on ITV, Channel 4's audience is pretty small, but it still adds up to a great many people. For example, 30 per cent of all adults watched one or more of the *Film on Four* series during the channel's first four weeks; that is a higher proportion of adults than read an average edition of the *Sun*, Britain's most widely read newspaper.

And Douglas added that the audience profile already showed proportionately more young people and more ABC1's watching than did ITV's, and that advertisers appreciated the worth of that to them. Adding some C4 spots to a predominantly ITV campaign would enable them to extend the reach of their messages. That is, when there were commercials to show. The IPA/Equity dispute did us great harm in our first months. There were very few ads. The public sympathized. They thought we must be doing poorly. Some of our films were in black and white, some of our programmes were repeats. Of course, the public thought, they are too poor to afford colour films or new programmes. Poor them; not worth watching. They stopped trying the channel. Growth slowed.

Sue Stoessl, Head of Marketing, warned me we might never reach a 10 per cent share of audience. That was the bad news. The good news was that it would not matter: the channel would pay its way comfortably at under that figure. In this she was quite correct; at 8 per cent of the total audience, Channel 4 would go on to take 17 per cent of the total audience of commercial television, substantially more than the proportion of their revenue they subscribe to sustain us. And Sue Stoessl knew, and always advised, that growth would be slow. There was an element in our practice which might hold back that growth but could not easily be wished away. Other channels' audiences grew because the schedule offered them programmes they liked and knew where to find, in uninterrupted succession to each other. We were wedded to diversity; prided ourselves on the unpredictable. If we abandoned that quirkiness to maximize audience we might find we had sold our soul for a mess of pottage. So patience had to be the watchword.

Another contradiction: we were a channel for everyone, 'For All of the People, Some of the Time'. But we also made a particular appeal to particular audiences. Trying to sweep everyone in militated against that. We were after younger viewers with *The Tube* and *The Comic Strip Presents* and *Whatever You Want* and, later, *Network 7*. We might have, and with hindsight probably should have, offered even more to younger audiences from the outset, at the expense of other age groups. Instead, though they were hardest to lure because most set in their ways, we sought to please older viewers also, with *Countdown* and *Years Ahead* and the Hollywood movies of the Thirties and Forties. In general, the mix worked. The channel's viewing profile, as the audience grew, remained flatter than ITV's, which was biased to the older age groups and to DEs. As television services proliferate, they will become still more specialized, aiming their offering at narrowly targeted audiences. A satellite service will offer television for teenagers only. Channel 4 aimed wider.

In search of growth, we loaded the schedule in our opening weeks with movies, and included as much comedy as we could lay our hands on. The Australian comedian Paul Hogan appeared on our opening night. Slick, rude, chauvinistic, he attracted some viewers and offended others. Well before the international success of *Crocodile Dundee*, he had made himself sufficient of a celebrity to advertise Foster's Lager. I thought his compatriot Norman Gunston funnier; neurotic, awkward, chin festooned with loo-paper blotting cuts from shaving, he interviewed Hollywood celebrities who gazed with horror and amazement at this uncouth, clownish representative of the media they had unguardedly agreed to see. Hogan and Gunston were early expedients. Cecil Korer brought us *Cheers*, which rapidly became a fixture on a Friday night. Our own black comedy *No Problem*, *Treasure Hunt* and *The Irish RM* moved us forward. So did the 'emphasis' on entertainment in Spring '83. So did *The Far Pavilions* in January '84. This glossy, safe mini-series was well viewed in protected slots – ITV holding back for once to help us with it. We reached a 7 per cent share of audience for the first time. Sue Stoessl and the marketing department set out to Boulogne on a trip to celebrate, arrived instead at Calais and can remember little else of how they spent the day.

In late 1984 the IPA/Equity dispute finally petered out. In January 1985 we offered *A Woman of Substance*, an adaptation of Barbara Taylor Bradford's bestseller made for us by Ian Warren's Portman Productions, with more than half an eye, it must be admitted, on the American market. It worked for us, and it worked for them. On three successive evenings our audiences soared way over the ten million mark. The final accolade came when the Central Electricity Generating Board, after the first two, anxiously inquired the break pattern for the third night. Peaking figures to them mean millions of lights and kettles switching on all at once. On the back of *A Woman of Substance* Paul Bonner scheduled *The Price*, a six-part serial starring Peter Barkworth, produced by Mark Shivas. An English industrialist's wife is kidnapped by the IRA. This changes her, and changes him. It was not nice, but it was riveting. The line on the graph moved steadily up.

By now, too, *Channel 4 News* was hitting its stride, all teething troubles behind. 'It will never work,' a BBC panjandrum had said when it started. 'You cannot do a news programme at 7 pm. BBC-2 tried it; hopeless. No one will watch.' It is true that *Channel 4 News*' audience is small; competing with *Coronation Street* and *EastEnders* it is bound to be. But so is the readership of the *Financial Times*. *Channel 4 News* does the job we asked it to do.

Sue Stoessl said not to put our would-be popular programmes on in mid-evening hours against other channels' strongest rating material. We put some of our educational programmes there instead. The IBA was asked by Parliament to ensure that a suitable proportion of our programmes was educational; they hoped that might be as much as 15 per cent. Quite how much we could manage we would have to see, being keen not to get tied down by precise quotas. However, from the very start Naomi Sargant found herself submitting for validation to the Advisory Committee to which she answered as much as seven hours a week of programming, fifty weeks of the year. Some of her colleagues at the channel objected to our need to fulfil this obligation, and would have wished it away if they could. They thought the educational output responsible, worthy, flat; bring on instead the wild men or the dancing girls. But the obligation was a statutory requirement; fulfil it we must. Naomi Sargant, with first Carol Haslam then Gwynn Pritchard to help her, spread her net wide and got on with it.

Of all the Channel's commissioning editors, Naomi had perhaps the hardest task; she had most to do, and least resource to do it. I promised that neither in scheduling nor in budgeting would educational programmes be underprivileged. We tried to place her programmes to their best advantage, and to give them adequate resource. But the volume required of her was prodigious; over and over again she worked the miracle of making the money go round. Naomi Sargant's aim was not to equip viewers to attain academic qualifications, but to foster in them a deepening awareness of the world and of their own potential in it. The channel would programme to build skills, to encourage numeracy, to foster an understanding of the arts, to inform critical consumers, to make us aware of health issues, to encourage activity in the immobile and the unemployed, to stimulate the handicapped and disabled, to teach us to cook and garden and do it ourselves; in all, in dozens of different ways, to help us get more out of life. In her time at Channel 4 Naomi commissioned 238 separate programmes or series, more than 2000 programmes in all; they were watched, and made use of.

The IBA agreed that much of our normal output could count as educational. Documentary series on *The Spanish Civil War* or *Vietnam*, or *China: The Heart of the Dragon*, were likely to tell those who viewed them at least as much about the world as if they had been commissioned under an educational rubric. General interest was of real educational interest. This principle was conceded, but the educational advisers wished to be consulted in advance. One test for validation was the provision of written back-up material; instead of the viewer just watching and going off to bed, the hope was that he or she might pursue an awakened interest in the subject. Channel 4 published a give-away magazine, *See 4*, to tell viewers what was going to be shown. Managed by Derek Jones, 200,000 copies of *See 4* were distributed every three months to public libraries and institutions of further education. At the end of a transmission, addresses displayed on the screen in London, Glasgow and Belfast indicated that a publication was available to help viewers follow up in print the interest the programme might have stimulated. This might be a free fact sheet – send stamped addressed envelope only; it might be a booklet at £1.25; or it might be a hardback, available at all good booksellers at £12.95. More tangibly than the telephone call to the duty ofice, the sale of follow-up publications registered the channel's progress in its customers' active use of it. Each season *4 What it's Worth*, Thames Television's consumer guide edited by Mary McAnally, drew tens of thousands of requests for further information. To take just a couple of examples, *The Modern World – Ten Great Writers*, to accompany the series of that name, appeared in the bestseller lists, as did Neal Ascherson's *Struggles for Poland*. The catalogue of leaflets, booklets, records, books and videos lists well over 100 titles.

> 23.05 *Five Go Mad in Dorset*, Mr Peacock, Romford, wanted to know name of music in this show.
> 23.06 *Five Go Mad in Dorset*, Mrs. Warren, Wimbledon. Absolutely disgusted by programme.

Several programmes we showed on our opening night – *Countdown, Channel 4 News, Brookside, Film on Four* – lasted. So did *The Comic Strip Presents. Five Go Mad in Dorset*, a jolly take-off of Enid Blyton's *Famous Five*, ruffled the feathers of the copyright holders in the weeks before. On the night, it got us off to a cracking start. That it was there at all we owed to the talents of The Comic Strip, and to the flair and judgement of Mike Bolland, hired as commissioning editor for young people's programmes but immediately coming up with comedy of style and invention. Comic talent seemed to seek him out.

A friend had prompted me to call in one evening at The Comic Strip in sleaziest Soho. Above Raymond's Revuebar, past the tit and bum, was a try-out spot for alternative comedians, too new or too rude to be employed on television. Alexei Sayle was on that night. French and Saunders were there too. I reeled a bit at the language, laughed a lot, and could see that these young talents had much to offer, if we could find a vehicle for them. More conventional comedy, on the other hand, I could not see our having much room for. Although at Thames I had rejoiced in Philip Jones's almost unvarying list of successes – and would cheerfully repeat *Man About the House* in the best slot I could find for it – I never really thought ITV's best efforts in this genre were up to the BBC's in quality. The ITV half-hour is four minutes shorter than the BBC's, and there's a break in the middle; that means that character and nuance are sacrificed too often to the plot and the horse-laugh. None of the sit-coms Channel 4 itself commissioned really excelled. Situation comedy is a conventional format; if Channel 4 was to succeed in comedy it would be in other ways. Mike Bolland tapped new talent in entertainment and was prepared to ride with the risks of it.

It was Bolland who gave us *The Tube* from Tyne Tees; a pioneering rock programme that was identified by many young people as Channel 4. *The Tube* was noisy and live and set new agendas for young people's music. It gave us Jools Holland and Paula Yates as presenters and, importantly, Muriel Gray. It was ambitious as regular rock shows go. Early every Friday evening *The Tube* lit up the screen.

Also in our first week on air, Bolland came up with *Whatever You Want*, and *Whatever You Want* came up with Keith Allen. Keith Allen thought he had it all, and was very nearly right. Self-confident to the point of arrogance but inventive with it, Allen was reporter, interviewer, presenter, and did everything he did with style. Keith Allen communicated, electrically, dangerously, and to working-class young audiences. He was also political. Reportage verged on agitprop. If *Whatever You Want* had started a little later, when things had settled down, it might have lasted longer. Keith Allen still writes for and acts in Channel 4 programmes, but his inventiveness on screen is missed.

Irreverent, shocking and, at its best, very funny, *Who Dares Wins* caused more upsets and heart palpitations at the IBA than any other show – the best comedy sketch show for a long time. And *Friday Night Live*, though it took three series to get there, in the end worked. When Harry 'Loadsamoney' Enfield walked on to the stage at the Mandela concert the crowd rose to their feet and roared. Along with Ben Elton, Enfield was a sort of Channel 4 star.

By grooming a young researcher, backing a hunch and giving him his own programme, *The Last Resort*, Bolland presented another of the stars of Channel 4 in Jonathan Ross. Jonathan, the boy you could bring home to mum but still fancy, brought freshness and fun to the chat show, and duly advertised a brand of lager in his turn. At the other end of the ratings spectrum was *Alter Image*, made, confusingly, by a company called After Image. This was an arts magazine in which each item was genuinely inventive. The principal inventors were Jane Thorburn and Mark Lucas. Sitting proudly, like a mother hen with her chicks, on a platform at the Museum of Broadcasting on East 51st Street, New York, with the makers of *Alter Image* at seminars for a six-week season of Channel 4's arts output grandly entitled *Extending the Medium*, I watched the audience gaze pop-eyed at Alter Image's inventive abstractions. 'You mean you really get this way-out stuff onto network television?' We did, and all made in a back room in Clapham. The British press, incidentally, commenting favourably on our success at the Museum of Broadcasting, reported that New Yorkers were queueing round the block to get in to screening sessions. This was true, but what the papers did not mention was that the screening theatre held only fifty-one souls.

If comedy on Channel 4 had to stand or fall by one example, that would have to be *The Comic Strip Presents*. Invented by the writer/performer and, later, film director Peter Richardson, The Comic Strip were with us on our first night. Merely commissioning them prodded the BBC into retaliation with *The Young Ones*. Sometimes okay, sometimes brilliant, the little films they wrote together and played in were, in Mike Bolland's phrase, a sort of small-scale, vulgar Ealing comedy of the Eighties. They are now, in a way, the backbone of British comedy; every single one of the Strippers is a star. The angry young men and women of the Eighties will no doubt be the mainstream of the Nineties. At Montreux in 1988 Peter Richardson picked up the Golden Rose for Comedy for *The Strike*; the miners' dispute according to Hollywood.

Duty Officer's Report – Easter Sunday, 3 April 1983
    22.30 *King Lear*. Lady viewer to object strongly to the swearing in the play. On a day like today there is no excuse for this sort of thing; it's just blasphemous.

The arts on Channel 4 began with performance. Given *Arena* and *Omnibus* on BBC, and on ITV LWT's *South Bank Show* edited and fronted by Melvyn Bragg, it did not seem a good idea to me to offer a regular single-subject format at the same length and in the same slot each week; enough was enough. (My successor, Michael Grade, disagrees; a fair whack of the arts budget now goes on *Signals*.) However hard to schedule, we would find space for the major event. We began with *Nicholas Nickleby*, specially reworked for television. A live theatre performance does not show up well on television; performances geared to the back of the upper circle have to be scaled down for the camera, and for viewers at home. So *Nickleby* was remade for television, on the stage of the Old Vic. *Lear* was too, at Granada's studios in Manchester. When we worked together on *The World at War* I said to Laurence Olivier that I hoped he would yet give us a Lear. He doubted he could do it. By 1982 he was too old and too ill to subject his body to the punishment a stage performance of Lear would have inflicted. But, for his brother-in-law David Plowright at Granada, he could and did record his part in the tragedy, one speech, one scene at a time. The rest of the cast was very fine. Channel 4 was able to give *King Lear* a peak-time screening, which was more than ITV – first time round at any rate – could easily do. So Larry's Lear graced our screen.

> 12.09 *King Lear*. Male. Congratulations to C4 on the performance,
> however felt that the production had been 'chopped up'
> unnecessarily. Also bad planning regarding placing one of the
> ads. Immediately Gloucester had his eyes plucked out there was
> an ad for donors to donate their corneas to science.

Michael Kustow had a taste for the big event. After the Royal Shakespeare Company's *Nickleby* he proposed Peter Hall's National Theatre production of Aeschylus' *Oresteia*. This was done in the hammering anapests of a new verse translation by Tony Harrison, and with music by Harrison Birtwistle that rose and fell under the actors' declamation. It was also done in masks, as in ancient Greece. Channel 4, unlike the BBC or Thames, had no facilities of its own. The National Theatre, therefore, set up a production company to record the *Oresteia*. Peter Hall insisted on recording four separate stage performances – the masks and the declamatory style made stage performance in this case acceptable – on four separate cameras, thus leaving himself with sixteen different full length tapes to edit to a satisfactory whole. Poring over them off-line at his home, he took weeks and weeks over it. The final edit, too, was expensive. The show went over budget. The National Theatre decided not to act as its own production company again. Peter Hall took the *Oresteia* to Epidaurus; past and present met and merged. Andrew Snell of Landseer went with them; a revealing documentary resulted.

21.25 *Oresteia*. Lady to say that she does not approve of ethnic
programmes!

Peter Brook's *Tragedy of Carmen*, filmed in Paris, followed, and after that
the *Mahabharata*. From the National Theatre again came Bill Bryden's *The
Mysteries*, earthy and uplifting. From the National Theatre of Brent we
got the *Nativity* and *Mighty Moments from World History*. (When they did
The Ring in a tent in Edinburgh, Tamara, not that keen on Wagner, was
sport and comedienne enough to be dragooned into playing a Valkyrie.)

We did *Opera on 4* from the Met, from the ENO, from Verona – *Viva
Verona*. Andy Park bought Philip Glass's *Satyagraha* from Stuttgart –
opera in Sanskrit. We showed Unitel's wonderful range of films by Jean
Pierre Ponnelle; my favourite was his *Cenerentola*. Audiences ranged from
the low hundred thousands to two and a half million for Rosi's film of
Carmen, with Domingo. We did twelve operas a year; the letters of
appreciation were touching. Gillian Widdicombe made all of it accessible
with her expert subtitling. She also prodded us into commissioning
recordings of Kent Opera's production of Michael Tippett's *King Priam*,
and later, unusually, a studio version of his *Midsummer Marriage*. I bought
Straub's film of Schoenberg's *Moses and Aaron*. It is usually the orgy that
catches attention. But the Welsh composer Bill Mathias told me that in a
Cardiff hotel at breakfast the morning after the broadcast a farmer said to
him: 'Did you see that wonderful film last night? Such beautiful music –
and theology too!'

Andy Park gave us *Sinfonietta*, visual treatments of six twentieth century
chamber masterpieces from Ives to Varèse, and Peter Greenaway's films
of *Four American Composers*, including Steve Reich and Philip Glass.
Kustow ambitiously caused Greenaway to collaborate with the artist Tom
Phillips on *A TV Dante*. Eight episodes of the *Inferno* were completed.
With that and with *Dancelines*, original dance commissions, Kustow came
nearest to inventing new forms rather than simply translating theatre work
to another medium. He bought in classical ballet for *Dance on 4*; and
Kylian, and Pina Bausch and Twyla Tharp, and Richard Alston, Merce
Cunningham, Trisha Brown, Janet Smith. And Michael Clark – all bum
and bravado. Michael Kustow, in fact, behaved as a patron of the arts in
a grand manner. And television spread our bounty, out of London, far
and wide. Viewers living in Wick and Worcester, Ambleside and Argyll
wrote in gratitude for the feast we were able to put before them.

22.55 *Pina Bausch: Bluebeard's Castle.* Gentleman to say that he can't
understand why such an inane programme is being shown and
furthermore why he has been watching it for the past two hours.

On a Sunday afternoon in the summer of 1985 I drove to Oxford. In a
downpour at Oxford City's ground – normal soccer attendance 300 – 3000
had gathered to see the Oxford Bulldogs play the Reading Chargers. There
were hot dogs and hamburgers to eat, Coke and beer to drink. The game
was American football. Desmond Morris had told me to go; he went most
Sundays. But I still found it difficult to believe my eyes. American football
started on Channel 4 in November 1982. Two years later there were fifty
teams in Britain, organized in leagues, pulling modest but friendly crowds
who relished, as I did, the spectacle and their part in it. American football
once a year now fills Wembley Stadium, though the pre-season warm-up
game that we see here – however good the teams, they come to London
to practise – is only a taster for the real thing.

Adrian Metcalfe, commissioning editor for sport, and Cheerleader Productions and producer Derek Brandon put *American Football* on Channel
4, and made it work. To do so they used every technical trick in the
book. I prefer sport straight on television, unedited, unprettified, without
intrusive commentary. Cheerleader adopted the other approach. Using the
angles and replay the US networks' coverage afforded him, Derek Brandon
gave it the works. To the sound of pop hits, quarterbacks threw, wide
receivers leaped, tight ends crashed, running heroes touched down for
glory, and bounced, signalled and postured in celebration. Audiences for
the sport grew. *Superbowl*, live into the night, became a national event.
Newspapers, which came to jeer, ended up reporting the game as if it was
ours, a welcome strike against insularity in sport. Large men in padded
shoulders and crash helmets started to appear on poster sites advertising
anything you cared to name. Life was imitating television. Baseball next.

The most grateful of our viewers were fans of cycling. When Adrian
Metcalfe came up with *City Centre Cycling*, I curled a lip but agreed because,
as he pointed out, it could not be an altogether bad thing to have the
traffic stopped of an evening in one of six British cities, while cyclists
chased each other lap after lap round the centre, commending Channel 4
to its citizens and advertising the city, and Kellogg's the sponsor to our
viewers. But I did not really fancy it, and I still don't much. It's the same
view over and over again of Birmingham's Bull Ring or Glasgow City

Chambers. What I did fancy, and always had since I first read Geoffrey Nicholson's reports in the *Guardian* and the *Observer*, was the Tour de France. That was real spectacle; the plains of France, the cobbles of Belgium, the steep cols of the Pyrenees and the Alps, the finish on the Champs Elysées at the Arc de Triomphe. And now there were British riders – Bob Millar from Glasgow, King of the Mountains – in with a chance. Paul Bonner and Adrian Metcalfe both demurred a little when I said we ought to cover it. But in the end we found a way; French time being a vital hour ahead of ours, we could with the aid of Phil Liggett's expert commentary just manage an edited report early each evening. Some skipped work early to get home in time to see it.

F. T. Bidlake was a much-respected speed cyclist of the inter-war period. In 1986 after the Tour de France I was solemnly, delightfully, presented by the British Cycling Federation with the F. T. Bidlake Memorial Award for Services to Cycling. The Chief Executive of Channel 4, I did not have the heart to tell them, cannot ride a bicycle.

'Virgin Airways Fly Wide Bodies Across the Atlantic', says the full-page ad, featuring a large Japanese gentleman with very little on. The same image has served for Olivetti, and for Ferguson TVs. I do not know what it was about Sumo wrestling that persuaded me we ought to do it. It may have been a traveller's tale, or a picture in a magazine, or a newspaper report, but something suggested that Sumo, with its strange ritual, should be pursued before someone else had the idea. Nothing happened; I grew impatient. Eventually, at New Year 1987, Channel 4 screened Sumo; the preliminary scattering of salt, the flaunting of twenty-odd stone of force-fed muscle, all the foreplay prolonged before the frenetic few seconds of skilled combat. Sumo is different. Offering it we were certainly, as the Act of Parliament requires, catering for interests that ITV does not. Even Norman Tebbit might have approved of this one.

Duty Officer's Report – Sunday, 10 April 1983
21.20 *Top Cs and Tiaras.* Mrs Hawthorne, Bromley, Kent:
      Simply gorgeous. Can we have some more please?
21.22 Male: Very nice – enjoyed it, tremendous stuff.
21.23 Male: Can we have some more. Smashing!
21.24 Female: Amazing. Absolutely delightful.

Middle-of-the-road viewers, fans of middle-of-the-road music, have a constant appetite that goes unsated. They hunger for Big Bands; Bert Kaempfert, and James Last; for the Palm Court; for operetta; for classical pop. Julia Migenes-Johnson, before she sang *Lulu* at the Vienna State Opera or *Carmen* to Placido Domingo's Don José, appeared in half a dozen shows for us – *Top C's and Tiaras*, devised and directed by Bryan Izzard. Though made on a shoestring they went down a treat with the fans. But they could not be a call on our air-time week in week out, I thought. Other priorities claimed our limited space. But some day, on radio or television, someone should cater, day in day out, for the neglected middlebrow.

Monday, 11 April 1983
23.48 *Malcolm le Grice*. Gentleman viewer:
Take this bloody rubbish off!

Every Monday evening in *The Eleventh Hour*, at 11 pm, Channel 4 showed the stuff with the best claim to meet Parliament's command that we encourage innovation and experiment in the form and content of programmes. In themed series, collated by Alan Fountain and his colleagues Rod Stoneman and Caroline Spry, a stream of strong viewing challenged the way we see and think about the world. On that April Monday *The Eleventh Hour* presented *Normal Vision*, a study of the independent film-maker Malcolm le Grice, jointly commissioned by us and by the Arts Council, and followed that with *Finnegan's Chin*, a 1981 BFI film written and directed by le Grice. Le Grice is a formal inventor. In successive weeks *Eleventh Hour* showed films about and films by other independents: Jeff Keen, Phil Mulloy, Margaret Tait. All were unlike the normal run of television; austere, abstruse, complex, combative these films gave us, as art should, to pause and consider. In June 1984 I went to Orkney to mark the opening of the IBA transmitter that carried our signal there. A calm, grave lady introduced herself. It was the film-maker Margaret Tait. 'Her films,' our blurb says, 'deal with looking and remembering, and the poetic and musical resonances that can occur between images. Living in Orkney, she also offers a rare, unglamourized vision of Scotland.' Now, quietly she pointed out that, since the transmitter was only now on stream, her neighbours had not seen her films or the film about her. I promised to repeat them.

The Eleventh Hour and its companion series *People to People* redress, its promoters claim, imbalances not only on television as a whole but within

Channel 4 itself. *The Eleventh Hour* offered images of women on film, gay films, the new cinema of Latin America, emergent film from Africa and the Third World. *People to People* gave us workshop series on working lives, in factories, hospitals, on the land. On *The Eleventh Hour* films by Godard, films on Nicaragua, films by women, films in Poland. You might be affronted by an *Eleventh Hour*, or bored; you could not easily claim to have seen it all before. Claiming kinship with Eckart Stein's *Das Kleine Fernsehspiel* on ZDF, which also displays an eclectic, independent adventurousness, *The Eleventh Hour*, by purchase and commission, contributed to the development of British independent film-making, in fiction and in documentary. By laying that work beside the work of film-makers from other and very different societies, *The Eleventh Hour* genuinely enlarged the range and scope of British television.

Most at risk if Channel 4 falters, independent film and video have claimed their place on public air-space and justified the claim. Ken McMullen's *Ghost Dance* and *Zina*, Phil Mulloy's *Through an Unknown Land*, Stuart McKinnon's *Ends and Means*, Ron Peck's *Empire State*, Lezli-An Barrett's *Business as Usual*, Hugh Brody's *1919*, Amber's *Seacoal* made pointed connections on our screen. We were asked to provide a 'distinctive' service. These were it.

When I first met independent film-makers they feigned indifference to television's audiences. Now they could reach out to them, as my colleagues acknowledged: 'The films Jean-Luc Godard made in the '70s reached 100 times the audience through single screenings in the 1985 season *Godard's Cinema* at the edge of the television schedule than through many months in the art cinema circuit.' Earnest, and a little lacking in humour they may have been. All the same, without *The Eleventh Hour* and *People to People*, Channel 4 would be the poorer, and would have a far less convincing claim to innovation. The two series, and particularly *The Eleventh Hour*, deserve – what I sought for them – a protected place in the channel's schedule, and an established and guaranteed claim on the channel's budget. The day I really worry about Channel 4's future will be the day their future is threatened.

Wednesday, 13 April 1983

22.50 *20/20 Vision*: Regular female caller, anon:
>
> C4 is disgusting, all communism, sex, cruelty to animals.
> She's not writing to Mrs T. any more as she has done nothing to close C4.

12

All at 4

IN the early days of Channel 4 there was a genuine camaraderie among us all. I had experienced this before on long-running programmes in which common endeavours – shared defeats and celebrations – cemented a team relationship. I had never known it before in an entire company. We were new, small as television companies go, and had a sense, not completely paranoid, that others were against us, waiting and watching for us to fail. It helped that we shared a common purpose. Even the ferocious arguments at the commissioning editors' weekly programme review meetings served to keep us together. We cherished the freedom to disagree passionately about means if we agreed about ends. We were a happy few, in 1984 two hundred employees in all; in 1988, broadcasting many more hours, three hundred. All worked hard. I never knew everybody by name; secretaries, because we paid low salaries, came and went pretty rapidly. So did junior engineers. But I knew most people and tried to foster the sense that everyone's contribution mattered. On anniversaries, or at the turn of the year, I sent handwritten notes to 'All at 4'. On each 2 November, our anniversary, accompanied by the Head of Personnel, Gill Monk, and her assistant, I went round the building presenting everyone with a packet of sweets, a flower and, if permitted, a kiss. At the front door in Charlotte Street, Charlie Maggs called everyone 'Darling'. 'Go right in, Mr Isaacs my dear,' he said to me one day before we went on air when the builders were in, motioning me up the stairs on to which a moment later crashed a large block of masonry, narrowly missing the Chief Executive, his objectives as yet unrealized. At our 1984 Christmas party at the Tun

Room at Whitbread's Chiswell Street Brewery, Paul Bonner successfully assembled our '4' ident from its component parts; this was more than I could have done. At Christmas 1985, Charlie, in tux and spotlit splendour, sang 'It's A Wonderful World' and brought the house down. There was a good feeling about.

But the apple of concord had a worm in it. At a very early stage the Board discussed tenure for commissioning editors, and was against it. We saw Channel 4 as different from other broadcasting institutions which employed permanent staffs and appeared to ossify with them. Much bright television talent turned freelance and changed employers often. Those who stayed throughout their working lives with one employer were likely to include the weak as well as the loyal. In any event, television throve on new blood and on new ideas; nothing so drab as the creative department that had to find each year an assignment or two for Buggins, because it was Buggins' turn. The Board of Channel 4, half envying the power of patronage it was bestowing on each commissioning editor, determined that no one on the commissioning side should have a job at the channel for life, or even on the permanent staff. All, it was made clear from the start, would be offered short, fixed-term contracts, usually for three years in the first instance. All accepted. I supported this policy; it was not right that large public patronage should remain semi-permamently in the same few hands. I stand by that. It was also argued that innovation, our statutory charge, could only result from relays of new people. This is less certain. The ideas we would latch on to as catalysts for new programmes were, after all, to come to us from others. A commissioning editor's job was to spot new ideas, nurture them, translate them to the screen. It was at least arguable that some security of tenure would enable that job to be better done than the inexperience of process and insecurity of mind that rapid flux and turnover would produce. But no one put that forward. I was, incidentally, quite clear that the Chief Executive was a commissioning editor also; I, too, must serve a term and go.

If the policy was fair its implementation was harsh. A decision was taken in mid-1983 to begin the process of changing and replacing commissioning editors immediately. To establish the point of principle we must make a start at once; some commissioning editors were not to have their contracts renewed to make clear to all that no one was a fixture. Mentally I kick myself daily for being party to this. But I was. The hastiness stemmed, I believe, from the tensions on the Board itself throughout the early part of 1983, with the Chairman in particular pointing scathingly to individual frailties, wishing to see some cut down to size, and political imbalance corrected. Whatever the reason, the result was cruel. The principle was right; its implementation could have been delayed. I later argued and had it agreed that within ten years the entire commissioning body would be replaced; but that within that decade each editor might be offered two contracts, even three. This practice, though still impermanency, was more acceptable, and is now implemented.

As it was, when it was announced to commissioning editors, the policy came as a bombshell. Real hurt was done to morale, if only because the Board's decision – to which I was party and they were not – had understandably but offensively been arrived at without their being consulted. Commissioning editors always argued for a greater collegiality in our decision-making than I, by temperament and practice, allowed.

In those days, up to mid-1983, I saw each commissioning editor separately to discuss and approve each of his or her recommendations for commissions. These bilateral, linear moves were reported to Programme Review, attended by them all, before passing for formal ratification to the Programme Finance Committee. By now it had become obvious that every commissioning editor could not sensibly report directly to me as Chief Executive any longer. We made a change. The majority now reported to Paul Bonner, the Programme Controller; Liz Forgan, David Rose, Michael Kustow and Adrian Metcalfe continued to report to me. This arrangement worked pretty well.

The names of those whose contracts were now not to be renewed could not be pulled out of a hat. I had to decide where to start, knowing that whoever was told to go would take dismissal as a personal vote of no confidence rather than as an impersonal turn of destiny's wheel. The first who went were Cecil Korer, Paul Madden and, a year later, Andy Park. Sue Woodford left also, at her own volition, to go with her family to New York. Paul Madden probably still thinks his black spot was owed to the hassle over Ken Loach's *Questions of Leadership*. That did not help him. I did have a rationale, though, for each hard choice. In his case, we possessed a large store of purchased documentaries which must be transmitted before it made sense to commission more. For some years we could well do without a commissioning editor for single documentaries. Paul Madden continued, as a consultant to the channel, to make himself responsible for our use of the archive, concocting with Mairede Thomas a selection each

Christmas, usually adding a reminiscent documentary also. He kept charge of animation. With *Mr Pye* and other pieces, he turned independent producer. After a longish gap Nick Hart-Williams, who had once run The Other Cinema, came in and gave our single documentaries a new status and perspective.

Andy Park had given us, and had in the pipeline, some of Channel 4's most imaginative commissions, including backing Robert Ashley's minimalist serial soap opera *Perfect Lives*; *Juno and Avos*, a rock opera from Moscow; and *Max Headroom*. But there was also a stock of jazz for which I learned late I had no early slots. And there were aspirations that seemed long in the fulfilling. Andy, who had come to us from Glasgow, now returned to his home there, promptly signing up with BBC Scotland, for whom he produced John Byrne's prize-winning six-part drama series *Tutti Frutti*. And that was just for starters. Cecil Korer retained a consultancy for us, selecting episodes of *The* – awful – *Gong Show*, and was commissioned, as in all such cases it was agreed a departing editor might legitimately be, to make some programmes as an independent. Mike Bolland took over as Senior Commissioning Editor for Entertainment Programmes, with marked success.

And there were other changes. We were fortunate to hire Farrukh Dhondy to replace Sue Woodford in charge of multi-cultural programmes. A writer himself – he had created for us *Tandoori Nights* – Farrukh laid about him with a will. Caroline Thomson came in to assist Liz Forgan by taking charge of *The Business Programme*, which later expanded into *Business Daily*. This was a bit awkward, for she was the daughter of the IBA's Chairman, Lord Thomson of Monifieth. But she got the job on merit, and did well. Liz Forgan was later appointed Assistant Director of Programmes. Under her there came David Lloyd, from the BBC. He had care of current affairs, including eventually *Channel 4 News*. He brought into being a new reportage series, *Dispatches*, building a welcome plurality of input into the current affairs strand.

David Benedictus assumed, under David Rose, responsibility for drama series. David Benedictus wore odd socks, had lots of ideas, but less ability to decide between them or to make the right ones happen. He spent ages and ages and some £30,000 – my fault, I should not have let him – commissioning treatments and scripts of Anthony Burgess's *Earthly Powers*, which, beginning with a Pope in bed with a catamite, is not all that likely to translate easily to the television screen, let alone attract co-production monies from cautiously clerical German or Italian partners. But he did give us one triumph; *Porterhouse Blue*, adapted by Malcolm Bradbury from Tom Sharpe's book, well directed by Robert Knights and starring David Jason. That won a prize or two, including an International Emmy.

In 1985 Peter Ansorge replaced him and moved things along steadily. He started with *A Very British Coup*, which worked here and sold around the world. The late Ray McAnally gave a charged central performance as Harry Perkins, the threatened Labour Prime Minister. For once I made a contribution here, suggesting that we invite Alan Plater, the adaptor of Chris Mullin's novel, to give us not a single *Film on Four* but a three-part cliff-hanging serial. It worked. Peter Ansorge also pushed on with our membership of the European Co-Finance Consortium, an association of six European broadcasters which Justin Dukes had helped bring into being. I had doubts about this, fearing dilute homogenized productions which often characterize such arrangements; 'Europuddings' was my name for them. But, resolutely holding out against all feeble options, Peter Ansorge instead persuaded our partners to help fund *The Manageress*, with Cherie Lunghi as the Italian woman in charge of an English football team. 'Television to Talk About,' indeed.

John Cummins, the most arrogant young man I think I had ever met, was employed as a researcher on *The Tube* when he interviewed himself into the job of commissioning editor for youth programmes to replace Mike Bolland. He gave us *Baby Baby*, Paula Yates's guide to parenthood, which broadcast well, and Paula Yates's guide to sex, *Sex with Paula Yates*, which did not get broadcast at all, because its casual style and prurient content detracted from its supposedly serious purpose. It was John Cummins, through Jane Hewland at LWT and Janet Street-Porter, who came up with *Network 7*, a post-modern primer of youth journalism, all fast, flash graphics and shortening attention spans. I thought it rather fine, live from its studio base of a disused warehouse on Canary Wharf. Alan Yentob must have thought so too; BBC-2 hired Janet Street-Porter to do the same sort of thing for them. After John Cummins departed, Steve Garrett for Channel 4 outdid *Network 7* with *Club X*.

Gwynn Pritchard, very level-headed and sympathetic with it, came to assist Carol Haslam and Naomi Sargant with their vast output. Later he replaced them both. Carol Haslam, after a year at the London Business School, applied for and got the job of Chief Executive of ITV's and BBC's

European satellite venture Super-Channel. It never caught on, and she moved on again. Naomi Sargant left Channel 4 in 1989 at the end of a demanding term. Naomi had given up tenure at The Open University to come to us; hers was a distinguished contribution to the record.

John Ranelagh had charge of religion. He caused to be made *Jesus the Evidence*; *Seven Days*; *In the Steps of St Paul* with – a real find, this – Karen Armstrong. He worked in science also, though he would never allow the word 'science' to be uttered without joining 'engineering' to it. His pantechnicon series *Equinox*, co-ordinated by Patrick Uden, was our only successful venture in the field. John Ranelagh wrote a hefty and serious study of the CIA – he admires that body and its achievements – while with us, taking only a short leave of absence. And he commissioned *The Other Europe*, a critique of Communism in action in Eastern Europe. This broke new ground; not many polemics from the right reached our screen. John Ranelagh was a fierce protagonist in arguments within the channel; hard where others, including me, were soft, holding out for editorial authority against liberal permissiveness, he did not mince criticisms of his colleagues. He tried for a top job in RTE, Irish Television, almost talked himself into it, and talked himself out again. He got the number two job on Denmark's new Channel TV-2, but did not last quite long enough in it to convey there all he might have learned, by disagreement as much as by agreement, here. He would have much liked to run Channel 4's news and current affairs. He may yet astonish us all.

Bob Towler, from the IBA's research department, once a lecturer in theology, replaced John Ranelagh in charge of our religious output. Rosemary Shepherd was hired to commission children's programmes. (Michael Grade, when I left, decided there were not adequate funds for her to do the job properly. She left.)

Paul Bonner, as the end of his second term approached, accepted an offer from ITV to become Director of the Programme Secretariat of the ITV companies. There his skills as a listener and conciliator, his innate sense of fairness, would stand him, and them, in good stead. We had worked well together from the day we started, both believing that as few layers of authority as possible should supervene between the programme producer and the transmission decision. Later commissioning editors were arranged in groups, each including a senior, supervisory figure. Some reported to Liz Forgan, and some to Mike Bolland. What this model gained in immediacy, however, it lacked in clarity. Michael Grade predictably abolished it. Hierarchy was bound to assert its claim in the end. The commissioning department now has a new structure and a new boss. Liz Forgan was appointed to the Board as Director of Programmes in 1988. Beneath her are two Controllers; John Willis, from Yorkshire TV, of Factual Programmes, Mike Bolland of Entertainment, and beneath them two groups of commissioning editors. (David Rose, as Head of Drama, still responsible for *Film on Four*, answers directly to Michael Grade.) So, with that exception, three layers of authority between the producer and the Chief Executive.

Another major change of structure was prefigured in my day, and enacted after my departure. Four senior colleagues were appointed to the Board as executive directors: Liz Forgan, Colin Leventhal, Frank McGettigan and David Scott. This acknowledges senior management's role in running the company, promises continuity and gives them, under the new Chief Executive, a voice and a stake in the future.

Others have departed: Pam Masters to the BBC, Ellis Griffiths to British Satellite Broadcasting (BSB), Sue Stoessl to consultancies in her expertise – making connections between programmes and audiences, Justin Dukes to industry, in which he will assume large responsibilities. Naturally enough, as the world moves on, few of those who were in at the start are there still.

*   *   *

In July 1986 the Peacock Committee, set up to inquire into the future of the BBC, recommended that the BBC should not take advertising, but that, in the interests of furthering competition, Channel 4 should have the option to sell its own air-time. The IBA and ITV were aghast; the remit, they thought, would suffer from this ending of ITV's monopoly and competition between us. So would ITV's fortunes. The cornerstone of the system that brought Channel 4 into being and sustained it was that our funding was determined as a proportion not of air-time sold only on our channel, which would have been hard for us and death for S4C, but as a proportion of air-time sold on both channels. This meant that however ITV and C4 divided the commercial audience our income was ample and secure. But now it looked to Peacock that the income to be earned on C4 alone might suffice to fund us. There could be an end to the ITV monopoly.

Channel 4's Chairman, Edmund Dell, had had his contract renewed for a second term. Justin Dukes reproached me for not objecting to the renewal – though I had no veto. But increasingly Edmund was at odds with the IBA, seeking every opportunity to loosen the bonds that tied us to them. Now he welcomed Peacock and advocated a surge for freedom. Edmund Dell was against the monopoly, and against the link with ITV. His position was clear and formidable. But he was in a minority. Lord Blake supported him on the Board. Others, including the ITV representatives, were adamant for the status quo. Whatever protection statute might offer, or might otherwise be contrived, I could not see that the remit could be as well fulfilled if the channel were to be private and to compete.

Justin Dukes commissioned a report by Professor Alan Budd of the London Business School on the channel's viability if we sold our own advertising. Budd reported, though he took no account of certain necessary additional costs, that at just over 14 per cent share of total ITV advertising revenue we could do it. When this report was received Edmund seized on it as a case made out. We could and should compete. I knew that it would be harder to maintain diversity in the schedule if every commissioning decision is made in the light of the need to earn revenue. It might be possible to get by that way. But why risk it? If it's not broke, don't fix it. But it looked as if Government, or at least Downing Street, was determined to fix it; some change was inevitable. In this circumstance Justin and I sought a middle way. We were in favour of keeping the status quo if we could. If we could not, we wanted to keep the Peacock option open; to sell our own advertising, alter our relationship with the IBA, but not be privatized outright. On 16 December 1986 the Board unanimously passed this resolution:

> The Channel 4 Board is content with the present funding arrangements
> based on 17 per cent of net advertising revenue. If, however,
> Parliament should wish to alter the structure of broadcasting, the Board
> would not rule out in advance alternative structures for Channel 4,
> and would be prepared to discuss such changes on condition that any
> new arrangements ensured the maintenance of the existing remit.

From year to year the channel's income, based on ITV advertising revenue, grew – from £105.2 million in the year ending 31 March 1984 to £163.4 million to March 1988. Annual transmission hours in the same period expanded from just over 3000 to just over 5000. Staff numbers rose from 202 to 303. So the channel remained highly cost-efficient; overheads never exceeded 10 per cent of our income. In the year to end March 1988 patronage to Channel 4 reached 75 per cent of available viewers each week, and 91 per cent each four weeks, so nearly everyone was watching some of the time. Channel 4's share of audience in that year was 8.8 per cent, and of ITV's audience on the two channels, ITV and Channel 4, 17.4 per cent. With the subscription ITV paid directly to fund Channel 4, excluding that to S4C, fixed at 13.6 per cent in a previous year, that meant that in my time the Channel was, indeed, paying its way.

In November 1988 the Government published a White Paper, 'Broadcasting in the '90s: Competition, Choice and Quality',* setting out its plans for legislation. The verdict on Channel 4 was unequivocal. 'The programming remits of Channel 4 and S4C have been a striking success. These remits must be fully sustained.' Under the rubric 'Reinforcing Quality', the government spelled out its wish to see Channel 4 continue to provide a distinctive service within the independent television sector, and retain its commitment to all the qualitative objectives legislation had set for it. Not only the BBC was to concern itself with the range and quality of programmes traditionally associated with public-service broadcasting.

But on what structure of ownership the remit was to be pursued the document was less certain. It set out options; Channel 4 could be privatized and put out to tender; it could be linked to the new commercial terrestrial Channel 5; it could continue as a non-profit-making body, a subsidiary of the ITC (the body to be set up to replace the IBA), with freedom to sell its own advertising, but to avoid it being wholly dependent on those revenues in a highly competitive market, with a minimum level of income guaranteed: 'This would provide a safeguard against any erosion of the remit which might otherwise arise as the competition for advertising and subscription revenue intensifies.' This last solution in this precise form is unsatisfactory both to ITV and to those, like Edmund Dell, who queried whether a channel competing for advertising against ITV can possibly also be owned by the ITC, which will regulate ITV, without conflict of interest arising. The link with Channel 5 was never a runner. Outright privatization with profit as the goal, though of interest to the Treasury and to some in the industry, could clearly be seen to jeopardize the channel's heart and purpose.

In the statement he made in the House of Commons on 13 June

*Cmd 517 (HMSO)

1989 the Home Secretary, Douglas Hurd, spelled out the scheme the government intended to embody in legislation. The remit was to be protected, but the channel was to sell its own advertising. Channel 4 was not to be allowed to become an independent commercial company, subject in the market to shareholders' pressure. It was anomalous that it be owned by the ITC. After 1993, therefore, if Parliament agrees, Channel 4 is to become a public trust, licensed by the ITC, selling its own advertising. It will be expected to exist on a baseline revenue of 14 per cent of terrestrial net advertising revenue (NAR). If revenue falls below that the ITC will have power to top it up, not, as originally suggested from a reserve, but by levying on the ITV companies up to the value of 2 per cent of NAR. If Channel 4's revenue exceeds 14 per cent of NAR, the surplus is to be split equally between C4 and C3, as ITV is then to be called.

Channel 4 will want to know how the trust that will control its fortunes will be appointed. It is crucial that those who make the appointments to the trust, and those appointed, have the Channel's independence, particularly from government, ever in mind. The Channel will also want to be sure, while welcoming the financial safety net, that the arrangements to fix its income do not cap potential growth. But Channel 4 ought to be broadly satisfied that government has taken steps to ensure it can pursue its qualitative and pluralistic objectives, go its own way.

When Willie Whitelaw ceased to be Home Secretary we invited him for a farewell lunch, an opportunity to express our gratitude to him for the legislation that had set us up, for his part in our birth and growth. I thought we ought to give him a present. I knew he loved golf, and of his prowess at it. I was first aware of him as a politician when he contested East Dunbartonshire in 1950. His election address contained the vital information that his golf handicap was a low one. And he had since served as Captain of the Royal and Ancient Golf Club at St Andrews. I determined to give him a No.4 iron, but made of silver. Justin Dukes aided and abetted me in this impulse. The clubhead was cast, and put in a box ready for the presentation. I mentioned to Edmund Dell, who would preside at the lunch, what I had laid on. He was aghast. 'Out of the question; you must be mad.' Punctiliously he explained, as a Privy Councillor should, that Ministers of the Crown were not allowed to receive valuable presents. Quite right, but I had forgot it. Willie Whitelaw received a far more modest memento of his association with us. The Channel 4 Golf Club is now the proud possessor of a valuable trophy.

If Whitelaw's successor, Douglas Hurd, does succeed, against all the pressures from elsewhere in government, in enacting legislation to safeguard Channel 4's future on the lines set out in his statement of June 1989, he too will deserve the gratitude of all at 4. A silver ink-stand, perhaps?

I3

Allsorts: An A – Z

LOOKING back, I most regret not broadcasting sport live without commentary, not persevering only with sub-titled foreign fiction, rather than descending to dubbed versions of the same, though that did attract more viewers, and failing to pre-empt the BBC's swift bid for *Heimat*.

I take most pleasure in the variety of what we showed. Here are twenty-six liquorice allsorts – a very personal, strictly alphabetical choice.

After Dark –
Open-ended talk. Lifted by an astute producer, Sebastian Cody, from Austria's *Club Zwei*, it began at midnight and went on till it finished. The aim, discussion between people with burning experience of the subject; e.g. the murderer and the judge. A participant might wait long to utter but in the end his turn came. Viewers could fall asleep in front of it, wake up and find the discussion just hotting up.

Open Media Ltd.
comm. ed.: Mike Bolland, Seamus Cassidy

26 Bathrooms –
Peter Greenaway's A-Z of British bathrooms, and what we do in them; everything, it turns out, except cook. In Greenaway's alphabet, Q is for a Quiet Smoke and V is for Violin Practice. Stylish pictures of eccentric interiors; the inhabitants clothed and unclothed.

Artifax
comm. ed.: Michael Kustow

Callas Sings Tosca –
The 1964 ATV *Golden Hour* black and white recording of Callas as
Tosca, Tito Gobbi as Scarpia. Introduced in high patrician style by
the then General Administrator of the Royal Opera House, Sir David
Webster, this glorious excerpt from Puccini's 'dreadful little shocker'
made a memorable reappearance from the archive.

ATV
comm. ed.: Jeremy Isaacs

Da Doo Ron Ron –
Documentary on record producer Phil Spector, who refused to appear
in it. Binia Tymienicka's film was remarkable for being the only
portrait of anyone in the music business to contain unfavourable
comment on its subject by his friends and associates.

Da Doo Ron Ron Productions
comm. ed.: Andy Park

Every Picture Tells a Story –
James Scott's portrait of his painter father William Scott's childhood
in Greenock and Enniskillen. The Chief Executive of Channel 4
acquired a picture by William Scott as a result.

Flamingo Pictures
comm. ed.: Michael Kustow

Flashback –
Visual documents; newsreel as evidence of social change, presented by
scholarly producers Taylor Downing and Vicky Wegg-Prosser.
Intelligent television history.

Flashback Productions
comm. ed.: Naomi Sargant

Ghosts in the Machine –
Video; artists explore a new medium. Genuine inventions, weird,
collated by John Wyver; sometimes hilarious. Very little Channel 4
did was visually innovative; this was.

Illuminations
comm. ed.: Michael Kustow

Handsworth Songs –

Powerful and imaginative film essay on the themes of 'race' and 'civil disaster' in contemporary Britain. Scenes of riot in Handsworth intercut with archive. This film found the voice and visual language to make its point.

> Black Audio Film Collective
> comm. ed.: Alan Fountain

Ian Breakwell's Continuous Diary –

Late night, for a fortnight. The peculiar vision of artist Ian Breakwell. Filmed and live. Humorous, bleak, bizarre.

> Annalogue Productions
> comm. ed.: Paul Madden

The Best of C L R James –

Not the best actually; that is in his books. But the welcome appearance on British television screens of the celebrated West Indian Marxist historian, author of *The Black Jacobins* and of one of the best books on cricket ever written, *Beyond a Boundary*.

> Penumbra Productions
> comm. ed.: Sue Woodford

Kitum – The Elephant Cave –

Kitum; a cave on the slopes of Mount Elgon in Kenya. After nightfall, elephants make their way in the dark up a steep trail to the cave's entrance and disappear inside. They go there to lick salt. Derek Bromhall developed the techniques that enabled him to film this in pitch blackness. If not seen, not believed.

> Genesis Films
> comm. ed.: Carol Haslam

Lowest of the Low –

German journalist Günther Walraff made himself up as a Turkish immigrant worker. Jorg Gfrorer, with a hidden video camera, filmed him. A bitter, shocking exposé of how German companies exploit *Gastarbeiter*.

> Kaos Film and Video
> comm. ed.: Nick Hart-Williams

Maids and Madams –
Many white South African children are brought up by black South
African women who, to survive, must look after the madam's children
and neglect their own. Apartheid begins at home. Mira Hamermesh's
film dissects the emotional relationship of black maid and white
madam.

AFP
comm. ed.: Liz Forgan

The New Enlightenment –
The ideology of the new right in America and Britain collated by
David Graham. When the Prime Minister challenged the Chief
Executive of Channel 4 to name a single series which had supported
her point of view he named this one. 'Ah yes,' she said. 'But that is
the only one.'

Diverse Production
comm. ed.: Liz Forgan

Open the Box –
Six-part series about television, produced by Michael Jackson. In 'A
Part of the Furniture', transmitted on Monday, 19 May 1986, through
a camera hidden in the TV set, we see what goes on in the room when
people watch television; quite a lot.

Beat Ltd.
comm. ed.: Carol Haslam

Perfect Lives –
TV premiere of an opera for television by Robert Ashley, in seven
parts, transmitted on consecutive nights, a post-modern version of
the mythology of small-town middle America. Our funding got this
made. Wake up, USA!

The Kitchen, New York
comm. ed.: Andy Park

Quilts in Women's Lives –
The archetypal Channel 4 programme title.

CS Associates
comm. ed.: Naomi Sargant

Rod and Line –
Michael Hordern read from Arthur Ransome on angling. Rivers and
river banks themselves give pleasure; add Ransome's prose in
Hordern's voice and you come close to bliss.

Granada
comm. ed.: Paul Bonner

A Sense of Place –
Ulster poets in Ulster places. Three fine films by a poet of film, David
Hammond.

DBA Television
comm. ed.: John Ranelagh

The Trial of Richard III –
Trial by television; but no charges of contempt of court. Richard III,
unavoidably absent, is put on trial for the murder of the Princes in
the Tower. For four hours lawyers and witnesses debated his guilt or
innocence. Two million watched. The jury acquitted.

London Weekend TV
comm. ed.: Paul Bonner

Up Line –
The most substantial work by Howard Schuman since *Rock Follies*, an
'edgy comedy with thriller overtones'. Under-rated.

Zenith
comm. ed.: Peter Ansorge

Video From Russia –
Shown, appropriately, in *People to People*. An American documentary-
maker invited men and women in the streets of Moscow, Kiev and
other cities to give their views. They did. A harbinger of *glasnost?*

Dimitri Devyatkin
comm. ed.: Alan Fountain

Wales – The Dragon Has Two Tongues –
Two views of Welsh history, those of broadcaster Wynford Vaughan-Thomas and historian Gwyn Alf Williams. Describing each other as 'a marshmallow historian' and 'a Marxist nag-bag', Wynford and Gwyn Alf put forward their conflicting accounts in combative fashion. Moved history on television a small step onward. Colin Thomas was the producer.

HTV Wales
comm. ed.: Naomi Sargant

Xerxes –
An old opera by George Frideric Handel, dazzlingly produced at the English National Opera by Nick Hytner. Stylish visuals, starry cast.

Thames TV
comm. ed.: Michael Kustow

Yan Tan Tethera –
A new opera by Harrison Birtwistle composed specially for television, commissioned by BBC-2, dropped by them, picked up by us and simulcast by Channel 4 and BBC Radio 3. The sheep were wonderful.

Landseer
comm. ed.: Michael Kustow

Zastrozzi, A Romance –
Stylized four-part film serial adaptation of Shelley's Gothic novel, *Capture, Conspiracy, Seduction, Murder*. Made in Bristol by independents. Witold Stock's photography very fine, but *Zastrozzi* might have been more effective as a *Film on Four*.

Occam Ltd.
comm. ed.: David Benedictus

14

Leaving

In July 1984, less than two years after Channel 4 went on air, I received an Honorary D.Litt. from the University of Strathclyde in my home city of Glasgow. At the Holiday Inn and in my cousin Esther's garden Tamara complained of pain. She had had a mastectomy eight years earlier and had ever since been dreading that the cancer would return. We had thought we were over it. Now back pain. The first scan showed nothing. At the end of August a conventional X-ray revealed that the bones in much of her body were pitted by tiny tumours. The specialist told me she would not live life's full term. How long? Impossible to say, anything from three years to ten. It would depend on her morale.

In September Edmund Dell reported to the Board that my contract would run out, after five years, at the end of 1985. He offered me another five years. I preferred a three-year term only, keeping me at Channel 4 till the end of 1988. This was agreed. I would then be fifty-six, and would have worked in broadcasting for thirty years. I thought that by then it might be time to do something completely different.

And there were other reasons for making a move. Channel 4 was well and truly launched; by the end of 1988 we might hope to have achieved a share of audience that would enable ITV to earn back annually the funds they contributed to our upkeep. We would be paying our way. I would not wish to leave before that end was in sight or, better, firmly secured. I would not wish to stay long after we had attained it. Running the channel then would be neither so demanding nor so exhilaratingly satisfying as getting it started had been. Besides, it would then be someone else's turn.

In January 1985 Tamara had ended a course of radiotherapy. She and I went then to her home country, South Africa. We stayed at the Cape as guests of the hospitable Menells. From Glendirk, above Wynberg below Table Mountain, we looked down to the sea at Muizenberg. For only the second time since she left in 1957 to make a new life in a politically cleaner society Tamara went back to the landscape of her childhood. On the beach at Muizenberg, for some the centre of the universe, the breeze lifted Kipling's 'white sands'. Lovingly she inspected every remembered stone.

In the autumn Sir Claus Moser, Chairman of the Board of the Royal Opera House, whose guest we had sometimes been there, came to see me in my office at Charlotte Street. He asked me if I would consider joining his Board. I was astonished and thrilled. I leaped at it. In December I was appointed. Late in January Tamara and I – she had much music in her, more than I – sat together with our guests, a director's privilege, in the Royal Box. Six weeks later the cancer erupted within her, and she was dead. We had been together for twenty-eight years. She had been my constant loving support. It was time to move from the home we had shared, and to move on, perhaps, in work also.

Alasdair Milne, Director-General, was in trouble at the BBC; *Real Lives*, when the Home Secretary asked them not to show it, divided the Governors. A lost libel action, settled too late and expensively, lost him further ground. A new Chairman, Marmaduke Hussey, was appointed. Rumour suggested that there might be a change there sometime soon. But before that could occur, the Board of Covent Garden prepared to find a successor to the General Director, Sir John Tooley, though he was not expected to end his term till the summer of 1989. Both Sir Claus Moser and Sir Denis Forman, his Deputy, urged me to allow my name to go forward. The BBC job, if it came up, was the pinnacle of my profession. But it was not on offer. The Royal Opera House, at the end of 1986, was declaring a vacancy. The BBC was not. Undertaking to be a serious candidate I put in for the job. In January I was interviewed. A new Chairman – though he had not confirmed acceptance – Sir John Sainsbury, now Lord Sainsbury of Preston Candover, sat in at the Board. After a lengthy interview they offered the job to me, subject to one proviso. Sainsbury was not yet satisfied he and I could work well together; we must meet first and talk before the offer could be finalized. I agreed to go to his home in the Boltons for a drink at 6 pm on Thursday, 29 January

1987. That afternoon came the news that Alasdair Milne was to leave the BBC. John Sainsbury and I met and got on. 'I believe we can work together,' he said. I agreed. We shook hands. For forty-eight hours my purpose held. But voices both within the BBC and without urged me to put in for the DG's job. I thought I might not forgive myself if I did not apply. The BBC made it plain that the search for Milne's successor would be over in a month. I asked Claus Moser for a month's grace. Generously he granted it.

My colleagues at Channel 4 knew I was in for the BBC job – not that I had applied for or been offered the Opera House job. They wished me luck, and hoped I would not be successful.

The press touted my candidacy. The bookmakers laid short odds against me. Folk at the BBC wished me well.

I enjoyed a preliminary conversation with the Chairman of the Governors, Duke Hussey, and Deputy Chairman Joel Barnett, and fancied my chances more than I should have done. The formal interview at Broadcasting House at ten in the morning was prefaced by a chat with Personnel about arrangements.

'We hope for a decision about five o'clock. Can you be by your telephone from 6 pm? If you get it, the Chairman will call you. If not, I will.

'And do leave time tomorrow morning for the media.'

The interview itself was less encouraging. 'Mr Isaacs,' said the Salvation Army trades unionist, President of the AUEW, Sir John Boyd, 'Mr Isaacs, you do not seem to me like a man who takes kindly to discipline. Now I see by your smile that you take that as a compliment. But I can assure you that some of us here see it as a criticism.' I ought to have known that was that, but the commissionaire wished me luck and hoped to see me back again.

I was not at home at 6 pm. I was by 7 pm. No call then, nor at 8 pm, nor 9 pm, nor 10 pm. At 10.25 pm the telephone rang. 'Jeremy – ' the voice told me I had not been successful.

'Who have they chosen?'

'I'm sorry. I can't tell you that. The Chairman will ring you in ten minutes or so. He will tell you himself.'

Paul Bonner rang a few minutes later to say, somewhat incredulously, that it was on *Newsnight* that Michael Checkland, the non-programme candidate, had been appointed Director-General. Shortly after that Duke Hussey came on.

'Jeremy, I expect you have heard what's happened.'

'Yes.'

'We very much enjoyed listening to you, and were very impressed by what you had to say. Trouble is, we were very impressed by what everyone had to say. Fact is, I am slightly surprised at what we've actually done. . . . '

I thanked Duke Hussey. He rang off. My brother Raphael and friends were with me, including Gillian Widdicombe, whom a year later I was fortunate to marry. We all had another drink. Later, I rang Claus Moser at the Dolder Hotel in Zürich and told him I would go to the Royal Opera House.

From every floor in Charlotte Street came messages, cards, flowers to say that someone was glad I was staying. By the weekend the news had leaked that I was not. It was not clear when I would go to the Royal Opera House, but it was only a matter of timing. In that disappointment of my colleagues' hopes, a bond severed. Edmund Dell suggested I go immediately, which would have allowed him to preside over the choice of my successor. But I did not want to go straightaway. In any event, John Tooley was not then due to leave Covent Garden till mid-1989. It was possible he might go a year earlier, at the season's end. Lead times are long in opera planning; I might have a role there, say, from Easter 1988. It was left open exactly when I might leave Channel 4. Edmund was out himself, due to go that July, 1987.

The Authority had appointed a new Deputy Chairman to replace Dickie Attenborough, George Russell. Now they were looking for a Chairman. I put up the name of Sir Peter Parker, who added an interest in the arts to proven industrial leadership. Oddly, and depressingly, the IBA turned him down at the last minute when he refused to undertake to abstain from any political activity in the forthcoming general election; Peter Parker supported the SDP. They took this refusal as his ruling himself out. He thinks they ruled him out. Flailing around, they now invited Dickie, who had been too busy to continue as Deputy Chairman, to take on the chairmanship. With *Cry Freedom*, his film on the life of Steve Biko and Donald Woods' friendship with him, mostly now behind him, he just about could. We warmly welcomed that. But he too looked to find my successor early rather than late, which I accepted.

In October 1987 over two consecutive evenings Channel 4 showed *Shoah*, Claude Lanzmann's nine-hour film on the Holocaust, built on interviews with survivors, perpetrators, witnesses, without a single frame of archive film. 'The old images,' said Lanzmann, 'have been used so many times that they do not speak to us any more.' He filmed the railway lines at Treblinka and Birkenau. 'The film works through this mixture of things that are permanent and things that have vanished.'

'At the end,' wrote Philip French when it was screened in London the previous year, 'you feel shattered, but not numb, because this great film makes you think, and feel, and want to learn more of this inexhaustible subject.' I never doubted that we would show *Shoah*, and that millions would watch it. They did. For two nights a commercially supported television channel did without commercials. The freedom to put such a work in the schedule, whatever the affront to those who had no interest in it, marks out a broadcasting system which has its priorities right.

In October 1987 they advertised my job. From inside the channel Justin Dukes, for real, and Liz Forgan, more as a signal of future ambition, applied. So did Anthony Smith, and Roger Graef, and Brian Wenham, who had now left the BBC. At first it was agreed that I should be on the sub-committee of the Board that would make the selection. Then I came to realize that was wrong. Neither the selectors nor the candidates should have to look to me during interviews. I suggested who should sit on the panel of Board members. Dickie agreed it. I asked to be consulted at some stage. Of course; that was understood. Laxly, I never pressed for any single candidate but prepared to give my views on each of the shortlisted candidates and to argue that Justin Dukes, whom some would totally rule out, could work in double harness with the likeliest editorial figure, a duumvirate as he and I had been, with perhaps seniority granted the other way round. I saw the list of applicants. I saw the shortlist. I stood by my telephone to be asked my view. I never was. Instead, on the Monday following the decisive weekend, Dickie asked me to meet him at the National Film Theatre. He told me that the five directors who formed the sub-committee had unanimously alighted on Michael Grade.

Michael Grade is to some a charismatic figure. I had seen a good deal of him at close quarters as fellow Directors of Programmes in ITV – he at LWT, I at Thames. He was a highly competitive figure who had once tried to hijack the Football League contract, shared by BBC and ITV, exclusively to ITV. He had gone to work in Los Angeles, then to the BBC as Controller BBC-1. He became Director of Programmes, and was to be Managing Director. Wearing, as he put it, a BBC hat that summer and autumn he had advocated privatizing Channel 4, though it was hard to see that it was any of his, or the BBC's, business. Now, feeling himself encroached on by the appointment of his old subordinate at LWT, John Birt, as Deputy Director-General under Checkland, he had an eye open for a move. (Ironically I had asked John Birt over lunch to confirm that he was senior to Michael Grade, not just Editor-in-Chief of News and Current Affairs, but responsible to the DG for all programme matters and therefore now Grade's superior. If that was the case, and it was, what was he going to do to assert himself in determining the overall tone of BBC programmes?) Michael Grade did not formally apply for the job at Channel 4. He let it be known he was available. The selectors were flattered, and overcome. I explained to Dickie, and later that evening to the Board, that I opposed this appointment, and why. I said that he was a competitive and commercially-minded television executive who would seek to take the channel downmarket, make it more popular, prepare it for privatization. I was alone in my view. I hoped I was wrong. I asked that my dissent be registered. I was asked if I would go at the end of the year to make way for him, and agreed to do so.

The next morning, momentarily tearful, particularly in reference to Justin's disappointment, I talked to my colleagues of Michael Grade's coming – the news had leaked late the night before – and of my departure. Michael came in to meet the press, and the Board. Outside my office we met. We shook hands. I wished him well, and said: 'I am handing on to you a sacred trust. If you screw it up, if you betray it, I'll come back and'- I meant to say 'thump' but looking him in the Adam's apple said – 'throttle you.' He promised he would not.

I was very critical about him. He was the opposite about me. In the Channel Four Television Report and Accounts for the year ended 31 March 1988 he wrote of 'a triumphant final year for the channel's founder Chief Executive'. I hope the channel will continue to prosper under Michael Grade, and will maintain its course. There is no good reason, except their own choice, why he and his strong team should not continue the work and surpass the achievement of those who came before them. But they will not have such fun, nor such reward.

I am often asked if what I handed over in 'trust' is still intact. I believe it is, though I do not see enough of the output to be sure. If I had to set benchmarks for the maintenance of that trust, for the continuation of the channel's distinctive purpose, they would be simple and few, going back to the programme objectives that marked our output from the beginning:

> an hour-long news, with a cool agenda;
> programmes from many different countries, preferably subtitled not dubbed;
> low-budget feature films as the key element in fiction;
> uninterrupted, unmediated opinion, across the political spectrum;
> *The Eleventh Hour*, and other voices from outside the system;
> the single show, in generous quantity as well as series;
> surprises, which means, for me, stuff that Michael Grade has thought of, and I never would.

If these are sustained in the schedule, there will be no need for me to practise unarmed combat. I shall keep my hands to myself. In any case, the trust I handed over is a public, not a personal, trust.

Channel 4 owes its nature and purpose to a consensus arrived at after years of debate; to the partnership of a regulatory body and a department of state; to statesmanship and an Act of Parliament; to a tolerant marriage between enlightened commercial broadcasters and responsible independents; to a dedicated team of people serving an ideal in which they believed. In the new dispensation that impends, that purpose must be sustained for the public benefit.

When Channel 4 was about to be born, David (Lord) Windlesham described it as a lovingly crafted steam train brought into being just as the jet plane was about to overtake and replace it. It is true that technology is transforming broadcasting, but the merits of the old system, of BBC and ITV, do not deserve to be casually thrown away. Like them, Channel 4 sought to satisfy a wide range of needs throughout the nation, the hallmark of public-service broadcasting. So long as it can fulfil those needs, cater for viewers' wants, so long it will deserve to be sustained. Broadcasting is not for those who control the airwaves, or for giants who own media. It is for listeners and for viewers, and it is up to them to make their needs and wishes clear to those with the power to shape the television services we use today.

Channel 4 set out to supply, as Parliament asked, a distinctive service. The funds were there; it was up to us to use them wisely. We set out to offer information, opinions and ideas, and laughter and pleasure in art, and anger and tears of pain and pity, and, if by drawing on others' talents we possibly could, new understandings.

We needed to be easy enough on the eye and ear and mind to please some large audiences, and precise and tough enough to stretch and satisfy the appetites of individuals with strong personal preferences.

We broadcast our fair share of junk, and our fair share of quality. We bought and commissioned from as many as we could for the sake of as rich a variety as we could encompass. We encouraged programme-makers to do their thing, rating diversity of judgement as important as quality of product.

We allowed ourselves to provoke and annoy and, sometimes, to be worthy and dull. We aimed to please, but not to please all viewers all the time.

Whatever we did, whether it was Brazilian soap opera, Chinese movies, Glaswegian ribaldry, modern dance, opera in Sanskrit, open-ended talk, news, cinema, gourmet cooking, faking pictures, exotic games, sombre documentary, the voice and utterance of the dispossessed, we did with all our heart and mind and strength. We tried for surprises. We sought to offer new choices, to push forward boundaries, to move the medium on a little. We had a go.

In the job I did at Channel 4 I had inestimable advantages; a clear brief, a free hand, a guaranteed income. We always had good chances of success, of calm after the storm.

Appendix

A Submission to the Minister of Posts & Telecommunications

1. The fourth television channel is a public asset which should be used and not wasted.
2. ITV has a strong claim to the fourth channel on simple grounds of parity with the BBC, and to enable it to provide complementary programmes on two channels. But ITV's interest is not necessarily the public's interest.
3. The government should only make available a fourth channel for use if by doing so it will lead to a wider choice of programmes, add to the services which broadcasting provides, and offer the possibility of a genuinely new experience on British television.
4. All these conditions could be fulfilled by allocating the channel not directly to ITV but to the IBA, provided the IBA defines more clearly the purposes to which it would wish to see a fourth channel put, and provided it can satisfy you that it will see those purposes fulfilled in its regulation of the channel.
5. The IBA should finance the channel by a levy upon the television companies.
6. The IBA should appoint a Controller of the Channel who, while working in harness with the Programme Controllers Committee which schedules programmes for ITV-1, would nevertheless have sole authority, under the IBA, to schedule programmes for ITV-2. It is essential that this authority should reside in one person. Only if this condition is fulfilled will it be possible to select programmes strictly on merit, and to build into the system the flexibility the BBC

possesses, and which is markedly absent in ITV's schedules today.

7. The Controller of ITV-2 should invite offers of programmes for his schedules from all the ITV companies, and from independent producers, in broad proportions agreed with the IBA, and subject to periodic review.

8. ITV-2's schedules should contain some entertainment programmes. But there should be a heavy emphasis, heavier than has yet been suggested in submissions to you by the Television Companies or by the IBA, on 'service' programmes catering for the interests of minorities of viewers. I have in mind programmes for viewers as consumers of goods and of services, and with interests in health, education, the upbringing of children, business and trade union practice, the environment, Parliament, and an endless list of hobbies and sports.

9. ITV-2 should carry nightly an extended programme of background news analysis and a Parliamentary Report, both provided by ITN.

10. ITV-2 should regularly, once a month or once a fortnight, devote an entire evening to one event. Not just plays, operas or ballets, but lengthy debates and discussions on matters of public importance, including, should Parliament ever decide to allow cameras into the House of Commons, Parliamentary debates.

11. The ITV companies should continue to receive all the advertising revenue for transmission in their areas, but the showing of commercials should be less dispersed through the evening's programmes than in the case of ITV-1. There would be a considerable further source of revenue available on ITV-2 from advertising aimed at viewers with specialist interests.

12. Many of the programmes would, deliberately, be less expensive per hour than the programmes presently provided on BBC-1 and BBC-2 or on ITV-1. All the same the programme service I am describing would cost something of the order of £25 million a year. But this revenue is available in the ITV system today, and it continues buoyant.

13. It may be asked why the ITV companies should be expected to provide a 'service' channel of this sort. The answer is that they enjoy a monopoly public franchise and earn a more than reasonable return on their investment. As the price for the continued enjoyment of

that monopoly, the government is entitled to ask them to provide this new service.

14. To sum up. ITV should have access to ITV-2, but only on terms that guarantee the public not a mirror-image of BBC-1 and BBC-2, but a widening of the range of broadcasting. In making it possible and obligatory for them to do so you, Minister, would be authorizing the provision of an additional service to the British viewing public, while exacting a proper price for the enjoyment of a public franchise. A Government which effected this extension to British television would convey a lasting benefit of which it might be properly proud.

JEREMY ISAACS
25 June 1973

Index

Index

Index

Index

Index